WITHDRAWN

THE OSTERMANN HOUSE

D1404949

J. R. KLEIN

DECATUR PUBLIC LIBRARY

FEB 0 1 2018

DECATUR, ILLINOIS

Copyright © 2017 J. R. Klein
All rights reserved.

ISBN: 1544815050
ISBN 13: 9781544815053

Also by J. R. Klein

FRANKIE JONES

And again, for Jeanne

This is a work of fiction. Names, characters, places, and incidents are drawn from the author's imagination or are used fictitiously. Any resemblance to persons, living or dead, events, or locales is coincidental.

ACKNOWLEDGMENTS

With particular thanks to my wife, Jeanne, for her valuable input and discussions, and to my agent, Carolyn Jenks, for her encouragement and insightful comments.

PROLOGUE

Houses, I think, are a lot like people. They have moods, emotions, tempers—they have personalities. And old houses... well, they're like old people. Set in their ways, somewhat predictable if perhaps persnickety at times, but consistently obvious nonetheless. Or so it seems. Old houses have wrinkles that don't hide well, creaks and aches that are easily heard and spotted even with the application of the best makeup. But then, too, old houses can fool you—they know the tricks. They know how to give off a warm and kindly smile when they want to.

That said, a house, of course, is not alive. Rather, its temperaments are built in, acquired across a period of time. Donated with good intention—although not always with a good outcome—by each previous owner. It is the owner, after all, who creates the house, changes it, molds its personality—its psyche. From each owner, something is left behind so that it becomes a collage of many disparate pieces. But if it has had one owner for a long time, the residue of that owner is everywhere.

You knew this the moment you set foot in the Ostermann house.

CHAPTER 1

Winning the coin toss was by no means a victory. I was the one sentenced to spend a day in Krivac following a lead from Ted Zelinski. Audrey would head down along the coast toward Corpus Christi. Little did we know that our lives were about to change forever.

I remember the afternoon well. Late August, hot, quiet, moody. I remember driving down the barren country road outside of Krivac. I remember the earthy smell of rolled hay from the fields. The turbulent sky filled with thick clouds tumbling and turning and spinning. A red-tailed hawk circling overhead—floating, hardly moving.

Pulling to a stop along the road, I glanced at the blue-and-white Jameson and Zelinski Real Estate sign. It wasn't the first of those I'd seen in the past three months. Before leaving Zelinski's office, he handed me the key to the house, saying he had been there earlier in the day and had left it open and that I should give the key a turn on my way out.

I swung the car into a gravel driveway. In front of me stood a two-story wooden farmhouse with a sharp-pitched roof and a large porch that spanned the entire front. Weather-worn paint, bleached by decades of harsh Texas sun, covered the outside. A stone chimney rose up the left side. Rivulets of ivy clung here and there to the house. The windows were flanked by thick brooding shutters, some closed, some partly open. A pair of Texas live oaks, green and healthy and as love-ly as you could imagine, arched tall over the house. Rising out of the ground, like the gnarled and twisted arm of Asmodeus reaching hopelessly for the sky, was an aged well pump with a gooseneck spout and a long handle, all much worse for wear. Farther on stood a white barn fronted by a pair of wide doors. Beyond all this, a pasture sprang into the distance where a copse of trees fanned across the back of the property, wrap-ping everything into a simple and neat package.

Getting out of the car, I could not help but stop at the barn. Nothing fascinates a city kid more than a barn, and I was no exception. There it was, looming before me as grand and beautiful as the Taj Mahal.

I went to the house and entered the living room, bare and still but for a few thin sallow curtains hanging next to the windows. The air was close and stale. I was hit with a blanched odor of old wallpaper, old paint, old dust, a hint of dry rot. A giveaway the place had been vacant for a hell of a long time.

As I turned, standing in the doorway of the dining room was a man. I backed up a step. Lean and tall, every bit of six-two, he looked at me with eyes as blue as artic snow and a face as worn as the house itself. His brow was thick and flat and wide. He wore denim overalls and a faded plaid shirt and a green John Deere cap bludgeoned from years of wear and tear. Short gray stubbles sprouted aside the rim of his hat and across his chin. He stood motionless, hands in his pockets, as though waiting to be introduced.

"Who the hell are you?" I asked.

"Blacek's the name. Charlie Blacek," he replied in a slow and deep drawl.

"What are you doing here?"

"Saw yer car out front and figured someone musta come by to see the place. Didn't mean to scare you none."

"Well, you did." I drew in a breath and tapped my chest. "You scared the hell out of me. I thought the place was empty."

"Sorry for that. Like I said, don't mean no harm." He pulled a pack of Chesterfields from his overalls and recovered a cigarette.

"You might wait on that, what with all the dry wood in this place."

He slipped the cigarette into the pack and put it in his chest pocket. "You thinkin' to buy the place?"

"Not sure," I said. "Just here to take a look."

"Well, look all you want, but some things you won't find with yer eyes."

"Oh? Such as?"

He didn't explain. Jingling coins in his pocket, he said, "This here's the old Ostermann place, but I guess you know that by now. If you wasn't from around here, and I somehow suspect yer not, you wouldn't know anything about it. But if you was from here, you'd know plenty...and I mean plenty." He stepped into the living room and looked at the walls and up at the ceiling. "It's old, all right. Likely over a hunnert, at least that much I reckon."

"A hundred and seventeen, so I'm told."

"Hunnert and seventeen. What d'ya know about that. Heck, I'm eighty-one and in all these years never been inside this place. That's why I had to come over and take a look. Live right down the road a lick. Lived there my whole life, in fact. Was born there, even. And never in all that time been in the Ostermann house. Not sure I've even been on the property. The Ostermanns...yup, they kept to themselves, all right."

I'm a pretty good judge of character. My instincts told me this Charlie Blacek fellow was probably as harmless as a cricket—a cricket in need of someone to chirp to. From the looks of the area when I drove in, listeners were few and far between.

"Michael Felton," I said, moving closer and extending a hand. Blacek gripped it with a palm that knew labor, rough and callused and almost too big for me to wrap my fingers around.

"Nice to meet you," he said, flashing a wide smile full of yellow teeth. "Like I said, I live down the road a bit. Got a stretch of land and a dozen head of cattle and a couple a hens and a sweet old German shepherd named Max with a hip near as bad as mine. The missus is gone now...passed on three years ago this November."

"Sorry to hear," I said, feeling a touch of sympathy for the old guy. I walked over to the fireplace—wide and deep and black. It had a marble mantle as fine and smooth as polished bone. This was no ordinary fireplace. You could roast an entire pig in it. I stuck my head inside and peered up the chimney. "House seems in pretty good shape to me, from what I've seen so far."

"Louise and her husband, Herman, owned it forever," Blacek said. "Can't say I remember anyone else ever living here. Ever. It was always Louise and Herman and their two sons. Herman died a while back and now it's just Louise. Kids is gone, grown and gone, and Louise is up in her eighties. Much too frail to keep up a place big as this. They took her out. Moved her to a home near Austin is what I heard. Don't know that as a fact but believe it to be so."

Wide strips of pine fitted snugly together with not so much as a sliver of space between them made up the floor. It crackled faintly like dry autumn leaves when you passed across it. Chestnut-brown hardwoods, never polished, never painted, trimmed the interior doorways. Age had given them dignity. The wooden window frames too, smooth and tawny. One wall had been papered eons ago. The others were painted, white probably. It was hard to tell. They had faded to a dull gray. Flakes of paint hung here and there from the ceiling.

I raised a window and nudged a set of stiff shutters and viewed the unkempt pasture dotted with bushes and thin saplings—spiny volunteers that sprouted across the field, quivering in the tremulous breeze. Clouds folded in a sepia sky like batter in a mixing bowl. The sun fell behind a cloud, sending pallid light into the room.

Blacek sniffed the air that drifted in the window. "Smell that? Uh-huh, that's rain. Coming for sure. Yup, it has that smell—that smell and that sky. See it? They call it *niebo diabla*... sometimes just *niebo*. It means 'the devil's sky' in Polish." I thought he was joking but it was clear he was utterly serious. "You can spot it right away. It has that funny color, that strange green cast. Kinda ugly, sorta sickly lookin'. Haven't seen one like that in a long, long time. If you grew up around here, you'd know about it. The old-timers hated it, used to say it was bad luck. Heard it a lot back when I was a kid. They'd look at the sky and shake their heads and say *obracając ciemno... obracając ciemno*." The words rolled off his tongue. "'Turning dark' is what it means. But it's more than just turning dark, though. What it really means is—"

"Well, sounds like a lot of nonsense to me," I said. "Nothing but storm clouds."

"Course it's nonsense. But doesn't stop people from believing it."

Even now, empty as the room was, you got the feeling it had once been meagerly furnished. You could imagine a chair, a sofa, a desk. A bookshelf, perhaps. A lone picture on the wall. Little else. A few scant and drab curtains hanging in stark stillness. Someone sitting there late in the day, bathed in the flat light from the window. I felt a small surge of sadness pass over me as I wondered about the years—decades, to be sure—that the space had belonged to someone else, to the Ostermanns. But I didn't know the Ostermanns, not as Charlie Blacek had described them. So, for me, it was the smell of oldness; the wood and the walls; the chilling stillness of the room; the tired, yawning fireplace; the floor that spoke as you crossed it—all of these things for no legitimate reason left me with a quick and strange sense of remorse.

The second floor was plain and simple—three good bedrooms, a small but sufficient bath, closets. At the end of the hall was a door to a narrow staircase that rose steeply to the attic.

Blacek looked up the stairs. "This one's all yers," he broadly announced, smiling an inconsequential smile and crossing his arms.

On the wall inside the door was an ancient light switch—one of those Pleistocene electrical relics with a knob you turn to feed juice through a scary cloth-coated wire up to a ceramic light fixture that dangles in the middle of the room. With sedulous care, I touched the knob between the tips of my thumb and fingers, ready to have every last follicle of hair on my body frizzled. I gave a slow twist. A pale glow lit the room above me.

At the top of the stairs I was enveloped in suffocatingly hot air that was baked into the attic by the terrible August furnace above the roof. I looked around the room. Gray light seeped in through two opaque windows, one at the west end, one at the east end. A pile of bric-a-brac and a stack of newspapers lay along the wall below the west window. In the middle of the room was a wooden milk crate and an old tilted and gimpy rocking chair. In it slumped a large doll with red lips and rosy cheeks and a thin gingham dress. Its hinged jaw was pivoted closed and its eyes were shut as if cast in a long and unfettered slumber.

Thick two-by-twelve beams made up the A-frame. Looking at these, I noticed areas of charred wood. I stood on top of the crate and focused my flashlight onto one of the spots, rubbing my thumb over it. As best I could perceive, it was the residue of a flame of some sort—a candle, maybe. The other spots were the same. Their sooty remains were geometrically oriented on the ceiling, suggesting the candles had been strategically located. Beyond that, I could tell little else.

Crossing the room, I peered out the west window onto a broad pasture of thin grass. I pulled a newspaper off the stack, a small local rag from the Krivac area, opened to the Real Estate section. In the left column, an ad had been circled in red ink: "Historic Ostermann House for Sale—Jameson and Zelinski—Krivac." It was dated June 2014. More than two years ago.

I went to the east window and glanced briefly at the barn. Starting for the stairs, I was stopped short in my tracks. There before me, sitting straight up in the chair, was the doll. Its chin had dropped and its mouth was agape as though caught in a moment of surprise or alarm. Its shiny-black agate eyes were wide open as though trolling me while I meandered through the attic. I all but expected its tiny elfin fingers to reach for me. "It's a stupid doll," I uttered and took to the stairs.

Down into the kitchen, Blacek at my heals. A surprisingly large space with a mineral-stained porcelain sink, linoleum-lined counters, a decrepit two-burner stove, and an ancient refrigerator dating to the forties or so. An old wooden table and two old chairs burdened with years of use and layers of worn and chipped enamel hugged the wall.

Above the sink, a window that hadn't seen a cloth in years looked out at the barn. Cabinets with glass-paned fronts— nice things that gave a glint of elegance to the room—hung on each side of the sink. To the left was a narrow pantry with a tier of shelves and two orphaned cans of Campbell's soup. Next to the pantry was a door—tall, narrow, half-closed. I gave the knob a tug. Three dry hinges groaned and stuck. Another tug and it opened.

"That fella there goes down to the cellar," Blacek proclaimed. "Coulda told you that the second we came in here. Root cellar. All the old places had 'em. Used 'em for storing food. You know—onions, taters, carrots, rutabagas…that stuff. You like rutabagas?" He fiddled with the Chesterfield pack in his breast pocket for a second, then tucked it safely away again. "Nope, never see cellars in houses much anymore. Kinda too bad, I think."

Blacek had that pegged right, about the cellar. The newer houses were built on slabs, most of the older ones were on blocks. You would never dig a hole in the ground and stick a house on top of it. Not in Texas, you wouldn't.

"You need to go take a look," Charlie Blacek said, directing a nod toward the stairs. "Cellars can be good places, but they can be bad places, too." He didn't explain what he meant. "Need to know what yer gettin'."

"You been down there?" I asked.

"Me? Nope. Came in just before you did, while you was out there pokin' around by the barn."

I grabbed the railing along a set of steep wooden stairs and started down.

"You be careful, now. No need in gettin' hurt," Blacek called from up above. "And watch out for the…" His voice trailed off as I stepped into the cellar.

What a place. As dark and mysterious as a mausoleum. Still and lifeless and filled with chalky air. The walls, rugged as in the catacombs, were made of craggy irregular stones that formed the foundation of the house. The room had a bare dirt floor. It bore a mustiness that comes from years of accumulated detritus deposited in miniscule amounts over time. Dampness hung in the heavy air. There was an old can of motor oil, and a couple of cans of paint, and a shovel and a small rusty pick, and an ancient kerosene lantern, but there was no evidence the room had been used in years.

A patch of dirt on the floor and part of the wall was stained black. Ageless Ball canning jars rested on a plain wooden shelf. I picked up a jar, shook off a layer of dust, returned it to the shelf, and walked on. A cobweb stroked my brow. Sweeping it away, I moved into the caliginous shadows. Stopping in the center of the room, I looked back up the stairs. Even the light from the kitchen seemed unwilling to venture very far down.

I walked along the damp wall until I came to the far end. As I stood in the glum darkness, a tingling sensation whipped down my spine. The skin on my back twitched. For a split second I felt as if I were not alone, as though something—someone—was nearby, right there next to me. I waved the light around the room and poked the paint cans and the old lantern with my shoe. Crouching, I rubbed a finger over the patch of blackened earth. It had an odd gritty texture.

I moved farther in, stopping several times to pan light across the walls and ceiling. Then it came—three clicking sounds. I held as motionless as a cat on the hunt, waiting for a reason to move. Once more, three clicks. Where they had come from, I had no idea. Little of anything in the room could have caused them. And then again—three more clicks, just like the others. Were they coming from the wall? Not possible. From behind the wall? Less than possible. I cupped my hands against the stones and listened, but heard nothing.

As I started to turn, a blast of vertigo hit me. I stopped, caught my balance, and rubbed my eyes, shaking my head. Fast as it had come, the sensation was gone. What had caused it? The dark and murky cellar itself? That alone was more than enough to give one's head a spin.

But something even more striking happened. A rancid, putrid odor hit my nostrils. I pulled back and fanned my hand across my face. Like the vertigo, the smell was gone in seconds. That was the strangest part of all because vertigo comes fast and leaves fast. But odors? I touched the side wall. It was warm, yet the room was temperate and cool.

I heard Blacek's size thirteens treading across the floor above me. I climbed the stairs, looking over my shoulder the whole way up.

"Well, you survived," Blacek said, with something akin to relief as I stepped into the kitchen.

We wandered out to a small pond in the middle of the untailored fields. At long last Blacek pulled a cigarette from his pocket and snapped a match in front of it. He took a drag and let it out slowly. "So where're you from, anyway?" he asked, popping a question that seemed to have been bugging him from the beginning.

"Houston."

"Houston, huh? Guess you don't know much about this area then, do you?" he replied.

"Krivac, you mean?"

"That's right, Krivac...little old Krivac, Texas. Population nine hundred and sixty-three, if you believe that sign out on the edge of town, and depending on what happens at the clinic during the night." He knocked an ash off the tip of his cigarette. "Fact is, Krivac doesn't get a whole lotta folks looking to move in. It's not that kinda place. Understand, now, there's nothin' wrong with it. It's just that…how would you put it? There's not much interest in these small towns nowadays. More people movin' out than movin' in. And the ones that stay…well, they get pretty set in their ways. Don't like change. Nope. Like everything the way it is. And be aware—they's always a good dose of superstition in these places. Like the funny ideas people had about the Ostermanns. No changin' that." Blacek watched the rolling clouds. "Course, every now and then we do get a few folks like you coming out from the city looking for a place. It doesn't always go so well, though. Pretty dern quiet out here, wouldn't you say? Yup, pretty dern quiet. Some folks can't take it. The quiet, I mean. Drives 'em a little…sorta stir crazy." He looked at me to catch my reaction. "Well, nuffa that."

"So who owns the property over there?" I said, viewing the field next to us.

"Clausens. They ranch it."

"No cattle, no crops anywhere," I remarked. "Just a lot of land. A bit odd, isn't it?"

"Not really. They have some cattle on the other end, I think. None on this side. Seen a couple of brown bales— hay, that is—out in the field. Says something's going on over there. Have this part fenced off, though. Ever see such a good fence? Clausens keep it in right nice shape, don't they? Nice posts, brand new barb. No need to worry about cattle or nothin' wandering over here, that's for sure. You know what they say—good fences make good neighbors."

"And across the road, what about that?"

"Another family. Not sure who."

I looked at the far end of the property. "That's strange. What's out there?"

"Out where?" Blacek said, squinting and fingering a stretch on the corners of his eyes, cigarette swaying from his mouth. Smoke drifted from his nose.

I motioned to a path that snuck through a strip of bushes.

"That? Goes to the graveyard."

"Graveyard. For what?"

"Dead people." A fugacious grin washed across Blacek's face. He tossed the stub of his cigarette on the ground and snuffed it out with the tip of his shoe, giving it several quick twists. "Ah, it's not much all in all. Kinda in disrepair from what I hear. Just a dozen or so graves. A few from the Ostermann family and some of the folks before them. Herman's out there, Herman Ostermann...buried. A little beyond that, there's an old Indian burial mound."

We turned and headed back to the house. A warm misty rain began to fall. I locked the front door. "Give you a lift down the road, Charlie?"

"Thanks, but no thanks. Walking's good for the old ticker, they say." He delivered one of his smiles and pulled a cigarette from his pocket and lit up. He removed his hat and rubbed a thick palm across sparse gray stubbles and stared at the house for a while, then placed his hat on his head. "Well anyways, if yer thinking of buying the old place, think real well. That's what I say."

CHAPTER 2

Like most things in life, this started simply enough. Houston, May 2016. I came blowing in the front door at ten thirty one night from Monclair University where Audrey and I were professors. Bushed, wiped out, used up, I aimed two dead eyes at Audrey. In barely more than a moan, I said, "Dammit, Aud...if we're going to bust our ass like this all day and half the night, we need a place we can get away to. That's all there is to it."

It had been one bad semester, the kind that goes on forever. Five desperate months in purgatory. But now, at last, it was nearly over. *Requiescat in pace.*

And so, on that night at the end of the spring semester, we hatched the idea of buying a house in the country. We made a list of the minimal requirements. It went something like this: not too close to Houston, not too far from Houston, an hour or two by car, out in the country, clean air, a bit of land, peace and quiet, the more isolated the better.

For a full three months we went over every speck of land a hundred miles north, west, and south of Houston, and ended up with nothing but a disgustingly long—no, make that *depressingly* long—list of useless houses. Unbelievable trash heaps going for a hundred grand. Lavish estates for a million plus. It was a numbing experience. Absolute, sheer drudgery. Being trapped with a loquacious real estate agent for four or five bromidic hours was not our idea of fun. Given a chance, they can make your average car salesman seem like Pope Francis. Worse yet, we had ruined a perfectly good summer. Funny how things go. You start off doing something, get yourself committed to an idea, and you can't come up with a good reason to quit.

August arrived. The fall semester was coming at us like a freight train. Soon we would once again be buried under an avalanche of courses and classes—never mind my book contract that was sucking wind. It was time to shit or get off the pot. No more traipsing across empty Texas back roads. We had all but given up on our house search. *Que sera, sera.*

Saturday morning, the last weekend in August, I had just cracked two eggs into a frying pan when the phone rang. "It's Ted Zelinski," I said.

Audrey rolled her eyes. With a single short sigh, the sparkle of the morning fell from her face.

"Hey, what's up, Ted?" I asked.

"Michael, have I got a hot one for you, have I ever." His voice burst with glee. "What's the chance you can make it out here today?"

"Not sure," I said, leaving ample room to maneuver. "I'll check and get back."

By now, Ted Zelinski was nigh a member of the family, that brother-in-law you can't quite like and can't quite hate. The one that brings cheap wine—screw cap—to a dinner party. Or no wine at all.

Many an afternoon had we trundled through one house after another with Ted Zelinski. He ran a small real estate office out in the Texas borscht belt—two hours west to Schulenburg, ten minutes to Hallettsville, a mile out to the small blithe town of Krivac. An area settled late in the nineteenth century by a wave of Polish, Czech, Russian, and German immigrants who had flooded in with the dream of land. Vestiges of them lurked everywhere. In the culture, in the food, in the genes—the faces.

Much as we didn't want to blow another Saturday with Zelinski, we decided to take him up on his offer. Audrey suggested we divvy up the chores, double down on our chances, go for broke and then probably forget the whole sad affair once and for all.

Hence…the coin toss.

CHAPTER 3

Zelinski was sitting with his feet up on his desk reading the newspaper when I returned to his office. A window AC unit purred like an electric cat.

"I was just coming out to see you," Zelinski said, springing from his chair. "How'd it go, Michael? Some water to wash away that Texas dust?" He pulled an Ozarka bottle from a small refrigerator.

I tossed Zelinski the key. "All locked up."

"So tell me—what do you think about it...the Ostermann place?"

"Not sure. What's the deal with the price?"

"Like it? You'll never get a bargain that good again. Ever!"

It didn't jive. I pulled out my cell phone and punched a string of numbers into the calculator. Ninety-four thousand five hundred dollars. Sixty-three acres. I stared at what came up as if I were looking at my Mega Millions number. Turning the phone to Zelinski, I said, "There it is, Ted, fifteen hundred bucks an acre. When have we seen land going for that?

Never. And that's without the house or anything else. Just the dirt."

Zelinski leaned proudly back, hands clasped behind his head. "That's why I wanted you out here today. This is the bargain of the century," he boasted. "Old lady Ostermann needs to get rid of it. Sorry to put it so bluntly, but it's the truth. She doesn't want it hanging over her. It's that simple. And as soon as I heard about it, I thought, it's yours. It's got Audrey and Michael Felton written all over it. Every last inch of it."

"You have dozens of listings in that window out there and all of them are two times, three times, four times as much," I said.

This was mere music to Zelinski's ears. If anything, it perfectly reinforced his initial supposition about the house being a colossal steal.

"How long has it been on the market?" I asked. I told him about the newspaper in the attic with the Jameson and Zelinski ad.

He dodged the question. In a low and hidden voice, he said, "Look, I'm gonna level with you, Michael. I always have, haven't I? See, we don't do much selling over here in Krivac. This is a satellite office for us. A year from now, it'll probably be gone. Schulenburg is where the real money is. Schulenburg and Hallettsville. Shiner, even. You list a corner strip mall out there and you come away with a big bucket of clams. I like the commercial stuff. Oh, sure, I'm happy to turn over a ranch or a house now and then, but I want to do it as quickly as I can. And, of course, I'm happy to help you folks out. And here, look what happens—you come out of this big winners, and I mean big. Bingo, you hit the jackpot."

Something still wasn't right. The more Zelinski prattled on, the less convinced I became. Something was rolling around in that cabeza of his, and he wasn't saying. Picking up quickly on my feelings, he searched for another approach.

I said, "I ran into a character out at the house. A fellow named Charlie Blacek. Ever hear of him?"

"Blacek? Sure, who doesn't know Charlie Blacek? He rides that ancient tractor of his into Krivac every few weeks for groceries—'fixins,' he calls them—fixins and a couple of sixes of Lone Star."

"Nice old guy. Talked a lot about the Ostermanns. Seemed to think they were a little strange."

Zelinski tipped forward and laughed. "Strange? Strange?" he gushed. "Everyone out here's a little strange. Find me someone that's not. This is Krivac, for Pete's sake."

"Is there something about the house we should know? We have more than enough weirdness in our lives just working with college kids. Surprises we can do without."

"Okay, here it is. The weirdness is that I could sell that place for a lot more than what old lady Ostermann wants. That baby is solid as an English castle. The problem, though, is that it's way too old for the likes of most people out here. They come rolling in here every day—'show me something new, show me something new'—that's what I get. No one wants a fixer-upper anymore. But that place can be whipped together in a flash and it wouldn't take much work. Slap some paint around inside and out, a good cleaning, simple stuff like that. Do that and you got yourself a true-to-life Norman Rockwell. But do you want to hear something even more weird? Do you know I could sell that place for a heck of a lot more *without* the house? Get a load of that."

I wasn't sure I had heard him correctly. "Without the house," I said.

"That's right, without the house. You know, the Ostermanns and all that malarkey—the small-town superstition crud."

I thought about Charlie Blacek's similar comment.

"Or maybe someone would buy it up, tear it down, and roll in a great big double-wide. You've seen them, I'm sure. The trailers, I mean. What a shame."

"So what *is* the deal with the Ostermanns? And besides, they're gone now, so how could it matter today?"

"Old habits die hard, Michael. You know that."

"According to Blacek, and he seemed to know everything about the area, according to him—"

"Well, I wouldn't put much stock in what Charlie Blacek thinks," Zelinski retorted, clearly wanting to leave Blacek out of the equation. "All right. What I *can* tell you is…okay, yes, some folks out here had funny attitudes toward the Ostermanns. I heard it, we all heard it. But it was only because they were so reclusive. Funny thing is, I never actually met Louise Ostermann herself...or Herman, for that matter. Hardly anyone had. What happened was that one day this fellow walks in here—sharp, dressed to the nines—and says he wants to put the house on the market...the Ostermann house. Never saw him before; no idea who he was. But a sale is a sale, right? It all checked out legit. And so..."

Zelinski stopped speaking. He reached for his Ozarka bottle, took a small sip, and set it slowly on his desk as though contemplating some deep thought. He had the look of one who would be happy to have this conversation done with, finished. Happy to hear the words, "Okay, Ted, I'm sold. We'll take it." But I was not in the least ready for that. Not now, maybe never.

"Where was I?" he asked, picking up his water bottle.

"And so..."

Zelinski smiled. "Yes. Well, it is true, people thought the Ostermanns were...I don't know what they thought, if you need to know. But the fact is, this is not about the Ostermanns. It's about the house and the land and the barn. What a package. We spent three months—Audrey, you, me—plowing through every kingdom and every rat hole this side of Valhalla. Scores of houses. Nothing we've seen even comes close to what you're getting from that place out there. You and Audrey wanted quiet, right? Well get ready, it's just you and the ants. Now don't get me wrong. I know what you're thinking, Michael, but I'm not trying to talk you into it. I always say that buying a house is the second most important thing you do in life. The first most important thing is a fill-in-the-blank—everyone makes up their own top list. But house buying comes in second every time."

Zelinski was on a roll again. He wanted a sale—that was obvious as hell. If I'd learned anything at all about him, I knew that he was no piker when it came to peddling houses. But what I couldn't figure out was why now, and why the Ostermann house? This wasn't the first "bargain of the century" he had shown us.

"Do this," Zelinski said. "Think about it. Come back tomorrow. Bring Audrey and take another look."

The rain was coming down straight and steady. I headed out I-10 thinking about the house and Ted Zelinski and Charlie Blacek. Yes, the house was a close fit to what we were after, with or without Zelinski's hard sell, his blue-light-special promos, which were hard to reconcile given that he was not the type to let a pearl slip away for peanuts. Not Zelinski! What was he up to? Was he trying to sell the house or dump it? Why? Even stranger, I had the feeling he wanted us to buy it. Yes, *us*...me and Audrey. Not Peter Piper or Old MacDonald or anyone else. *Us!*

Of course, Zelinski was probably right when he said the house would be easy to whip into shape. A good cleaning, throw some paint on the walls, new furniture. It was a fixer-upper, after all, and a little fixer-upping is all it would take. And yes, the price was...well, was beyond good. The land alone was worth a lot, a hell of a lot more than what Louise Ostermann wanted. That was instantly clear. And even if, God forbid, the old house and barn were to go up in a blaze, the value of the land would stay high. Possibly even increase as Zelinski had claimed.

So what was the deal, then? The place could have untold problems, of course. Face it, there could be a thousand and one things wrong with it. Perhaps the old lady hadn't paid her taxes. Perhaps the beautiful pine floors and hardwood trims were teeming with termites slowly boring through in one big, all-you-can-eat, gastronomic smorgasbord, ready to bring down the roof. Or was it...was it that Zelinski couldn't get anyone in the area to bite?

I slipped Bob Mamet into the CD player to drown out the *slap-slap, slap-slap* of the windshield wipers and turned my attention to the highway, trying not to become roadkill in the thick bumper-to-bumper, eighteen-wheeler, six-lane, white-knuckle, rain-drenched traffic—gripping the wheel for all it was worth.

CHAPTER 4

I walked across campus, weaving my way under the shade of glorious old Texas live oaks and across brick sidewalks and through arched passages toward the Humanities building of Monclair University, Houston's fine and fabled old school.

On Sunday, Audrey and I paid a visit to the Ostermann house as Zelinski had suggested. We picked through every inch of it, top to bottom. Holding a small powwow afterward, Audrey recommended we grab it and get our lives back to normal again...and, who knows, maybe even end up with some down-home peace and quiet—country style.

I resisted telling her about the noises, the clicking sounds, I had heard in the cellar, and said nary a word about the foul smell or the rush of vertigo that had sent me wobbling. I knew what she would say. She'd say it was just the clattering and clanking of the old water pipes, the staleness of the dirt floor, the crepuscule darkness of the room itself. I figured there was no point getting into a big stink about it given that I myself had no idea what had really happened.

Nor did I mention the doll with the rolling eyes and bobbling mouth I'd encountered in the attic—the doll that, I should add, was gone on my second trip to the house less than twenty-four hours later. As was the newspaper with the Ostermann house advertisement. Also gone. Who had taken them and why, I had no idea—but for sure they had been there on my first visit to the attic and were gone the second time around.

We made an offer to Zelinski, undercutting what Louise Ostermann wanted by full ten thousand. You could see the grief in Zelinski's face even though he had little wiggle room on the matter. Take it or leave it was my feeling, and the better part of me was hoping Ostermann would leave it.

Moving past a swarm of students on their way to classes, my cell phone rang. I pulled it from my pocket. It was Ted Zelinski. We talked for a few minutes. I thanked him and called Audrey. "Hey, hon, just got a buzz from Zelinski. Crazy, but the old lady took our offer."

"Oh, Michael, that's great," Audrey said in a flat voice that, if not teeming with joy, was at least filled with relief.

Two weeks later, we returned to the house to meet with the inspectors—a structural engineer, an electrician, and an exterminator for the termite inspection. The house was probed and poked inside and out like a marine recruit at an induction physical. By the end of the day, the reports were in.

The structural engineer, a short rotund man in his fifties with a face mottled by the sun and a scar of two inches or more that angled from just below his hair line to above his eyebrow, said, "Here, let me tell you about this place. First off, it's an old house, probably more than a hundred years."

"A hundred and seventeen, to be exact," I said.

The engineer nodded. "She's built on a stone foundation with a cellar—something you rarely see out here anymore. Thick stone foundation. From there, it's mostly wood frame. Wooden siding covers the outside. Most of the inside was at one time paneled with simple wooden slats. You can still see some of 'em in the upstairs closet. They were probably painted or maybe even covered with cheap wallpaper or thin fabric. That was common in a house like this years ago. Anyhow, along the way, someone put up drywall. It's old drywall from back in the fifties, I'd say. You can tell from the type of nails they used. The walls are sturdy, just a crack here and there, nothing serious. They haven't moved a lick in all the years. Nice and plumb...nice and even. That's good. The floors are original. Wide strips of pine. They're in pretty good shape. Someone may have put cheap carpeting over them at one time. Then it was torn out. The fireplace is good; the flue's open. I burned some paper...draws real well. The second floor and attic are fine, nothing unusual. Old bathroom and kitchen. Course, you knew that. But there are a couple of things I gotta show you."

"Oh? Like what?"

"Follow me."

He led the way into the cellar to the back wall where he aimed the beam of a DeWALT 12-volt flashlight onto the stones.

In the dim light, the scar on his face was more evident than ever—a shadow filled the groove forming an asperous line.

"See that there? It's the outline of an old doorway," he said, targeting light along the edge of it.

"Where?"

"Step back a bit."

We moved a couple of feet away. Sure enough, like viewing a Monet painting from a distance, I could make out what had probably been an entrance of some kind.

"You think that was an old doorway, huh?"

"Oh yuh, no doubt about it." He again ran light along the edge of it. "You could miss it easy, though, especially with that shelf there across the front, blocking the view."

"A door to what?"

"Nutha room." He tapped the back wall with a mallet, did the same on the side wall, then tapped the back wall again. "There you go. Notice the difference? Nothing but air behind this fella. Says there's a room back there, all right. Look at the stones they used to wall it off. They're different from the ones in the rest of the foundation."

Sure enough, the stones on the walls around the basement were a mishmash of sizes and shapes, probably collected from the property when the house was built long ago. You used what was close by, what was accessible—that's how you did it back then, the engineer explained. The stones in the doorway were slightly different, newer and cleaner. Someone had brought in a load of them to close up the entrance. It was a good match, but far from perfect.

"What do you think is behind it?" I asked.

"Won't know till you open her up...assuming that's what you plan to do. No need to do it now, though, far as I'm concerned. This isn't the first one of these I've seen in my days," he said, aiming his mallet at the entrance.

"It won't be a problem for the house, will it?"

"Meaning what, structurally?"

"Uh-huh, if we went in there?"

"Nah, that foundation there is a Sherman tank. But I suppose if you wanted to, you could open it before you sign the papers. Personally, I doubt you'll find much, so I wouldn't give it a whole lotta thought." The discovery seemed to have made his day, like stumbling across an arrowhead unexpectedly on a path in the woods. "Just the same, you need to be real careful down here. These places can trick you. That's how I got this little zipper here, down in an old cellar." He pointed with the handle of his mallet to the scar on his forehead. "Tripped and hit a rock on the wall. Big one with an edge sharp as a scalpel. Wife says it improved my looks." He slipped the mallet into the loop of his carpenter jeans. "Nuffa that. Got something else to show you."

He took me up to the coat closet by the front entrance and pointed to the floor. "That there's a trap door."

"Seriously...a trap door?" I said, squinting.

He got on his knees and pointed to a square about two feet by two feet. "Watch." He pulled out a screwdriver and pried the lid up, tilting it back on a set of rusty hinges.

Amazed, I stared into the hole. "Where's it go?"

"Corner of the basement. No stairs or anything down below. Just a small opening to the basement."

"Strange. What's it for?"

"Your guess," he said, looking up at me. "Could be a million reasons. May have been the original entrance to the basement before they put the door and the steps in the kitchen. In my book, that's not likely, though, cuz normally you access the basement from the kitchen, *not* from the front closet. You know, root cellar and all. Wouldn't make sense to go in and out of the basement from here, would it? So in all likelihood, this thing's been here a long time. From the very beginning, probably, but I can't tell you why. Anyway, *there it is.*" He set the lid down and gave it a tap.

"But aside from those few anomalies, everything else looks pretty good. Roof's okay. No evidence of leaks. No evidence of water coming into the attic. Even so, I'd get the shingles replaced sometime soon. They're a good twenty years old. Well, that's it," he said. "No surprises; nothing bad going on here. In fact, overall, this is a real solid old place."

So, too, with the electrician. "A few deficiencies, but nothing glaring," he said. "Most of the house has the original wiring from decades ago. Eventually, y'all might want to have the whole thing done over electrically. If nothing else, I'd get that light fixture in the cellar replaced sometime soon. And the one in the attic, too. Haven't seen a switch like that since chickens did have teeth. In general, though, the house is safe. Not in any imminent danger."

Then came the termite inspector. He walked us out to a corner of the barn. "Just one little area out here," he said. He reached down and held up a half dozen ant-like creatures that wandered aimlessly across his palm. "These here is termites. You'll find more out by that old woodpile next to the barn." He climbed out of his coveralls. "But the house itself is fine. Clean as a tin whistle, as if the critters are afraid to go near it," he said with a full-throated *ha, ha.* "Dudn't matter, though. We got a saying out here. There are only two kinds of houses: thems that got termites and thems that's about to get 'em. For now, this place is pretty much in the second category. But I'd say get her treated all around just for good measure. That's my recommendation." We walked to his truck. He paused and gazed up at the house. "Quite a joint. Been by it a thousand times, passing down the road, but never—" His words broke off, as though he'd intended to say more but stopped. He retrieved an invoice from his hip pocket, handed it to me, and shook my hand. He gave a nod and left.

After everyone was gone, I took Audrey to the cellar and showed her the doorway the engineer had found, outlining it with my hand as he had done with the beam of the DeWALT.

Audrey looked around the cellar, sizing it up from what little she could see in the dim light.

My feelings about the house still unsettled, I said, "You don't think Zelinski knew about this, do you? That it had something to do with him trying to unload the place so cheap? We can still get out of it if we want."

Audrey shook her head. "Did the engineer say what's inside there?"

"No, of course not. He had no way of knowing."

"So we won't worry about it, then."

Odd logic, I thought.

"Okay, and what if it's filled with bones of dead bodies? *Then* what?" I asked.

"And what if it's filled with bags of gold?"

Better logic.

"Well, I never told you this, but the first time I was down here, I noticed a foul odor like something rotten coming from over here by the wall," I said.

Audrey sampled the air. "I don't smell anything."

"But you do have to admit, the whole thing is more than a little bizarre."

CHAPTER 5

By the beginning of September, the papers were signed and the house was ours. We bought simple furniture, painted the house inside and out, removed wallpaper, and hung curtains. The porcelain bathtub and kitchen sink were resurfaced. The old stove and refrigerator were chucked—back to Ralph and Alice Kramden, COD. Hardwoods were cleaned and waxed. I dealt with the electrical switch in the attic and the light fixture in the basement and came away with all my synapses still connected. The pump in the yard was given a generous layer of fire-engine-red Rust-Oleum. A security system was installed.

Now, my curiosity could wait no longer. In the cellar, I swept a rag across the back wall by the old doorway, wiping off years of dust and pulling away chips of mortar. With brighter light in the room, the shape of the entrance—six feet high and three feet wide—was fully evident. I removed a second stone, then a third. A big black hole gaped at me. Slowly, I stuck my arm into the void as far as my elbow and promptly pulled it out. Bending over, hands on my knees, I looked in but saw nothing. Nothing but motionless lampblack and empty air. I reached in again, this time to my shoulder, waited a second, and waved my arm in a wide circle. Nada. Poking my head inside was out of the question. Too much like a guillotine.

Audrey needed to see it. "Hey, honey, take a look at this," I said, calling up to the kitchen.

"Take a look at what?" she asked.

"Down here...and grab a flashlight."

Audrey stood in front of the hole, arms crossed. "Man, just like the engineer predicted. How weird is that."

"Yeah, weird indeed. In a hundred and seventeen years, people do a lot of weird shit, I suppose. I can't tell what's in there. Go ahead, put your hand in."

"Are you *nuts*? I'm not sticking my hand in there," Audrey said, backing away.

I worked on a stone, inched it forward and set it on the ground and wiped my face with the front of my shirt. Finally, I had opened a space a little bigger than the width of my shoulders. Just enough to squeeze through.

"All right, here goes." I looked at Audrey and sucked in a long breath and released it. "*Arrivederci*," I said, as I wiggled in headfirst.

I was barely inside when Audrey said, "What do you see?"

"Hand me the flashlight."

"Now you don't think the wall's going to cave in, do you, Michael?"

"Well, if it does, you've got a hell of a lot of excavating to do," I called back.

"What do you see?" Audrey asked again.

The yellow-white stream from my flashlight poked at the darkness. I was standing in a room maybe ten feet by twelve. The air had a lifeless chill to it—the intractable stillness of a tomb. It reminded me of a basement room in an old abandoned Victorian house that we played in when I was a kid in Chicago—the Hutchison place. The house sat vacant for a half-dozen years while the details of a grubby divorce were being worked out. We loved going into it, playing hide-and-seek throughout its fifteen empty rooms, up in its dark and bleak attic, down in its remorseful cellar. Everything about it spooked the shit out of me. Now, here was a room straight out of the Hutchinson place right smack in our cellar.

The moment I entered I felt a noticeable but subtle presence to the room—that odd feeling you get when you're in someone else's space, that sensation that makes you think you're not alone when you know you are.

A tingling shiver passed through me, then was instantly gone, exactly as had happened when I'd been in the cellar before we had bought the house.

Suddenly, I thought I heard a voice. Or was it just Audrey speaking to me from outside? No...no, it wasn't. "Shh," came the word, soft but sharp. My heart tickered. I stopped and listened for a moment and laughed and moved on. It was my shoe rubbing on the dry dirt floor. Had to be. I stepped deeper into the room. Again, "*Shh!*" it ordered. Was it *shh*, or was it *shoo*? I wasn't sure. Turning, I looked at the small square gap I had come through.

"What's going on, Michael?" Audrey called.

"Nothing. Looking around."

I ran the beam of light across the walls. They were made of the same random collection of stones and large rocks used throughout the basement, telling me it had been part of the original house, not some add-on that had come later. On each side wall was a heavy circular ring, big steel beasts about six inches across. I pulled on one, carefully at first, then with all my might. It didn't budge a fraction. Whatever its purpose, it was meant to hold a lot of weight.

I aimed the light on the ceiling above. Several thick beams—tarnished from age or possibly even smoke, I couldn't tell which—held wooden planks that extended across the ceiling. I searched the room for evidence of its last visitors, hoping it would provide a clue to its original purpose, its former use: a footprint, a nail, old storage remains left behind, a newspaper that could be dated, things like that.

"I'm coming out," I said. "The place is empty. I can't tell what it was used for, but whoever sealed it off didn't leave diddly."

At that moment, my eye caught the dull reflection of something half-embedded in the dirt floor. I reached down and picked up a metallic object about the size of a silver dollar. I aimed the light beam onto it and rubbed it with my hand.

It had a peculiar shape: nine flat edges each connected by spokes to a central portion.

"I found something. Here, take the flashlight." Squeezing through the opening, I handed the object to Audrey. "Check it out," I said, dusting myself off. "I have no idea what it is. Maybe an old coin or old charm of some kind."

It had the appearance of a finely minted piece of jewelry. On one side were odd symbols that resembled the letters of an archaic alphabet. On the other side, out on the edges, were three shooting stars with long streaking tails flowing behind them. It was remarkably heavy for its small size—probably three or four times the weight of an old Spanish doubloon I'd once owned.

Audrey fiddled with the object. She turned it around in her hand and bounced it up and down in her palm. "Bizarre thing. Funny shape," she commented. "Some kind of nonagram, you might say."

I told her about the grody feeling I'd had when I entered the room. "From what I can tell, it's been closed up for a long time. And there are these large rings embedded into the walls opposite each other. Big heavy dudes. I couldn't tell what they were used for. And the ceiling has dark blotches here and there. You know, soot from candles or something, sort of like what's in the attic. It was hard to say from down below in the dark." I patted dust off my sleeve and shirt and hair. "There's no doubt the room was part of the basement at one time, but let me tell you, it's a little fucking dungeon. I'd feel a whole lot better if we just opened it up. Can't really hurt...can it?"

In the afternoon, I went into Krivac to get a paint refill at a small Sherwin-Williams store on Main Street. Coming out, I saw Charlie Blacek putter down the road on his old green tractor exactly as Ted Zelinski had described, something destined for the Smithsonian if ever there was. He swung wide and pulled to the curb next to my car.

"Well, if it isn't Michael Felton," Blacek said, pushing in the throttle on the small dashboard. The engine coughed twice and stopped. "In here for some fixins, too?" He climbed slow and stiff off the tractor.

"House fixins," I said. "Paint."

Blacek sported one of his grins. "Yup, seen yer cars out front of the house, and Zelinski's sign is gone in the yard. Guess that means y'all bought the old place, huh?" He snagged a cigarette from his pocket. "Everything going okay? No surprises?"

"Nope, none. None but a room we found in the cellar."

Blacek bent forward at the waist, eyes opened wide. "Room? What kinda room?" he asked.

"In the basement along the back wall. One of the inspectors found it. It had been closed off with stones some time ago," I said.

Blacek waved an arthritic finger at me, brow turned sharply down. "Wouldn't go in there if I was you."

"Oh? And why is that?"

"Some things are meant to stay closed up, *that's* why. Someone closed it off and that someone had to be Ostermann himself. And he did it for a reason. Take my word for it. I know a few things about this stuff."

I wanted to laugh. It was pure superstition of the kind Charlie had doled out the first time I'd met him. I gave a wink. "Thanks, Charlie," I said in good humor, not telling him I had already opened the room and had already been inside. I climbed into my car and drove off.

In the middle of the night, I was awakened by something tugging at my sleeve. I turned to my left to find Charlie Blacek standing next to the bed. My heart revved. There he was, complete with denim overalls, faded shirt, and John Deere hat.

Lying flat, eyes full of sleep, I watched. It was Blacek, all right—head to foot. But his face was grayer and older and even more lined than ever, jowls as saggy as a basset's. His teeth were near brown and his eyes were thick and covered with opaque white cataracts. Purple clotted blood dripped from his nose.

He spoke, saying, "Didn't listen when I told you not to go in there, did you?"

Sleepy or not, he had my attention now. "You didn't say that," I uttered in a low, defensive voice, staring, feeling pinned to the bed. "What you said was—"

"What I said was, *don't* go in there!"

Thinking I was dreaming, just talking to the empty air, I squeezed my eyes shut for a couple of seconds and opened them to find the image of Charlie gone.

I got up and slinked my way to the bathroom, took a leak, and looked out the window at the light from the white moon that cast itself down onto the barn and glistened off the pond. The sky was clear but for a few high clouds. The wind, what little there was, rustled the leaves of the oak tree that stood guard by the back porch.

Starting down the hall to the bedroom, I had a sensation of being watched. Crazy, but I didn't turn to look, not immediately. Rather, I merely stopped and listened for a second and then, slow and even, rotated and glanced over my shoulder.

At the end of the hall near the far window was another image, this one of a pale and hazy man, someone I had never seen before. Dead yet healthy looking—both. It made no sense, but that's what I saw. It, he, whatever it was, stared at me with dark trenchant eyes. Eyes as dark and black as its hair and the black suit it wore and the black tie. I blinked and shook my head as if to clear my vision. Everything about it, everything but its face and eyes, was cloaked in shimmering vagueness.

"*Shh!*" it said. It was the same voice, the same word, I had heard in the cellar. It started down the hall toward me. Seemingly frozen in place, I watched as it passed by, turned at the stairs, and started down. For some intractable reason, I followed. Halfway down, it stopped, looked at me, and went on. Through the dining room, into the kitchen, and down into the cellar...it, me. The wooden cellar steps creaked and moaned—not when it passed across them, but when I did.

We arrived at the bottom. It had not turned on the light, nor had I, yet the room was visible in a thin veil of glowing illumination that emanated from the apparition before me. It turned and looked at me once again and headed to the back wall and proceeded straight through it. I twisted myself in through the small opening I had made earlier in the day. Once inside, the light from the form, the apparition, no longer penetrated the darkness. Instead, there was only a voice. Brusquely, it said, "This is the Ostermann house. It belongs to Ostermann. You could have left it the way it was, but you didn't. Now it's yours…now it's yours…*now* it is yours…*shh.*"

With that, the shape lit brightly and then dissolved like strands of smoke that fall apart in the open air.

I went upstairs and rolled into bed and fell asleep the second I hit the pillow, as though drugged.

In the morning, Audrey was already up and downstairs when I awoke. I lay in bed thinking about what had happened during the night. I had had a dream. So what? A long unsettling dream spurred no doubt by my visit into the cellar room earlier in the day, but a dream for sure. Nothing more, nothing less. A dream that for reasons unknown included Charlie Blacek, who probably had morphed into that other…whatever it was. But isn't that exactly how dreams go? They start out in one direction and quickly veer to the right or the left with no purpose. They have no logic; there is no timeline. It's the mind running in a frenzy of wild uncontrollable ADHD. Odd as the dream had been dark at night, it was good for a laugh in the morning. I felt better, because when you came right down to it, I was no worse for the wear and I only remembered a few specks about it at all.

I scuffed my way into the kitchen, gave Audrey a kiss, and reached for a mug from the cabinet. "How'd you sleep, hon?" I asked.

"Like a baby."

"Didn't pee in bed, did you?"

"Hope not. Say, you weren't down here last night, were you?" Audrey said.

"Down here?"

"In the cellar."

"No, of course not." I poured a cup of coffee. "What makes you think that?"

"Dirt…dirt from the cellar on the kitchen floor."

I rested the cup on my lip and smelled the coffee and took a sip and looked out the window at the barn. And thought.

Chapter 6

Three days later in Houston, I went over to the anthropology department and paid a visit to Dr. Philip Pollard, an archeologist Audrey and I had known for years. I showed him the nonagram, hoping he might shed some light on its origins.

He held it up and examined it with a magnifying glass. "It is intriguing. Very well crafted, I must say. It doesn't appear to be forged—pounded from a piece of heated metal is what I mean. Or poured into a mold. The whole thing seems to be silver or perhaps platinum. But if so, it's only coated. It's much too heavy to be solid silver. But the presence of silver would say a lot…let's just say it would help rule some things out. It would suggest that it's not particularly ancient, for example."

Pollard studied the object with the intensity of a stamp collector in possession of a rare acquisition. "The inscriptions are certainly…well, different. Some kind of zodiac-like writing or glyphs, but I can't really place this in any particular context."

"What's the deal with the shooting stars, Phil? What do you make of them?"

"These?" he asked, turning the piece over. "Not much, really. Nearly every culture that ever existed has used stars one way or another. Even the US flag has fifty of them. And right here in Texas, too. The Lone Star State. But the spokes are interesting to me." He counted them, enumerating each one as he went. "...seven, eight, nine."

"Why nine? Why not six...or twelve, or eight...or whatever?"

He glanced at me through his magnifying glass, his eye as big as a walnut. "Uh-huh, and why did the Egyptians build the pyramids?" He returned to the nonagram. "But I do know you can make a lot out of the number nine. It's one of those numbers that's had symbolic meaning for thousands of years. In some cultures, it represents finality or judgment. That's probably because it's the last whole digit before the number ten. It's also been used to describe the perfect movement of God. Nearly every religion going back to prehistoric times has placed special emphasis on the number nine. It pops up all over the place. Like the nine circles of hell in Dante's *Inferno*."

Pollard stopped talking as he examined the edge of the nonagram, holding it close to him. "But there's more to it than that," he continued. "About the number nine, I mean. More than people just incorporating it into their belief system. The number nine is mathematically unique in a very real way." He took a piece of paper and set it on his desk. "If you take any positive integer, any whole number, and multiply it by nine, you get numbers that always add up to nine. For example..." He wrote out the numbers 25 x 9. He punched these into a calculator and wrote down 225, then wrote 2 + 2 + 5 = 9.

"Give me another number," he said.

"Forty-six."

Pollard wrote 46 x 9 = 414. Then 4 + 1 + 4 = 9.

"Crazy," I said. "All right, try this. One thousand, two hundred, and eighty-eight."

Pollard wrote 1,288 x 9 = 11,592, and then 1 + 1 + 5 + 9 + 2 = 18. "Now we add the last two digits." He wrote 18 = 1 + 8 = 9. "You get nine."

"Huh," I said, intrigued. "Okay—five, eight, five, seven."

And wrote 5,857 x 9 = 52,713, which gave 5 + 2 + 7 + 1 + 3 = 18. And, of course, 1 + 8 = 9.

I took the paper and wrote out 16,182 x 9, and did the calculation. It came to 145,638, or 1 + 4 + 5 + 6 + 3 + 8 = 27, and 2 + 7 = 9.

"No matter how you do it, in the end, that's what you get—the number nine. No other digit from one to nine will do that."

"Never knew you were a mathematician, Phil."

"I'm not, but my brother is. He showed me that." He waited a second and said, "Here, I've got another one for you. In this, you don't multiply by nine, so in a sense, nine doesn't enter into the calculation at all. Pick a number."

I wrote 52,883.

"Add the numbers."

I did, $5 + 2 + 8 + 8 + 3 = 26$.

"Now subtract 26 from the original number."

I wrote $52,883 - 26 = 52,857$.

"Okay, add the numbers."

I wrote $5 + 2 + 8 + 5 + 7 = 27$, and said, "Two plus seven equals nine."

"You got it."

I did it again, this time using 72,641.

$7 + 2 + 6 + 4 + 1 = 20$

$72,641 - 20 = 72,621$.

$7 + 2 + 6 + 2 + 1 = 18$, and $1 + 8 = 9$.

"The other significant thing about the number nine is that it precedes the number ten, as we all know. The number ten is every bit as important, if not more important, than nine. The two are inextricably linked because nine comes immediately before ten. We could go on for the rest of the afternoon talking about the number ten. In a nutshell, it has importance because it consists of the digits one and zero. The number one is regarded by many cultures as representing matter, or God, if you will. Zero represents chaos, emptiness, disorder. Together, they signify life and death—one represents life; zero is death. Nine leads into the number ten, and the use of nine is often considered significant for that purpose. That's how it was in many ancient cultures. When you come right down to it, ten is the number of real importance, but of course you need nine to get to ten. Needless to say, we have no way of knowing if any of this has anything to do with this fella here," Pollard said, referring to the nonagram in his hand. "But it's an interesting thought. You see here, that's the problem with archeologists—we do a *lot* of freebasing with very little evidence." He held the nonagram up to the window light, looking it over with great care. "Nine…uh-yeah. And don't forget, cats have nine lives," he added, with a broad Cheshire grin. "And so where did you say you found this?"

"In a room in the basement of an old farmhouse we bought out in the country. The room had been closed off. It's strange, and I'm not sure what to make of it. So far, there's nothing revealing about it. Just an empty room with an entrance that was covered over with stone and mortar. We don't know why someone would do that. You'd think they'd have a reason."

"You'd think so," Pollard replied, still hunched over the nonagram as he spoke. "Old houses are peculiar, though. Years ago, we had a great old place when we lived in New England. A big house. Inside the front hall closet was a hidden staircase that went down into the basement. A secret staircase to the basement for no apparent reason. But my archeological sensibilities forced me to hunt for an explanation. I researched the house for months. Traced everything back as far as I could. And what I found was that the old place had been built just that way—with a cramped little staircase barely tall enough to stand up in and no wider than the shoulders of an adult. It was part of the structure of the house from the very beginning…

and that's all. I couldn't find anything more about it, why it was there, or what it was used for."

"I'm planning to open up the entrance," I said. "Can't be any harm in that, I suppose."

Pollard agreed. He handed me the nonagram. "I'm at a bit of a loss," he admitted. "It could still be just some kind of trinket, I suppose. I can have it examined further, if you want. Maybe give it to Cynthia Osborne when she gets back in town."

"Ah, it's probably nothing important. I wouldn't bother." I gave the nonagram a flip in the air and stuck it in my pocket. "Thanks anyway, Phil. You know how little things can get your curiosity going."

A feyish smile spread across Pollard's face as he swung an arm toward shelves laden with artifacts of every imaginable size, shape, feature, and dimension.

I got halfway to the door, turned, and said, "While we're at it, Phil, have you ever seen an apparition?"

"Seen a what? An apparition? No, can't say as I have. What brings that on?"

"Oh, I don't know. Have you ever heard of anyone seeing one? You know, sort of like a...a—"

"A ghost?"

"I don't know that I'd call it a ghost, exactly."

"You know, they say ghosts do exist," Pollard said.

I laughed.

"Me, I prefer to call them spirits of the dead," Pollard said.

"Maybe we'll just leave it there, Phil. Thanks."

He gave a nod and a "You betcha."

On the next trip to the house, I set the nonagram on the mantle. It was, after all, part of the old homestead.

For no special reason, while I was heading down into the cellar in the afternoon, I counted the steps...seven, eight, nine. Hmm. I stood at the bottom, looked up the straight and narrow staircase, and counted again. Nine. Each one quite tall, taller than you might expect or need, as if to structure the staircase to hold exactly nine steps. It made going up and down far more challenging than if there had been, say, ten or so. They could have put in ten steps, easily could have. Eleven or twelve would have been better yet. But no, there were exactly nine. The height of each step and the steepness of the staircase meant a nosedive was in the cards for sure without a good grip on the railing. I should never have talked to Pollard.

Then to the staircase that went to the second floor. Once again, nine steps. Each one tall, just like in the cellar, but at least the entire staircase was stretched out making the climb easier—but nine steps nonetheless. And what about the attic? You got it—nine, very similar to the ones in the cellar.

Yes, I should never have talked to Pollard.

Chapter 7

Time slipped by. Before we knew it, it was early autumn. We spent every weekend at the house, painting, remodeling, doing nothing.

Then came the issue of what to do with the room in the cellar. Should I open it up or close it off again? And be certain that I did have second thoughts about going in after my night watching Charlie Blacek standing by my bed staring down at me, gross and ghastly. And my encounter with the image that had escorted me into the cellar. Together, they had a bigger impact than I thought they might. Maybe just best to let sleeping dogs lie. Of course, I knew I could never do that—the millions of years of deep-seated curiosity embedded in our psyche prevent it. I knew from the day the structural engineer aimed the beam of his DeWALT on the back wall of the cellar that I would be heading in.

It took more than two days to remove the stones that covered the entrance. It was obvious that if secrets were to be found, I would have to work for them. And work I did.

Except for the first loose stones, the rest had been put in to stay, not meant to be messed with for a good long time. I chiseled away at the mortar piece by piece, chip by chip. Once I had removed enough stones, I secured a temporary wooden beam across the top and supported it with two-by-fours to keep the whole affair from caving in as Audrey had worried about.

With the entrance open, I gave the room a thorough inspection and examined the spots on the ceiling. Without doubt, they were the charred residue of something that had burned down below. Intentionally burned. Burned with regularity. Not once, not twice, but often enough to leave their telltale remains. Even more unusual, they had been set to form an almost perfect circle.

The metal rings on the walls staring at each other like pairs of wide-set hollow eyes defied explanation except for the obvious possibility that they had been used to lift tremendous weight or...or to tie something—someone?—to the wall. There they were, mute and leaden. As I stood in the room encased within thick stone walls, it was easy to conjure up a host of scenarios involving solemn rituals conducted deep within the subterranean recess of the old house. Root cellar, my ass!

I built a frame and jerry-rigged it well enough to hang a door—a simple but solid off-the-rack Lowe's concoction—and ran an electric line in and strung it to a small light fixture. Rube Goldberg, to be sure, but plenty of light for the room just the same. Standing back and gazing at my artwork, it hit me. The room reminded me of a wine cellar we had once seen in an old farmhouse deep in Auvergne in southern France. Cold stone walls, dirt floor. Voilà—this would become our wine cellar. Its past provenance, horrid or kindly or whatever history it held, would now give way to the delights of many a fine wines waiting to please the senses.

One Saturday in October, I drove into Krivac to buy a saw at the hardware store. On the way out, I was approached by a white-haired woman who said she had overheard me talking to the store owner, or so she claimed. I knew she had been tracking me as I walked down the narrow aisles of the store waiting for me to leave.

I was barely outside when she said. "Excuse me, I'm Ruth McDonald. I heard you say you bought the Ostermann house."

"That's right," I replied.

"There's a lot to do, I bet. Fixing up the old house and all."

"Some. We're not changing it much."

We walked down a sidewalk shaded by tall trees until we arrived at the courthouse.

"Tell me, Mr.—"

"Felton," I said. "Michael Felton…Michael."

"Well…um. Well…exactly how familiar are you with the Ostermann house?"

"In what way? We had it thoroughly inspected, if that's what you mean. It seems fine. Very sound, in fact, for its age."

"Well, I don't want to be an alarmist, but the house has a...how should I say? Has a certain history. It *was* cheap, wasn't it?"

"Economical is how I'd describe it. Nothing's cheap these days."

She stopped walking and looked at me. "I guess what I meant is that the house is well known in the Krivac area going back many decades. And I've been here longer than I care to admit. Louise Ostermann lived in the house all her life. Was born there eighty-some years ago. She lived in it with her husband, Herman, and their two sons, Adam and George. George, the youngest one, was always known as Bud."

Oh crap, here we go—another history lesson about the Ostermanns! We sat on a bench next to a looming statue of Stephen F. Austin, the father of Texas.

"The Ostermanns lived there a long time. What's so unique about that?" I asked.

"It's not that so much as...look, I know most everything that's happened in and around this town in recent memory. It has to do with the stuff that occurred at the house over the years. Strange stuff, weird stuff. Some people say it all stopped about the time Adam and Bud left. That's why a lot of the young folk out here don't know much about the house. But I know unusual things are still happening. *Lots* of unusual things."

"You're going to tell me it's haunted, is that it?" I remarked, laughing. "It's almost Halloween, after all."

Ruth was unfazed by my attempt at levity.

"Then what is this 'strange stuff,' as you put it?" I asked.

"Well, for years people in the area claim to have seen glowing lights on the property. Others say the Ostermanns held meetings, gatherings of some sort out in the fields."

"Maybe it was a religious ritual, a coven of witches or Wiccans, for example. That wouldn't bother me."

"It wasn't that."

"How do you know?"

"Sometimes there were thirty or forty people. This always occurred late at night. Nobody knew who the people were or where they came from. How they got there was unclear because there were no cars, no pickup trucks. Not even a horse and buggy. And you never saw any of them in town, either."

Good God, what are these people doing, keeping tabs on everything that happens out on some rural farm? "I don't know what the deal is with the lights," I said, "but the rest seems perfectly normal to me. People getting together out on the Ostermann property…could be anything."

"When you get that many people coming out to an area like this, people notice. It's impossible not to. Where did they come from?"

I shrugged and shook my head.

"Have you talked to Louise Ostermann?"

"The sale of the house was handled by a real estate agent and a lawyer," I said. "There was no chance for us to talk to her. Or any reason to, for that matter."

Ruth went on. "To this day, you can't raise so much as a single head of cattle on that land, I'm told. Never see any deer, either. Or rabbits, or raccoons, or opossums. None ever on the property."

"That's not true," I said, peeved, telling her that on that very morning I had seen three big, healthy deer out in the pasture and the trees were full of birds. "I don't know what you're getting at."

"And that fence, the one over between your place and the Clausens'. Notice how nice they keep it."

"Good fences make good neighbors," I said.

"It's more than that. Have you wondered why it's always in shipshape? Probably the best stretch of fence in all of Lavaca County. Next to perfect, I'd say. Lavaca County, Fayette County, Gonzales County—anywhere in these parts. Not a single post missing, not a single strip of broken barb anywhere. Know why?"

"Surprise me."

"Cuz they don't want anything of theirs roaming over onto the Ostermann property, *that's* why. Don't want to recover one of their steer from your place and try to get it back into the herd. Anyway, it would be hard to do. Oh sure, you could march it down the road, but you wouldn't want that fella back in the herd with all the rest. Not after it had gotten... well, after being on the Ostermann property."

What a bunch of hogwash, I thought. I told her it sounded ludicrous.

Ruth looked at me with the face of an annoyed school-marm about to rap my knuckles with a ruler. "You're right," she said, her expression gradually softening. "I should never have brought it up." There was a long pause, and she added. "Well, anyway, it was…it was good to meet you, Mr.—"

"Felton."

She got up and started off.

I sat on the bench and stared at the ground, thinking about what she had said, when presently I heard, "Oh by the way, Mr. Felton, do you have kids?" It was Ruth McDonald again.

"No, it's just Audrey and me. Why?"

Ruth McDonald sighed heavily as though in deep relief, but never expanded on her query. "I live in town. You can find me here if I can be of help." She pushed a smile and left.

At first I hadn't planned on mentioning this to Audrey. Who the hell was this Ruth McDonald person, anyway? She struck me as one of those flakes I'd always associated with small towns but had never actually met. The kind who come up to you and start talking for no reason. We don't do that in the city; we keep to ourselves. On a bus or subway, we stare straight ahead, avoiding contact with everyone around us. After all, who wants to encourage a conversation with some guy wearing a T-shirt that says Ask Me about Redemption? It was different in the country, apparently. I wasn't used to the new rules.

"I think you have to take this with a grain of salt," Audrey said when I told her about my encounter in Krivac.

"Yeah, I know, Aud, but remember when I told you about Charlie Blacek's warnings the first time I met him?"

"Charlie Blacek, what does he know?"

"Yeah, but now here's this person saying the same thing."

"It's just small-town chatter, Michael. That's all. People butting into our business. It may be their way of testing us, the newbies. Their way of provoking us. Who knows?"

"You think so?"

"Sure, why not?"

I sat in one of the old kitchen chairs we had deposited on the back porch. "But what if there really *is* something to it?"

Audrey came over and straddled my lap facing me, arms on my shoulders. "How? In what way?"

"I'm not sure, babe. About the property, let's say. You know, maybe there's something peculiar about it. We didn't check into that when we bought the house, did we? And this stuff about the Ostermanns. What about them? Suppose they—"

"Look, we've been here for weeks and nothing weird has happened, has it?"

"What about the room we found in the cellar? That was pretty damn weird."

"Not really. Someone sealed it off, that's all. There could be a million and one reasons," Audrey said. "Don't forget, this is a small country town. What do people have to do out here? Someone cooks up a story and someone adds on to it and before you know it, pretty soon it's a legend. That's how I see it. We bought a house that's tied to an old legend. So what? Every house, if it has any years on it at all, has *some* kind of history to it."

I said, "This Ruth McDonald person brought up the thing about the Clausens' fence. You know, the one over there on the east side." I aimed a thumb in the direction. "Talking about how good the Clausens keep it. Funny, but Blacek said the exact same thing the first time I was out here with him."

"They like their fences in good shape. What's wrong with that? In fact, I did see someone, Clausen possibly or one of his people, fiddling with the fence this morning up by the graveyard. I gave him a friendly wave, you know, neighbor and all. He looked over, tilted his head a bit…Texas nod, I guess. Seemed nice enough, though. I think little Miss Nosey you met in town could have spun the whole thing just to see how you'd take it. Who knows, she's probably a lonely old woman who needs someone to talk to."

"I don't know…maybe you're right."

"Enough about the Ostermanns, okay?" Audrey said. "Tell me, did you get what you wanted at the hardware?"

"Yeah. Cool place. A great old store." I pulled Audrey close to me. "Did I ever tell you that you have fantastic eyes?"

"Ooh, now, let's see, about a thousand times, maybe."

"That's *all?*"

"Okay, two thousand times."

CHAPTER 8

Audrey had classes to teach. She left for Houston early Sunday night. I stayed at the house and worked on my book most of Monday, did some chores on the property, and repeated the pattern on Tuesday. I made good progress on all fronts and was pleased with what I accomplished.

In the evening I prepared a simple meal: steak on the grill, salad, baked potato. Afterward, I went to the front porch and sat in one of the old wicker chairs we had purchased at an antique store in Krivac. No sooner had I planted myself than I saw Charlie Blacek's John Deere putter down the road and pull into the driveway. He killed the engine—two short burps—and climbed the steps to the house. Wide yellow grin and six-pack of Lone Star under his arm.

"I'm bettin' you could use some company," he said, holding the beer up in front of him.

"Read my mind, Charlie. And I never refuse a man with beer."

"Not just beer…Lone Star Beer." He settled slowly into a chair, his face half-hidden in the shadows of the low-watt porch light. I made a quick study, trying to connect him up with what I had seen glaring down at me in my queer dream.

Charlie popped a can and handed it to me, foam fizzling onto the wooden porch slats. He opened one for himself. "Always say, good to get to know yer neighbors." Charlie's tone was more snoop than statement, but I didn't mind. "Here's to the house."

"To the house."

He snagged a cigarette from his breast pocket, placed it between his lips, and deftly struck a match with one hand and lit the cigarette, sucking in a long smooth drag. Smoke drifted from his mouth. "As nice a night as they get out here. This time a year, it's my favorite. Corn's in the bin, kinda like money in the bank. Good time to count yer blessings, innit? Me and Emma—that was my wife—me and Emma always liked these days best of all."

The sun was gone. The sky was long and dark but for the light from a big orange harvest moon slung low on the horizon. A flickering breeze flushed across the porch.

Charlie sat quietly for a while. "Reckon I need to apologize for something," he said, his voice open and sincere.

"Apologize? Apologize for what?"

"The other day in Krivac when I jumped on you about that room you said you found in the basement. Should've not said anything. Wasn't none of my business."

"Ah, forget it, Charlie. I have."

"I mean it. Country people don't like others pokin' into their business. It's kind of a creed out here. You do your thing, and I'll do mine. That's the rule."

"I get it," I said. "No problem." I took a swig of beer.

"That's good," Charlie said, and added, "So what'd you find, in the basement?"

I laughed so quick I choked on the beer. I wiped my lips across my sleeve. "Empty old room."

"You figure the Ostermanns closed it off for a reason?"

"Must have, but hard to know why." I considered telling him about the nonagram I'd found but didn't, afraid of what new neuronal adventure of Charlie's it might send us on.

"I heard when I was a kid that old man Ostermann had secret rooms in the house and that he kept people locked up in them. That's what I heard. Course, it was mostly kids' talk. No one ever knew if it was true or just a lotta baloney. One of Emma's friends when we were teenagers said she had proof of it. Course, she didn't."

"Well, this room was empty," I said.

"No bones or nothin'?" he asked.

"No bones or nothin'."

"They claimed Ostermann had people tied to the wall down there. Suppose that's why I reacted the way I did the other day. Didn't want you findin' somethin' bad if you went in."

Nor did I tell him about the large iron rings that were embedded in the walls. Best to let that dog lie, too.

He leaned back in his chair. "Figured as much. Rumors and kids' talk, that's what it was." He stared at the ceiling fan, watching it as a cat might as it rotated in an endless repetitive circle. "Who would ever believe I'd be sitting in this chair on this porch?" he remarked, eyes on the ceiling. "Eighty-one years, and now this."

The current from the fan pulled cigarette smoke up in a thin stream, spreading it into the dark night. I had quit smoking decades ago, but the smell of burning tobacco was at times a temptation even though I was long past the temptation phase. A cigarette and a beer—that part I still remembered all too well.

Charlie rubbed the tip of his cigarette against the inside of an old coffee can he brought from the tractor, a makeshift ashtray that he kept dangling from the dashboard on a loop of wire. He began talking about the graveyard. Not the small one where Herman and others had been tucked away but the Indian burial ground that was located a little ways beyond. You could tell Charlie was long on local history, that he lived in the past, and that he liked it that way. It was something I had noticed before in many people after they got to a certain age— the connection with the past and the reluctance—or perhaps just the inability—to occupy the present or probe the future. Maybe there just wasn't enough hope left for the future.

Charlie popped open another pair of beers and handed one to me. He took a sip and belched politely and snapped a match in front of a cigarette.

"The Waumtauk Indians ruled these areas at one time. They were a lot like the Tonkawa, another tribe here in Texas. The Waumtauk had their own special view of life and death. That burial mound out there is Waumtauk, pure Waumtauk. I know that for a fact cuz one of my grandmothers was Waumtauk. She told me all about them when I was a little nipper. Won't find no Waumtauk out here today. They're all but gone. Killed or run off or left. Lost their land. But believe me when I tell you, the Waumtauk is still here. Oh yeah, don't think they're not. As long as they're out there," he poked a thumb toward the back of the house, "as long as they're out there, they're still here. Some folks thought Herman Ostermann was Waumtauk, or part Waumtauk, but I know better. He may have known a lot about them, but he was no Waumtauk."

Now I realized that the Waumtauk was the real reason for Charlie's visit, companionship and beer notwithstanding, but I had no idea why it mattered.

Charlie's face was as pale as white chalk in the bated glow of the porch light. Speaking in a low and guttural voice that carried the moment, he said, "Let's just say it's no coincidence those graves of the Ostermanns and the others is right there practically next to the Waumtauk's." He never said what he believed Herman Ostermann had learned from the Waumtauk except to say that the Waumtauk never die. The burial is never a burial. The end is never an end.

Before I knew it, we had killed off Charlie's six-pack and a couple of hours with it. He pulled a silver pocket watch from his overalls, flipped the lid, and delivered a short murmur of surprise. Rising stiffly from the chair, he apologized again, this time for filling my head with useless nonsense. He lumbered off the porch and hung the ashtray back on the dashboard. From below the seat he recovered a crank, pulled the throttle halfway, went to the front of the tractor, and gave the shaft several short snaps until the engine sputtered, fired, and purred. He climbed aboard and signing off with a simple nod, made a large wide loop and took to the road at a good twelve miles an hour.

I sat for a while in the coolness of the evening. My watch said eleven-thirty. Charlie's tales had stirred my curiosity enough to entice me to trudge through the dark and murky pasture to the row of bushes that led into the graveyard. But it was not the graveyard itself that I was interested in. I continued on for a short distance, twenty-five or thirty feet, hardly more, until I arrived at a slight rise in the ground.

The moon, now straight up in the sky, sent creamy light onto the mound. Realizing I was standing next to an ancient burial site, I backed off and looked at it in the unfettered silence that surrounded me. For a second, I thought I heard a voice—a voice or…oh, shit—three clicks. They did *not* come from the Indian mound, of that I was certain. They came from behind me, from the Ostermann graveyard. Immediately, I felt the hot breath of someone standing at my back. Turning quickly, I found Charlie Blacek's big, angular frame not two feet away. He looked at me and in a gular voice said, "Knew you'd be out here."

Shocked and stepping back, my foot hit a rock, sending me flat on my ass. Charlie Blacek was staring down at me wearing the same red hat, the same plaid shirt, the same denim overalls he'd been wearing moments earlier. His forehead, eyes, and nose were shaded from the moonlight by the rim of his hat. A stern and unforgiving face glared at me. I watched and waited.

"That there's the burial mound, just like I told you back on the porch. But that land where the Waumtauk is buried has been violated. Oil from a well up across the way," he said, waving to the land farther on. "Oil from over there leaked down into the Waumtauk mound. The burial ground has been contaminated—ruined, as far as the Waumtauk are concerned. It has, yes—but remember what I said. The Waumtauk never die. The end is never an end."

I sat plastered to the ground wondering how Blacek had managed to make it across the pasture without my hearing him, how his tractor could have come down the road in the still of the night undetected. I rubbed my temples for a second. When I looked up, Charlie Blacek was gone—neither hide nor hair. Before me was nothing but the graveyard and the path through the bushes. In the distance stood the house with a few glowing lights. What was going on? What the *fuck* was going on? How could this be? Where had Blacek come from? Where had he gone? A gravestone in front of me ricocheted moonlight onto the grass. I climbed to my feet and clomped across the pasture to the house.

CHAPTER 9

In the morning, I had a diaphanous memory of Charlie Blacek's vexing visit the night before out in the graveyard—him staring down on me, and me on the ground looking up. Putting away a mere three beers over several hours out on the porch with him was hardly enough to make my head take a crazy spin. On any given night, I could easily polish off three beers with little detriment to my cerebral function.

I dressed and crossed the field to the graveyard to see in the daylight what I could not make out late at night, hoping to find evidence of my nocturnal visitor even though I knew there would be none. Maybe I wanted to see the graves, but probably not. I had no compelling desire to visit Herman Ostermann's grave, or any of the other graves out there. Some people find graveyards fascinating, historically interesting maybe. Not me. For me, they're morbid and depressing, a vivid reminder that we're here and then gone just as quickly. Yet, I went.

Yes, the old grave site was indeed in disrepair just as Charlie had said the first day we'd met at the house. It had once been surrounded by an elegant wrought-iron fence. Except for an occasional granite post supporting a section that remained nobly upright, most of the fence lay toppled in the soft grass, as still as the bones below the tombstones themselves. Something that looked like an old gate decorated with elaborate designs of cornstalks lay there as well.

I looked at the graves, five in all. Four were from the Weinlander family. Three children—Eliska, Milan, and Alexandr, ranging in ages from three to seventeen—passed one after another between 1893 and 1908. The father, Andrej, died at age forty-nine. The fifth gravestone read:

H. Ostermann
Departed from this World
August 19, 2007

Crouching down, I dusted off the surface of the stone and looked closely at the words. How odd, I thought. Why had the birthdate been omitted? It was a plain nondescript grave that marked Herman's exit from life, that and nothing more. In fact, it did not fully identify the individual as *Herman* Ostermann.

I walked over to the burial mound. It was roughly twenty feet across and encircled by a ring of large stones, some of which had sunk into the ground with only the top showing. By all accounts, a portion of the mound could be on the Ostermann property. But no matter where property lines had been set, the burial mound belonged to the Waumtauk and to the Waumtauk alone.

As I stood there, hands in the pockets of my jeans, I imagined the Waumtauk gathering near the mound, preparing to inter one of their own. My mind flashed to the comment Charlie Blacek had made while sitting on the porch the night before. The Waumtauk never die. The burial is never a burial. The end is never an end.

Two nights later, I paid a neighborly visit to Charlie Blacek to return the courtesy he had extended to me. But yes, of course, there were other motives—a little info about the Waumtauk perhaps. Charlie Blacek seemed to be a wellspring of local lore. How solid it was, I had no idea.

I pulled into Charlie's drive shortly after seven thirty. The sun was going down and the moon was coming up. I sat for a minute, staring at Charlie's house. It was a whole lot like ours, stamped from the same cookie cutter, and it looked thoroughly like the kind of place Charlie Blacek would live in, the kind of place he would have lived in his entire life. It was in need of a coat of paint, but was otherwise as sturdy looking as Charlie himself. The porch, unlike ours, was screened in. A ceiling fan crawled in a circle, slow as a tortoise. Yellow light from one of the front windows spread out onto the porch.

No sooner had I turned off the car than Charlie came to the front door followed by Max, his German shepherd. Charlie opened the screen and greeted me exuberantly. How many visitors did Charlie get these days, I wondered. I pretty well knew the answer.

Climbing up the three steps to his porch, I displayed a six-pack of Lone Star. "Beer delivery," I said. "Complete with a little friendly company."

Charlie's face lit. He offered a chair on the porch and plunked himself down in another one. Max came over, sniffed once or twice, and waited, hoping for a good ear scratch, which I afforded him. His eyes closed in delight.

Charlie talked for a long while about nothing in particular—tales of the past, tales of Krivac, his hopes for a good crop next year, God willing. Finally, with a beer behind us and a second in progress, I said, "Tell me something, Charlie. I'm interested in the Waumtauk. You said the burial is never a burial. The end is never an end."

He gave a firm nod as if to say, yup, that's exactly what I said.

"And you said the land out at the mound has been violated and…"

He snapped a match in front of a cigarette and drew in a soft puff. His crystal-blue eyes seemed to grow darker in the hollow and sympathetic porch light. "Did I say that?"

Now I was in a spot. Dare I try to explain that I saw him standing above me talking about the Waumtauk after I fell on my ass by the burial mound? And that he had vanished in a split second right before me? I think not. "When we were talking about the Waumtauk over at my place last night…"

"Well, yer right, it is true. That land is gone forever." He shook his head and knocked an ash from his cigarette into an old Campbell's Pork & Beans can next to him. "I was eight or nine, I'd guess, when it happened. Mamah was beside herself. She didn't go over to see what had happened because it was there behind the Ostermann place, and she had no plans to try to penetrate that place. But she heard about it. Everyone knew."

"People knew but did nothing?"

"Nothing to do. But even then, even as a boy I knew what it meant. It meant the spirits of the Waumtauk would be restless, and that's exactly what's happened. A lot of people tried to blame all the bad and evil that's happened out here in Krivac to the Ostermanns. And believe me when I say, plenty has happened. Lots of folk movin' out, not many movin' in. Remember? I told you that the first day you was here seeing about the house."

I nodded and said, "You mean it was all due to the Waumtauk."

"No, the Waumtauk don't interfere in people's lives. All's I'm saying is that the Waumtauk is restless." He pressed his lips together. "Okay. Nuff said."

I wanted to get more out of Charlie on this, but I could tell it was hopeless. He let his information out in bite-sized chunks like those individually-wrapped mini Halloween candies.

Chapter 10

The weather all week was cool, slipping back and forth from short bouts of rain to occasional episodes of broken sunshine. Late one evening after dinner, I poured a glass of wine and went to the living room. I placed logs in the fireplace, wedged paper underneath, and lit a fire. Immediately, the old dry wood I'd collected from the property burned and crackled musically.

From the window, I watched as a bemired darkness settled on the land. The barn was little more than a faint pencil sketch. Strands of gray light from the lagging sunset sky came in through the window, casting a vaguely mysterious quality throughout the room that was lit only by the flames of the fire.

Sitting in an overstuffed chair before the fireplace, I tried to clear out the troubling thoughts of the past ten days. It wasn't easy though, to forget about my conversations with Ruth McDonald and Charlie Blacek, I mean. I was pestered with an inner penetrating feeling that there might be some truth to their odd prognostications. Part of that fear that wells up inside you when you sense something's not quite right. Yet nothing strange happened, nothing out of the ordinary—not until one weekend late in October.

I turned on the CD player. Bach's Violin Concerto in A Minor filled the room. Flames leaped from the logs. So soft and gentle, they had a hypnotic effect on me—always did. I watched their erratic movement. The trance-like effect of the fire pulled my thoughts to Audrey. When we were apart even for a day, my thoughts always came back to her.

I remembered how we had met. How different and yet how similar we were. I had grown up on the west side of Chicago; Audrey, in Corpus Christi, Texas. We had both been married before, both while in graduate school.

My marriage had been rocky from the words 'I do.' It started slowly, then fizzled out altogether. A day without an argument is like a day without sunshine. You say po-tay-to, I say po-tah-to. You say to-may-to, I say to-mah-to.

Audrey's marriage, although seemingly made in heaven, quickly slipped down into hell. Her husband was handsome and loving—and an addicted skirt-chaser. Soon came the hang-up phone calls in the evening, the cryptic notes of secret meetings that slipped out of his pants pockets onto the closet floor. Both of our marriages soured fast, doomed from the start, consumed by trouble the way oxygen feeds the flames of a fire.

But even bad marriages aren't easily forgotten. A certain type of guilt remains. Sometimes it's the short stupidly-conceived marriages that are most problematic to our psyches. The remorse over our foolishness lingers on. We bury away the vestiges of these marriages the way we hide a bad grade on a test hoping no one will ask how we'd done. So it was. Audrey and I had joined the faculty of Monclair University as members of that enclave of divorced Americans.

One day Oscar Busey, the dean of the College of Arts and Humanities, said to me, "Michael, I've got the perfect person I want you to meet."

A chill ran down my spine. Oh, let's just torture me, I thought. The infamous blind date! But I did it to make Oscar happy. It turned out to be marvelous. We had dinner at a nice restaurant, staying for hours, talking and laughing. We were the last to leave. Audrey was great. She knew so much about so many things. Not the biology nerd I thought I would be sharing an evening with. And she was wonderfully attractive—stylish blond hair, hazel-blue eyes that brimmed with happiness when she laughed. The dreaded blind date turned into one of the best evenings of my life. We saw each other regularly for two years and then were married. Now, seventeen years later, nothing seemed more perfect.

We were about as well matched as a couple could be, even to the point of liking the same sports. Not that we were dyed-in-the-wool sports fans, mind you. Anything but, in fact. We didn't give a tinker's about football, baseball, basketball, tennis, soccer, golf, or most other sports. Only hockey—that was it. It had been part of my life from childhood, beginning with pond hockey that's played on every patch of frozen water in and around Chicago. On Saturdays and Sundays, a bunch of us would skate from morning until late in the afternoon when the lifeless winter sun faded out, turning the puck into a vague black spot.

Hockey kept me out of trouble in high school and, having sprouted to a six-foot-two 195-pounder, I managed to earn a scholarship to the University of Wisconsin, where I did my undergraduate work. As a Division I team, Wisconsin had a tough schedule against good opponents. It turned out scores of NHL players over the years—people like Chris Chelios, Adam Burish, Dany Heatley, Rene Bourque, Mike Eaves, Robbie Earl, Brian Elliott, Tony Granato, Joe Pavelski—the list goes on.

I had to work hard to keep my place on the team. But I succeeded. And as a third-line left-winger, I managed to knock a puck into the back of the net for the Badgers now and then. It was clear, though, that I was not NHL material, so I set my goals on doctoral studies in philosophy—something else I truly loved.

Throughout the years, I never totally quit playing hockey. In Houston, I joined an A-level recreation league—the beer and pretzel league as it's called. This was supposed to be a civilized game—no fighting, no checking—and for the most part it was. The league had a lot of skilled players, quite a few who had played in college and one or two who had made it to the AHL for a while. The skating was fast and the shooting was hard. It was also the only time I ever took a cut to the face. Full cages are required in college hockey, so you come away with all your chiclets and not many cuts. In the rec league, I had gone to wearing only an eye shield and one night caught a stick on the lower lip, resulting in five small stitches and a faint scar.

Then, too, a couple of mornings a week, I'd go to a rink in south Houston to the 7:00 a.m. stick-and-puck session for the extra exercise. Sometimes I'd stay and watch the morning practice of the Houston Aeros—the triple-A farm team of the Minnesota Wild—as they flashed across the ice. I'd picture myself out there, just one step away from the NHL. It was my middle-aged fantasy.

Audrey developed her own addiction to hockey. She loved everything about the sport: the skill and natural athleticism of the players, the speed. She loved it all—all but the fighting. For years, we had season tickets to the Houston Aeros and had witnessed the making of dozens of NHL players who emerged from the ranks of the AHL.

These things I thought about as I watched the darting flicker of the flames, sitting in the soft chair with my feet on the ottoman, eyes slipping closed. Several hours later, I was awakened by a noise. Stiff and achy from sleeping awkwardly in the chair, I rotated my neck and stared at the ceiling, listening with great attention the way you do when first confronted with an unknown sound. I tried to locate it, to place it. Had it come from outside? Inside? Part of the house itself?

The wind through the trees? The wind causing branches to rub against the house? Creaking of the old floors? An intruder! The sound gradually faded out. My wristwatch said 2:34 a.m.

Pulling myself from the chair, I proceeded through the living room into the dining room, stopping every couple of steps to look around. The front door was closed and bolted; the windows were shut. I went into the kitchen and peered out the window to the backyard. The trees were still and listless. The sky was open and dark.

Leaning against the kitchen counter, still dazed from sleep yet alert enough to piece things together, it all seemed silly—nothing more than a dream of some sort that had carried over after I awakened. As I turned toward the dining room, a burst of light flashed through the doorway in front of me—quick, bright, vivid, and fast.

"Jesus!" I blurted, pulling away.

This was no dream. This was real. Fool me once, shame on you; fool me twice…yeah, yeah, I know. I held the flashlight in front of me but left the light off as I stood facing the entrance to the dining room, my back to the kitchen window, trying to reconcile what I had just seen. Inching forward, I entered into an impenetrable darkness. I snapped the light switch and quickly scanned the room. I sucked in air and let out a quick deep breath. Everything was fine.

Each of the events—the noise, the burst of light—was by itself not disturbing. Easily rationalized, easily understood as one of those things that happen late at night. But together, they made me wonder. I thought for a moment, but there was little to connect my impression with hard evidence of anything unusual happening.

Moving back into the kitchen, I looked around one last time. My eyes landed on the door to the basement—ajar, opened two fingers. It could have been like that all along, but I felt certain it had been shut tight.

I pulled the door slowly open, turned on the light, looked at the earthy cellar floor below me, and inched my way down. When I got to the bottom, I noticed that the wine cellar door was open—not just slightly, but all the way. I always closed it, and I remembered doing so earlier in the evening after I conscripted a bottle of Rhône from the rack.

As I started toward the wine cellar, the kitchen door at the top of the stairs snapped shut. Snapped shut hard enough to cause the latch to click. I turned sharply and looked up at the door, waited a couple of seconds, then climbed the stairs one slow step at a time.

Turning the knob and nudging the door with my foot, there before me was a book, a research volume of Audrey's splayed out on the floor. I was sure it had been sitting on the counter when I came into the kitchen. Had it been on the floor, I would have picked it up, or maybe stumbled over it on my way to the cellar. Glaring at me from the opened page, one word caught my eye: *locus*. It had been underlined three times in red ink.

I set the book on the counter and went to the back door and gave a tug, checking it again, and proceeded through the rest of the downstairs for one last look. Opening the door of the coat closet, I stepped back in shock. The top of the trap door was up, tilted against the wall.

I shined the flashlight into the inky black cellar, the very place I had just come from. Next to the hole on the closet floor was a red pen. Perhaps the one used to underline the word *locus* in the book in the kitchen...perhaps. I set the lid down and pressed it firmly, went upstairs and scoped out the rest of the house, and climbed into bed. A long and strange dream awaited me.

I was in a dark and narrow passage that was cut through clay-like soil just high enough to stand in. Behind me, the tunnel dead-ended against a stone wall. In front was darkness—a mass of gray-black emptiness. I could see only a short way into the distance before blackness took over. I began walking, rubbing against the clay sides as I went. The walls were hard and uneven.

My vision oscillated in and out of focus. A low harmonic sound emerged from the walls and vibrated about me. I walked as if being pulled into the passage. As happens in my dreams, bits and pieces occurred in changing hues of various colors. The tunnel walls were at times pale green. Odors— some subtle, some strong—came and went. The smell of tar and damp clay. But most of all, a strange pungent odor, something otherworldly.

Moving forward through the tunnel, I found myself standing in front of an entrance to a room carved out of the clay. In parts, there were stone walls like the ones in the basement and the wine cellar. The room was bathed in dull, blue-green light. I felt oddly out of place, as though I had entered a new dimension. I wiped perspiration from my forehead.

My shirt was moist and sweaty. My body—diffuse, light, amorphous. At times I sensed myself floating. At other times my legs were stiff, locked in place, immobilized. Faces appeared and disappeared in front of me, images I did not recognize—except for the face of Audrey. She stared at me and then vanished, a two-dimensional, thin, gray form. A cloud that took shape and faded away.

Again, everything changed. The walls were suddenly gone. I was standing outside near the barn. The sky was cold and dead. Bursts of lightning swept across the sky. Suddenly, swarms of insects descended on me. Giant roaches as big as my finger landed on my arms and crawled under my shirt. I felt their sharp claws on my skin as they climbed up and down my back. I looked at my arms—the roaches had changed to spiders, hundreds of them, thousands of them. I wiped them frantically from my face and eyes. A voice came from nowhere, saying, "We are nine. You are one." I reached into the air, trying to find the voice, its source. Again it said, "We are nine. You are one." The dream ended.

CHAPTER 11

In the morning, I awoke feeling as if I had been pummeled by a heavyweight. It was because of that damn dream. I knew it was. One of those dreams that leaves you feeling exhausted no matter how deep or how long you slept.

I went to the kitchen and sat at the table for several minutes in a blind stare, then got up and made coffee. My thoughts were filled with the events of the night. From the window, I watched the morning mist vanish as a warm and generous sun spread across the field.

Sipping coffee on the back steps, I tried to reconstruct what had happened, attempting to make sense of it. The more I thought, the more foolish I felt. After all, none of it was very unusual. Not really. Strange sounds? They occur all the time. A flash of light? Probably nothing more than a reflection of the moon off something in the yard. The basement door shutting, the book on the floor? So what? A bad dream? Lord almighty, how many of *those* have I had? The opened trap door? I racked my brain, trying to recall if I had left it that way at some point in the past. True, I once considered putting a ladder down there as a second point of access to the basement if we ever needed it. But that had been weeks ago. I had long since closed the trap door—I was sure I had.

Beginning to feel better, I made breakfast of poached eggs, toast, and orange juice. My thoughts moved to the work I had slated for the day. Progress on the book went well. I stayed at it for several hours before closing my laptop and putting it aside. My plans were to spend the rest of the day on projects in and around the house, piddling in the barn, collecting firewood from the pasture, clearing an area of thick brush.

I went to the barn to retrieve tools. The morning was delightful—cool, soft, aristocratic. An easy and spirited breeze twirled through the air. Sparrows soared across the clear blue sky in snappy angular motion. The air was sweetened by the delicate fragrance of grass from the fields. I walked to the side door of the barn and lifted the latch to enter. The door didn't open. Must be stuck, I thought—jammed the way old doors become wedged closed. I leaned against it, pushing hard with my shoulder. The whole door frame shook a little, but the door didn't budge.

Looking at the latch, I could see the bolt that spanned the door and the frame. The door was locked, not stuck. I thought for a moment. This was the way I always accessed the barn, not through the large barn doors that I opened only when I wanted to let in light.

Had I locked the side door yesterday after leaving the barn? Possibly, but I had no recollection of it. Regardless, the key would be in the kitchen on the hook where we always kept it.

But the key was not on the hook. Nor was it in the dining room. Nor the living room, the bedroom, my pants pocket, or the half dozen other places I searched. I walked back to the barn and peered through the window, cupping my eyes. There it was—in the lock on the *inside* of the barn door.

This is impossible, I thought. All the windows and doors were locked and the key was in the barn. I backed away, thinking, searching for an explanation. The picture that emerged was not a good one. Last night, there had been noises somewhere in or around the house. Then the flash of light in the dining room. Now, the barn was locked from inside. Of course, of course…someone's in the barn. It all fit. There was no other explanation.

I tapped on the window. "Hey, I know you're in there," I called. "Come out. Just open the door. It's all right. I won't do anything. If you need food or something, I can give you some. Just come out so I don't have to call the police."

I waited and listened, expecting a response, a noise.

Nothing.

I called once more. Waited.

Again nothing.

A third time.

Still nothing.

I rejected the idea of calling the police. For now at least, that seemed unnecessary. I decided to break the window. Next to the barn was a thick board. I smashed the glass, waited a few seconds and called, saying I was coming in and that I was unarmed and that all I wanted was to open the barn. I removed chips of broken glass, put my shirt over the window ledge to cover the small fragments, and pulled myself inside.

The barn was dark. Only faint streaks of light from the window nibbled partway in. I went quickly to the door and unlocked it and flipped the light switch. Standing in the entrance, I called into the barn again. There was nothing but somber silence—somber silence and nothing else.

I knew that most of the barn was just empty space and that there were few places a person could hide. Even the hayloft, high up as it was, could be seen from below. I pushed onward into the cavernous space of the barn, talking assuredly to anyone who might be inside. Soon I had searched the entire barn, top to bottom, side to side, front to back—every last inch of it. It was empty.

There was no evidence of an intruder. Every window was shut and locked. The big barn doors were barricaded with the thick plank I always placed across them from inside, rendering it impossible to enter through those doors. The only way in and out was from the side door, and that door was locked with the key hanging inside.

Confused and bewildered, I went to the back porch and sat and thought. My conversation with Ruth McDonald in

Krivac came to mind. Was this the kind of thing she was talking about? Was this what we could expect—the "unusual stuff"? Bullshit! I wasn't about to let some townie fill my head with that nonsense. There had to be a rational explanation, something I had overlooked.

I stared for a long while at the gaping barn window. Fuck, now I had to go into town and buy a sheet of glass. With a hefty groan, I went into the house and picked up a tape measure and lugged my way back to the barn and calculated the size of the window.

I climbed into my car and headed down the rutted dirt road toward Krivac until I came to the two-lane highway that passes by the Walmart on the outskirts of town, glancing over at the whole gargantuan catastrophe as I buzzed along. It was impossible *not* to look at it. Impossible not to see the parking lot full of cars and trucks and people coming out with shopping carts the size of dumpsters loaded with tons of crud. Thanks a fucking lot, Sam Walton, I thought in my thoroughly pissed-off mood. Thanks for sucking business from downtown Krivac.

I pulled into town, passing century-old buildings. Solid structures, they were. Limestone and granite. Buildings that will outlast anything Sam Walton could slap together. Nothing will tumble these fine gems. Not the ferocious hurricanes that make their way deep inland, not the destructive Texas tornados. These beauties will last.

Each building displayed the name of its founder and the date of its creation: Stepok 1887, Morrissey 1892, Fulmer 1903. Down along Main Street, a string of small stores advertised

Dry Goods or Drugs. There were a handful of restaurants, three antique stores, a flower shop, a meat market, and the C&J Grocery—the family-owned store where we shopped. Somehow it had managed to survive the ferocious competition and ultracheap food prices that Walmart doled out. There was a small hardware store with no name other than Hardware. It was one of my favorite places in Krivac.

I went in and ordered a sheet of glass and picked up strips of wood, some putty, and a packet of nails.

"Fixin' a winda, eh?" the old codger behind the counter remarked.

"Uh-huh. The one in the barn busted."

"Them's the worst kind."

"Oh? Why's that?"

"Don't know. Always gives me trouble. Nothin' ever seems to fit right in my barn. How'd it break, the one in your barn? Mine broke when a rake fell through it. One a them there." He pointed to a row of long-toothed implements used to level a patch of heavy dirt. He left and returned with a sheet of glass wrapped in brown paper. "What about that key of yours? Want me to cut you another one?"

"Key? What key?"

"The barn key. Got yourself locked out, right?"

How the hell did he know that? "I'm not sure what you mean. I—"

"Someone got into the barn and locked you out. Wouldn't happen if you had a spare key."

"How'd you know I got locked out?" I asked.

"Charlie Blacek said so. He was in here a bit ago and told me all about it. It's true, isn't it, about the barn? Don't know how you can get locked outta your own barn," he said, shaking his head and putting the nails and putty in a small paper bag. "But however you did it, it's a good idee-er you get another key, especially if you live out at the old Ostermann joint. You do, don't you?"

Just what I needed—another yokel carping about the house, about to tell me my hair is on fire.

He looked at me, held a stare for a second, then turned to the cash register and totaled the bill.

I paid, picked up the window paraphernalia, and left, placing everything in the back seat of the car. I climbed into the front and stuck the key in the ignition and sat with both hands grasping the steering wheel, looking out the window. Was I going nuts, or what? Charlie Blacek hadn't come by the house while I was dealing with the key inside the barn. He couldn't have known anything about it. How could he? Yet, the old guy at the hardware store laid out all the details perfectly. Someone must have told him. It sure as hell wasn't me...was it?

On the way home, I passed Charlie's place. Max, his German shepherd, was out by the back of the house, which meant Charlie was somewhere nearby. I was tempted to swing into the driveway and chat with Charlie. But I didn't, thinking instead it was better to keep my distance for a while.

When I got home, I went to the barn, took a long rod, and poked the dirt floor all over, hunting for a hidden entrance—anything at all. Silly, but I did. I had to convince myself that there was no way in or out of the barn except by the doors and windows. And of course, nothing turned up.

Repairing the barn window no longer interested me. I wanted the whole affair as far behind me as possible now, so I went into the basement and started building a rack that would span the entire left wall of the wine cellar almost to the ceiling. I measured the dimensions and calculated how much wood I would need. I wanted a functional rack where we could stash away hundreds of bottles.

In the afternoon, I went to the C&J Grocery and that night had a dinner of fish, vegetables, and salad. I popped open a bottle of Bourgogne from the village of Pommard. Enjoy the country in style!

I sat for a long while out back listening to the song of the crickets and the sporadic screech of a distant owl. Very late, I went up to the bedroom and pushed open the window. A cool and kind breeze blew in. Silvery strands of moonlight filled the room.

The morning arrived with golden sunlight and the fragrance of clean country air. I sat in the kitchen planning the day. First, I would tackle the broken barn window. A good night's sleep had remotivated me. Second on the list was to spend a couple of hours working on the wine rack. I scrounged through the kitchen, looking for the barn key. Weird. It was gone again.

Hunting everywhere, I realized I had taken it up to the bedroom the night before. I pored through the small pile of things on the dresser, pulled the dresser out, looked behind it, shook out the clothes lying on the floor, looked in the closet, and searched the bathroom and a half dozen other places. Then it hit me. I went down the stairs and out to the barn.

The side door was locked and the broken window was as broken as it had been the day before. I peered inside. Sure enough, the key was in the lock inside the barn. This time, however, all I needed to do was climb through the open window and unlock the door. Once inside, I pulled the key from the slot and bounced it up and down in my palm like a prosecuting attorney holding a piece of incriminating evidence at a criminal trial.

But there was more. Inside the barn on the dirt floor next to the door was my Nikon camera. From what I could tell, it was undamaged except for a small dusty spot where it had rested on the ground. Walking out of the barn, I looked around the property, over at the house and out to the road and back across the pasture. I knew someone had gotten inside the house—probably even up to the second floor—and had done it without my hearing them.

Up in the second-floor window, I saw a glow of light surrounded by a hollow face-like image. It hovered several seconds in the window, snapped off, and was gone. This wasn't the first time I'd seen it. The same thing had happened a week or so before when I was working in the yard—a big orb floated in the kitchen window, watching me...watching me. It was freaky as hell and it stopped me dead in my tracks.

I stood by the barn, trying to come up with logical explanations. The light in the window was surreal and enigmatic and unnerving. It was similar to the image I had seen in the hallway on the night I had removed the stones covering the entrance to the hidden cellar room. But now as then, I was left without an explanation, with no tangible proof other than what I had seen...what I thought I had seen. Was it all in some way connected to everything that was happening?

Why the camera had been taken from the house and left in the barn was a different matter, one for which I could come up with at least a partial explanation. Perhaps it was intended as proof that someone had indeed gotten into the house, and had done so while I was there, right under my nose. The key in the barn again a second time, what about that? Could it be that I'd thought I had taken it up to the bedroom but hadn't? True, I remembered going upstairs, remembered pulling up the window, and remembered falling into bed. But maybe I merely *thought* I had taken the key with me.

If Audrey were here and claimed to have taken it upstairs, you could believe it. She was the one who never forgot little details. I was the one who always got things turned around, thinking I had done something when I hadn't. But she wasn't here, so the key *could* have been downstairs all along. On the kitchen table, let's say. And maybe I had forgotten to lock the back door of the house. Not likely, but possible—plausible. Then someone had come into the kitchen, picked up the key, grabbed the camera and set it in the barn, locked the barn from inside, and climbed out through the broken window. For no other reason than to fuck with me.

As I sat on the ground, leaning against the barn with the camera in my lap, my mind swirled—wondering what to do now. I knew that Louise Ostermann had been parked, as Ted Zelinski had so sweetly described it, in the Cumberland Care Center on Courtland Drive in Austin. What if I went out to see her, to talk to her? Ruth McDonald had asked if I'd spoken to her. Why? Was there something Louise could tell me? She had lived in the house a long time. It couldn't hurt to pay a visit. I mean, what did I have to lose? If you want information, go to the source.

I gathered a few things from the house, tossed them into the car, and went to close the barn door, giving the broken window one last glance. I stopped and stood motionless in utter disbelief.

"What the fuck?"

The window was repaired. I walked over and stared at it, my jaw agape, shaking my head and thinking. There were no chips of broken glass. No evidence that the window had been broken *or* repaired. It was the original old window. The same opaque, cloudy, dirty glass with the same gritty, rock-hard putty—as if it had never been broken at all.

I ventured into the barn. The sheet of glass, the putty, the wood, and the pack of nails I had bought at the hardware store the day before were still there—the glass still wrapped and taped in brown paper, leaning against the wall.

I left the barn and went to the window again and touched the glass, astonished. Could it be that it had never been broken? How? How? I tried to find an explanation. A dozen ludicrous possibilities thrashed through my mind, but none made a shred of sense. If someone was fucking with me, he was doing a hell of a grand job!

But this was way beyond the "fucking with" stage. It defied logic, defied reality. Or...or had I only *imagined* that the window was broken? Then I must have also imagined that the camera had been placed in the barn. I ambled across the grass, looked at the house and turned and looked back at the barn again. I climbed into the car and took off to find Louise Ostermann.

CHAPTER 12

The nursing home was as typical as a penny. If you've seen one, you've seen them all. Red brick, well landscaped—in this case oaks, palms, and mountain laurels. A coat of dark-green paint covered the window frames, giving the building an unnecessary feeling of oldness. Inside, floors polished to a shiny gleam led down wide halls. A guard was settled in behind a small desk. I told him I wanted to visit Louise Ostermann. Within minutes, a middle-aged woman wearing blue scrubs came down the hall. She requested that I keep my visit short, given Louise's tendency to tire. I was taken to the central plaza where the residents were brought during the day.

"Good afternoon, Mrs. Ostermann. You don't know me, but I'm Michael Felton. My wife and I bought your house in Krivac."

Louise looked up.

"You remember the house, don't you?"

Louise nodded.

"I was wondering if you might be willing to share some information about the place," I said. "It's a nice old house. It has a lot of character. I'm interested in learning more about its history. Do you remember how long you lived there?"

"All my life," Louise replied. "Eighty-one years. I never lived anywhere else...until they brought me here."

"And your family," I continued, "they were raised there also, is that right?"

"That's right."

"Your sons, Adam and Bud, are they still around?"

"They left."

"When was that? Do you remember?"

"Oh, some time ago."

"Do you know where they are now?"

"Adam left after he got out of high school, as I remember. He's somewhere out west. He never liked Krivac."

"Why's that?"

"He thought there was something strange about the town. He didn't like the people," Louise said, her voice thin and frail. "He used to say the people were crazy, that they had crazy ideas. He said they had a nutty way of thinking about stuff."

"Like what, for example?"

"The town thought the government was spying on them. The whole town believed it. Adam told me everyone blamed it on us. That's what he heard in school, anyway."

"Why would they blame it on you?"

"They blamed it on me and Herman."

"*Why?*"

Louise shook her head. "That's how it was."

"Did people ever try to break into your house? You know, people from Krivac, for example."

"Sometimes, now and then."

Egad! It was one of those questions you ask but don't expect much in the way of an answer. "Did they steal anything?"

"No, Herman kept them away."

"How did he do that?"

"I'm not sure...he had a special way of doing it."

"You don't know how, then?"

"No. He never told me too much about that stuff. It was something he rigged up or figured out. A way to keep people off the property. I...I don't know what it was."

"Who were the people who tried to get in? Did you ever find out? What did they want?"

"I don't know who they were, exactly. Some of the townspeople, that's all I know. We never bothered anyone. We always just minded our own business. But when I went to sell the house, the real estate person..." Louse paused, searching for a word.

"Ted Zelinski, you mean?"

"Yes, him. He said I'd never be able to sell it unless I did it cheap. He said no one would buy it...that's what he said. And he said if I didn't do that, the people in town were going to buy it, and they might even burn it to the ground. I didn't want that happening so I did what he wanted."

Odd. I thought back to the first day I saw the house. Zelinski claimed he had never met Louise Ostermann. That's what he said.

"And what about Bud?" I asked.

"He's gone, too."

"Do you know where *he* is?"

"I'm not sure."

"He doesn't keep in touch?"

Louise waited a moment and then shook her head.

"Is there some way we could reach Adam, maybe by phone or something, if we wanted to?"

"I don't have his phone number. I don't have his address, either. Maybe someone else does. I'm not sure."

"About the house, do you remember the basement?"

Louise looked straight ahead, not replying.

"The entrance to the basement is in the kitchen, remember?" I said. "Well, when we were down there one time, we found something interesting. Something a bit unusual. On the far wall opposite the stairs was a doorway to another room. It had been sealed up. Do you remember anything like that?"

Louise's eyes glanced at the floor. Her mouth quivered as if she were about to speak, but she said nothing.

I continued. "So out of curiosity, I removed some of the stones that covered the entrance."

Louise looked up at me.

"I went in the room. It was empty. There was nothing inside. I thought that was a bit odd...the room being closed off, I mean. I was wondering if you knew why that was."

I waited. Louise seemed to be formulating an answer. I couldn't tell if she was trying to recall something from the distant past or whether it was something she didn't want to discuss. Her mental strength seemed good for a person in her eighties. Her face had that aura you find in people with a clear intellect, the kind of pure insight some people carry with them no matter how old they get. She had brown, deep, sensitive eyes that displayed a sort of restfulness that comes from having put something aside, having dislocated oneself from an issue—a dilemma. I described the room again.

Louise began to speak. With careful deliberation, she said, "It was just an old, useless room, that's all. We felt we didn't need it, so Herman and Bud closed it off a few years ago—"

"*Oh*, Bud's been back to the house?" I said, struck by Louise's admission of this. "I thought—"

"No. That's wrong," Louise replied quickly. "No, it wasn't Bud. It was Herman who closed it off. Herman died a few years ago…he's buried out on the property."

"Yes, I saw the grave."

"There are a few other graves from the family that owned the house before my parents bought it. That's how it used to be. People buried their loved ones nearby. It just made sense to do that, especially in remote areas." There was a long pause, Louise continued. "We never used the room in the basement. Herman thought it was making the house cold during the winter. You know, it extends out beyond the rest of the rest of house; he thought it was bringing in cold air from the soil above it. There was nothing to keep it warm. That's all it was." She tilted her head and added. "I don't think about these things much anymore. Not very much. It's hard to remember so far back."

"Do you know what the room was used for?" I asked. "Before it was closed off?"

"It had no use. It was just for storage of old equipment and tools, things like that."

"Was the room there when you were a child?"

"Yes, but I never went down there. It was dark. That was before electricity had been put in all of the house. The room had a big door on it that my father kept locked most of the time. Anyway, I didn't like going into the basement; it frightened me. Later, when I was grown, it didn't bother me much, but even then I rarely went there. Herman would go down a lot."

"And the two boys, Adam and Bud, did they ever go in the room, maybe to play? You know, the way boys do?"

"Oh, no, never," Louise said in a soft but firm voice. "Herman insisted they didn't. He said it was dangerous." Then, as if to correct a wrong impression, she added, "You know what I mean...that they could get hurt playing down there, and we wouldn't know it."

By now, Louise was tiring, her eyes were beginning to slip closed.

I said, "I want to thank you for the information. I only want to learn as much as I can about the history of the house. All old houses have their own private history, I think. It's fascinating to find out as much as possible. There is one other thing, though. I found an odd little object in the house. In fact, it was right there in the basement room we just talked about. I meant to bring it but I forgot and left it back at the house. It's about this big." I formed a circle with my finger and thumb. "It's made out of metal of some kind. It has nine spokes that go from the center to the edge out on the rim." Louise looked quickly at me. "It has a bunch of unusual inscriptions on one side. They seem to be part of a language of some type. I'm not sure."

Louise shook her head. "It could be an old coin or something, I suppose."

"That's what we thought, but it doesn't look like any coin we know of," I said. I took out a pen and paper and drew the shape of the nonagram. "Here, this is what it looks like."

Louise watched. I could tell it was familiar to her. She said, "What are you going to do with it? Maybe you should get rid of it."

"Why should we do that?"

"Just get rid of it. It sounds like junk."

It was an odd answer. I had hoped to follow up, but a nurse came over and said it was time for Louise to return to her room. I thanked Louise and left.

Chapter 13

I headed back to Krivac, stopping to have lunch at a ratty truck stop outside Austin, thinking all the while about my conversation with Louise. Her revelation that someone—people from the town—had tried to get into the house was heavy news. As was her comment about Herman devising ways to keep people away. That the basement room had been part of the house from the beginning, and her explanation that Herman had sealed it off because it was making the house cold, was believable—compatible with the types of changes and modifications that occur in old houses over time. Rooms are added; rooms are removed. Nothing about that was strange. Her familiarity with the nonagram was probably the most interesting thing of all, particularly her comment that we get rid of it.

By the time I arrived home, the sun was tilting toward the horizon. I opened the back door and turned off the alarm. A half hour later, Audrey rolled into the driveway. It was great to see her. I needed a break...too much shit going on. She walked into the kitchen, gave a hug and a kiss, retrieved two bottles of beer from the refrigerator, and handed one to me.

"Let it be known: Texas drivers are totally nuts!" she said with a gasp, sitting at the kitchen table. "Geesh, it's good to be here. How was your week?"

"You do not want to know."

"Try me."

I gave her the lowdown on everything that had happened during the previous two days, describing the noise in the night, the key in the barn, my breaking the window to get into the barn, my trip to the hardware store, the codger's comment.

"I'm telling you, Aud, the whole thing was totally crazy. I went through every inch of the barn. There was nobody inside...not a single, solitary, freaking soul. I can't explain it. All I know is some jerk *somehow* got the key from the kitchen, locked the barn from inside, and vanished. Pulled a pretty slick Houdini, he did. And when I was at the hardware store, the old guy there started blabbing about getting another key made for the barn, saying Charlie Blacek had told him about what had happened. The guy knew the whole story about the barn—top to bottom, everything. He said Charlie had told him."

"Charlie must have known."

"How? He never came by. I never talked to him. It's hard to miss Charlie Blacek if he's anywhere in the line of sight. But if what the old fella at the store said is true, then Charlie had known about my encounter with the barn." I filled Audrey in on my dealings with Charlie Blacek—his occasional visits in the evenings with a six-pack of Lone Star, his tales of the Waumtauk, the old John Deere he puttered around on.

"So maybe you told the guy at the store that you got locked out. Maybe you mentioned it casually and forgot you told him."

"No, I know I didn't. I was thinking about it when I was there, but that's all. I mean, sure, that was the reason I went to the hardware store in the first place, because of the key in the barn and the broken window that I needed to fix. But I never said a word about the key, I'm a hundred percent sure. Good God, you'd think that guy could read my mind! Son of a gun knew everything, claimed he had learned it from Blacek. That's not all, though." I drew in a breath and let it out slowly. "The barn window, the broken one, well...it was suddenly fixed."

Audrey eyes opened wide. "Fixed?"

"That's right, fixed."

"Who fixed it?"

"Ha! Not me."

"Who, then?"

"This might require a few more beers." Waiting a second, I said, "All right, here goes...what happened was, I threw some things in the car and went to close up the barn. When I got there, I looked at the window and noticed it wasn't broken anymore. In fact, it was exactly the way it had been *before* I broke it. Exactly! *Same* dirty glass, *same* cracked putty, *same* old window."

"Michael, cut it out," Audrey said, treating this as if it were one of my goofy dead-pan jokes.

"This is no joke, Audrey, I'm telling you—"

"You're saying first the window was broken, and *then* it wasn't."

"That's what I'm saying."

"Well, you must have imagined it or dreamed it. That's all I can say."

"Imagined it? Hell's bells, Audrey, I didn't imagine it—I *saw* it. And I didn't dream it, either, unless I dreamed myself all the way down the road to the hardware store and back while driving my car. Check out the piece of glass and the rest of the crap I bought to fix the window. It's right out there in the barn. What I did was climb in through the window, the one with the busted glass, to get the key that was inside the barn. Not once, but twice. I have yet to learn how to transmogrify my body through a sheet of intact glass. It was broken. That I know because *I* was the one who broke it. But I *wasn't* the one who fixed it."

"All right, so you didn't imagine it and you didn't dream it. Now what?"

"Uh-huh, you tell me." I leaned back against the wall and took a slug of beer. "Some other things happened, too," I said, feeling suddenly queasy, like an innocent person about to be grilled on the witness stand in court. "Twice I saw the face of—I'm going to tell you this, but just sit on your hands for a second until I'm finished, okay? Wait until I'm done, because it's strange. I was working in the yard when I saw the face of someone—someone or something—in the window of the house. Twice I saw it. Once—"

But she did not sit on her hands, not for a second. Reactively, she tilted her head down, leaned forward on the table, and said, "Michael, *please*. What do you mean you saw a face in the window?"

"See. See, I knew you wouldn't believe it. I knew."

I sat there stewing for a long while, then got up. If nothing else, I could show her the stuff in the barn I had bought to fix the window. Surely that would convince her it was for real, that I was still sane, that I was not playing solitaire till dawn with a deck of fifty-one. "Follow me," I said.

We walked out the back door, down the steps, and across the stretch of grass to the barn under the now gray-black sky that hung above us. I pulled the key from my pocket, opened the barn door, and flipped on the light. We went inside.

"There you have it," I said, facing Audrey, referring to the wall behind me. "All the junk I bought to fix the window. Why would I do that if the window wasn't broken?"

"All what junk?"

"That stuff there," I said, directing a thumb over my shoulder at the wall where I had left the glass, and the wood, and the nails, and the new putty.

"I don't know what you're getting at, Michael, but there's nothing there."

I spun around and gaped at the spot where I had left everything. "All right, where'd it go?" I said rhetorically. I turned around, looked at Audrey, and walked across the barn in the pale glow of incandescent light. "I swear, it was right there just a few hours ago."

"Well, I don't know what to say. Whatever you bought isn't there now." Audrey walked over to the window. "This is the window that was broken? This one?"

"Yes, that one," I snapped, pointing at the window.

"Hon, the window's fine, and—"

"I know, I told you that in the kitchen, Audrey!"

She shrugged. "And there's nothing here from the hardware store."

"*Oh*, you think I'm losing my marbles, is that it?" I said. The implication was a little too close for comfort considering all the crap that had been happening.

Audrey looked softly at me. "No, of course not."

I wandered back and forth across the barn. "Let me tell you, there's something real fucking strange going on out here. Real fucking strange."

"Oh, Michael."

"You don't know it because you haven't been here. I've been here trying to crank out work on my book—*which*, I might add, is turning into a bit of a train wreck all its own given how little I've accomplished with all the shit that's happened." I went into the details of my visit with Louise Ostermann, and what she'd said about the attitude of the townspeople toward them, and how someone was always trying to get into the house.

Audrey came over and put her arms around my waist. "How's about we just forget this stuff for a while, all right?"

"See, now you're trying to pretend all this never happened. Don't placate me this way, Audrey. At *least*—"

"Michael, slow…down. I'm not placating you. If you tell me it happened, I believe it. Okay? What I'm saying is, let's give it a break. All right?"

I walked across the barn again and stood with my hands jammed deep into my pockets. Audrey was right. Anyway, we had more than enough right now to occupy our time. We didn't need to dwell on the undwellable. I looked at her and nodded begrudgingly.

Late that night, we climbed into bed. Audrey fell instantly asleep. The quiet of the country had that effect on her. It was a lullaby. I, on the other hand, lay catatonic in bed unable to sleep. I stared at the ceiling, revisiting over and over the issue of the barn. A certain type of clarity comes in these empty silent moments.

I was left with two opposing possibilities, each wrapped half in logic, half in absurdity, making neither particularly acceptable. Position one said that I had broken the window just as I remembered doing and that it had been mysteriously repaired. Position two said that it had never been broken and that I had imagined it or dreamed it, as Audrey had suggested. Dealing with the absurdity of each of these was a challenge, but of the two possibilities, I especially could not accept position two. I don't hallucinate, am not schizophrenic, and am not prone to imagining crazy and outlandish stuff. Furthermore, my dreams aren't *that* real, no matter what Audrey might think. Like it or not, for a second I wondered whether what Ruth McDonald had told me outside the courthouse might just be true.

Yes, I had been considering for quite a while the possibility that Ruth was more than the fruit loop I perceived her to be, that she might indeed have useful information. She did know a hell of a lot about the town and the Ostermanns. True, she might be "a lonely old woman who needs someone to talk to," like Audrey had said. And she might have wanted nothing more than to "butt into our business," as Audrey had also said. But even if that were true, it didn't preclude her information being valid, unfabricated. And it didn't mean her motives were suspect. Did it?

The trouble was, I was beginning to question my ability to…how should I put it? My ability to *perceive* what was actually happening—what had happened. Yet, like I said, I don't hallucinate and rarely have a bad dream. And when I do I know it's just a dream, for crying out loud. I stared at the ceiling as the tall oak outside the window cast wavy shapes above me. I felt my eyes close, my thoughts fade.

CHAPTER 14

Saturday morning arrived, bringing crisp clean air and a turquoise sky. I came down to the kitchen as Audrey was making coffee—barefoot, no bra, just panties—sexy, lacy things. I put my arms around her and kissed her on the neck. My hands moved over her waist, around front, creeping downward. That's all it took. We got as far as the living room, to the sofa.

After breakfast, we drove over to the Krivac nursery and bought a set of bushes and a tray of flowers for around the front porch. We spent Sunday doing very little. Just what I wanted. I was all for titrating out the amount of time spent on chores around the house, ready for the work time to wind down and the escape time to crank up.

In the evening we had dinner at a simple but nice restaurant near Hallettsville and returned to the house. It was the end of the weekend; Audrey needed to get back to Houston. I thought about working for a while on my book but scrapped the idea and poured a glass of wine. We sat at the kitchen table. The effects of the wine tempered my thoughts, for the moment making everything that had happened seem distant and remote.

We went out to the back porch and watched the last trickle of sun slip below the horizon. Audrey went upstairs to get a book. As I walked into the house, Audrey came into the kitchen. She looked me in the eye and let out a deep low sigh.

"Michael, I think you need to see this."

I followed her up to the bedroom. My laptop was sitting on the dresser facing away from me. Audrey moved to the front of the computer. I saw the tension in her face as she stared at the screen. She looked at me for a second and then at the computer again as if unable to detach herself from it. There, spread across the screen in big, red, italic letters, was the word

LOCUS

My eyes were glued to the word. Its strange message seemed to make the room close in on me. "You didn't do this, did you?" I asked, searching for something to say.

Audrey crossed her arms, refusing to even acknowledge the suggestion.

"Okay, I know you didn't. I don't know why I—it's just… it's this crap here, and the keys in the barn, and the barn window, not to mention what Louise told me. What the fuck's next?" I went to the window, rested against the wooden frame, and closed my eyes for a moment. Leaning on the sill, I looked out at the pasture and the dull sky, thinking about the word on the computer. Audrey was silent. "Why *locus*?" I mumbled, turning toward her. I remembered the same underlined word in Audrey's book, the one I had picked up off the kitchen floor in the middle of the night.

"Latin, maybe. Who knows?" Audrey droned. "'Site' or 'place,' something like that. It's used in biology, too, a part of the genome."

"Yeah, but how did the word get on the computer?"

Audrey shook her head in dismay. "Hacked in from a wireless connection, maybe. Your guess is as good as mine."

I reminded her that we didn't have Internet access at the house. Early on, we had decided against it. This was going to be our "cabin in the woods," so to speak. "Someone got into the house again. There's no other explanation," I said. I could tell Audrey was thinking the same thing. "We need to check the place out."

Not having a gun, I looked around for a weapon of some sort. In the bedroom closet was an old baseball bat I used to knock balls out into the pasture. I picked it up and started out the door into the hall. Audrey followed.

"Be careful. Stay back, Aud," I said, waving an arm at her.

"It could be dangerous. You'll need help."

"I'll be fine."

Down the hall I crept, arriving at the entrance of the second bedroom. I pushed the door open. The room was bathed in the thin evening light that came in through the window, filling it with an eerie glow. Edging my way across, I stood in front of the closet door, waited a second, and yanked it open. A shirt fell to the floor. My heart thumped. I gasped and stepped back holding the bat in front of me, shaking it and thrashing it at arm's length through the closet, poking everywhere in sight, pushing clothes back and forth, jamming the bat into the closet until I was convinced it was empty.

Into the other bedroom, the closets, the bathroom we went. All were empty. I opened the attic door. A trickle of light from the two small attic windows marred the room's darkness. I turned on the light. Twenty-five dull watts filled the room. I started up the wooden stairs, each footstep amplified by the silence of the house and the creak of the old pine. I didn't know why, but if someone was still in the house, this is where I expected him to be holed up.

I hadn't been in the attic in a long time. It seemed more crowded, more cluttered, many more boxes than I remembered. At the far end was a stack of boxes, about three feet across and four feet high. It reminded me of Lee Harvey Oswald's sniper's nest on the sixth floor of the Dallas Book Depository. I stopped and gripped the bat, squeezing the handle. I walked toward the stack, wound up, gave a huge whack against the side of one of the boxes, and looked quickly behind it.

Audrey came racing up the stairs. "Michael!" she screamed. "Are you all right?"

"I'm fine," I said, drawing in a long deep breath. "I'm fine."

Audrey followed me to the kitchen. I still needed to go into the basement. I grabbed the flashlight from the counter, turned on the basement light, and started down the stairs, proceeding toward the wine cellar. Halfway across, the small bulb that illuminated the basement flashed, popped, and went out. Now, except for the stream from the flashlight, I was in total darkness. I stopped and considered returning to the kitchen but continued on until I reached the entrance to the wine cellar. As I entered, a short, high-pitched screech filled the room. I pulled back and scoured the floor with the light just in time to see a mouse zip along the wall.

Sitting in a chair in the kitchen, I ran my hands wearily across my eyes. "Everything's all right," I uttered. "The house is secure; nothing's been tampered with...nothing but the computer." I looked out the window at the deep sky. "But you know, now that I think about it, the computer was down in the dining room and turned off when we left. I never take it up to the bedroom." I looked at Audrey. "And besides, if someone turned it on, they'd have to know the password. They couldn't get in without it. It would be hard to decipher even if you were a good hacker. So, I don't see how—"

"It's time to call the police, Michael."

"Call the police? How can we call the police, Audrey? I mean, what would we say? What could we possibly tell them? That the barn key became mysteriously locked inside the barn? Not once, but twice. That the computer was upstairs in the bedroom, turned on, when we came home? We can't do that. They'll look at us like we're crazy. They'll tell us we left the computer in the bedroom, that we just don't remember. It all sounds pretty thin unless you were here when it happened. And—"

"We tell them someone's been in the house, that they came in while we were gone, and that someone broke into the barn. It's up to them to investigate, isn't it? That's what the police do, don't they? Or if nothing else, there would at least be a record that we reported it. I think that's important. Or maybe they can look for fingerprints or—"

"Good grief, honey, they'll find hundreds of them. Thousands of them. Fingerprints from Louise Ostermann and all the people in her family, from ourselves, from the workmen who did the repairs after we moved in. Every clown who's been in this house in recent years. It just won't work."

"Fine. But we have to do *something*, Michael. If someone can get in the house when we're *not* here, they can get in when we *are* here. What the hell kind of place is this?"

"Aha…starting to believe me now, huh?" I said.

I got no reply.

"Look, the house is safe," I said, attempting confidence. "There's no one else here but us. *That*, I'm sure of. I checked every inch of it, top to bottom."

"Michael, the fact is, someone got in. Just like what Louise told you. They were messing with the house back then, and they're doing it now," Audrey said.

"Hold on a second," I said. "Let's just deal with what we know. And all we know is, yes, somebody did manage to get in a couple of times. Well, okay, three times—once when they took the key out to the barn, and once when they put the key and the camera in the barn. Now they got in and screwed around with the computer."

"For Pete's sake! Isn't that enough?"

"But it doesn't mean it's all connected to what Louise told me. We don't know beans about Louise Ostermann. She's... what? Eighty years old or whatever? Who knows if anything she says is true. We need to keep this as simple as possible. Let's just deal with one thing at a time, okay? One thing at a time. Forget about Louise for now. We'll have the alarm system checked. It must be defective in some way. Maybe the technician can tell us if it's been tampered with."

Audrey sat in the chair, shoulders slumped, eyes cast on the table. "Oh, God, Michael. That'll take days. I can't stay. I have to get back to Houston tonight for my class tomorrow. I've *got* to *go*."

"I know, babe, I know. Go ahead. I'll stay and take care of things. All right?"

Audrey left for Houston later that night.

CHAPTER 15

Sleep came slowly. I lay in bed motionless, tired, wanting to sleep but not able to—tuned in to each and every noise that emanated from inside and outside the house. And being an old house, there were many. By now, I had already come to know most of the sounds much the way you learn to recognize the nuanced rattles of a familiar old bike or car. Finally, I faded into an uncertain slumber. Three times, perhaps four, I awoke, listened for a while, and drifted off again. Late at night, I got up and ventured down to the kitchen, feeling a necessity to convince myself that the house was secure. The moon cast a dull-blue hue throughout the room. I drank a glass of water. As I stared out the window, I saw a dark, shadowy movement between the house and the barn. It darted past the house in irregular spurts. I inched closer to the window and peered out and saw the faint outline of a young deer standing motionless, locked in a solitary stance. It turned its head and stared at me as if seeking permission to trespass on our property. Then it leaped forward and was gone. I went upstairs and climbed into bed.

I slept longer than usual in the morning. When I awoke, the room was filled with warm yellow sunlight. I thought again about my conversation with Louise Ostermann, and my discussion with Audrey the previous night. Why would someone want to get into the house? There was nothing of any value here, no big-ticket items. Just a lot of books, a camera that had been moved around but not stolen, and a computer that served only as a vehicle for leaving cryptic messages.

Weirdly, I wondered if some asshole was out there who had become obsessed with the house, a kind of house stalker. Like those people who become fixated on a person and won't let them alone. Maybe the house held special significance for someone going back many years. Someone who had loved it. Or hated it. Suppose Herman Ostermann had been shitty to a kid who had wandered onto the property, and now and forever it was payback time? And what if that person knew how to get in and out in ways that were unknown to us? Some creep could enter, move things around, mess with us, leave, and not even set off the alarm.

But if someone had been breaking into the house way back to when Louise owned it, for example, there might be a record of it in old newspaper articles, in the police blotter. The papers should be stored in the library. It was worth a try. I also could go talk to dear old Ruth McDonald. Flakey or not, she seemed to know a lot about the house, assuming she was more than just a blowhard. She was certainly willing to talk about it when she approached me outside the courthouse.

I paged through the Krivac phone directory. Ruth McDonald's address was listed as 549 Maple Avenue. I knew this as one of the original streets that ran through town. I scribbled the number on a sheet of paper and stuck it in my pocket. I drove over to the Krivac library and asked to see old newspaper articles. They were in the east wing, I was told. The east wing turned out to be a small room just off the main library, which itself was nothing more than a slightly larger room. The librarian took me to an old microfiche reader.

"What exactly are you looking for?" she asked. "Maybe I can help."

"I want any information I can get about a house we own. It's out on the edge of town. It used to belong to the Ostermann family."

"Oh, my! The Ostermann house?" she said.

"That's right. I'm interested in articles from the newspaper—"

"That would be the *Gazette*, the Krivac *Gazette*."

"Yes, the *Gazette*."

"There might be a few articles, I don't know. Most have been removed, though."

"Checked out, you mean?"

"No, I mean removed from the library. They're no longer here."

"Who did that?"

"A couple of people, two men, came in and said they needed them."

"Needed them for what?"

"I don't know," the librarian said. "I just work here. It was about five...no, longer than that. Maybe seven or eight years ago, I guess."

Aye yai yai! "All right, give me what you have."

The first article, "Tract of Land West of Krivac to be Sold", was dated June 13, 1952. It stated:

> The property is part of a large piece of land that was owned by the Svoboda family until recently when it was broken up and sold in parcels that included the land north of it and the land to the south. A piece of land bordered by FM1346a and FM2771c will be sold in four to five sectors, each one of about a hundred acres.

It went on to describe the land in detail, including a small stream that ran east to west, transecting the acreage to be partitioned. It also explained that "a deed has been entered in the county courthouse." It sounded like our land, but it didn't make sense. We had deeds going back to 1899 and, according to those, the house was 117 years old. Of course, the article had been written decades ago. The roads could have been renamed since then. It occurred to me that this might not even be our property. I continued reading until I came to a surprising passage. I read it several times.

> A portion of the undeveloped Svoboda property will be sold to Herman Ostermann, a semiretired nuclear

engineer, and his wife, Louise Ostermann, who recently moved to the Krivac area and who plan to build a house on the property.

The paper had a picture of the property before the house had been built. The three trees in the picture were younger versions of the three oaks behind the barn now. So, too, with another oak that stood behind the house. It was how the picture would appear if neither the house nor barn were there. In fact, it would not have been possible to take that picture had the house and barn been there at that time. Okay, so maybe the house had been moved from somewhere else to where it is now. Why not? It's possible. But what about the basement? You don't move basements around. The house, maybe. The basement, no.

I scrolled through a second article from the *Gazette*. It also had a photograph and was dated October 26, 1953—a couple of months after the first article. The title read "Ostermann House Oldest in Area".

The house owned by Herman and Louise Ostermann is one of the oldest in the Krivac vicinity. The original edifice, constructed in 1899, has changed little since that time. A barn, also on the property, is believed to have been built in 1899.

The article described a house that was identical to the one we bought from Louise Ostermann. Even more convincing, the photograph showed the house, the barn, the three trees behind the barn, and the one behind the house. The caption below the picture read: "The house on west FM2771c owned by Herman and Louise Ostermann."

So first, the Krivac *Gazette* published an article in 1952 saying that the land where the Ostermann house now stands was nothing but empty pasture, and that the Ostermanns had moved to the area that year. But both Louise Ostermann and Ruth McDonald claimed Louise had been born in the house and had lived there her whole life—more than eighty years. Then, in 1953 the *Gazette* published an article saying that the house had been there since 1899. To make things even murkier, we had the original deed for the purchase of the property, dating to October 17, 1899 in the name of Jacob Weinlander. It demarcated the property boundaries exactly as they were when we bought the house.

Confusing as it was, none of it mattered much to me. I knew the Ostermann house was old, very old. The wood in the attic, basement, and walls was rock hard—so hard, in fact, that on numerous occasions I had bent large nails trying to pound into it. Moreover, remnants of cast-iron gas lines, once used for lighting before electricity had been installed in the house, remained. No one would light a house with gas back in the fifties, not even in rural Texas. Stupid small-town newspaper getting the details messed up, I concluded.

But then came the real bombshell. The year was 1971. The article's headline read: "Teenager Disappears on Ostermann

Property". I started reading. It gave elaborate details of how three boys had wandered onto the property with the intention of inspecting the graveyard and exploring an old school bus that was on the far end. It was a cool and drizzly December afternoon when Jeffrey Broding, Denny Schneider, and Clement 'Lefty' Robinson—all thirteen-year-olds from Krivac Junior High—entered the property from the back, walked over to the school bus, and climbed in. Jeffrey Broding sat in the driver's seat and twisted the steering wheel left and right, jamming in the clutch, attempting to shift the stiff gears. Schneider and Robinson got out and headed over to the graveyard, where they inspected the old tombstones. They called to Broding to join them but got no reply. When they arrived back at the bus, Broding was gone. Not a trace of him anywhere. The article said an intense search for the boy had begun, and that he had yet to be found.

"Shit, that's big," I muttered. I hunted but could find no more about it except for one little blurb two months later saying Jeffrey Broding was still missing. Whoever cleaned the files out of the library had missed the ones on the Broding incident, it seemed—something that in my opinion was significant. On the other hand, the odd information about the house and when it had been built seemed far more trivial. Only later would it have meaning to me.

I picked up my things and started through the library. As I passed the circulation desk, I asked the librarian if she knew, had ever heard of, someone named Jeffrey Broding.

"Jeffrey Broding? Of course. There's not a soul in town who doesn't remember the Broding incident. The young Broding boy, he went missing right out there where you live, out on that very property. Our family knew the Broding family very well. They left town, though…picked up and took off pretty quick after Jeffrey disappeared."

It was an extraordinary bit of information. Why would the family leave an area where their own child had disappeared? If it were me, I'd be there forever—looking, searching, investigating. I'd never give up. I thanked the librarian and left.

I drove over to Maple Street and pulled up in front of 549. It was every bit the kind of place I imagined an old-timer like Ruth McDonald would own: an imposing Victorian behemoth with a gigantic wraparound porch that covered the front and one entire side—the house of the seven gables. This one, painted an unflattering brown and white. I knocked on the door. An answer was not long in coming. Ruth opened the door about six inches and peeked out.

"Ah, it's you, Mr. Felton," she said, as if expecting someone else.

"Yes," I replied. "Did I catch you at a bad time?"

She swung the door open. "Not at all. I thought it was that fellow who keeps perusing the neighborhood trying to drum up yard work. Come in." Her voice became friendlier.

We walked through the foyer past a gigantic curved staircase with old mahogany railings. "Nice place," I commented, looking around. "I love these old houses. Tell me, how many—"

"Eleven rooms. If that's what you mean," Ruth said. "Five on the first floor, four on the second, two on the third. Not counting bathrooms and closets, of course. And three fireplaces. Two down here and one upstairs."

Ruth led me into the living room through a doorway parted by thick felt curtains of maroon and deep lavender with purple fringe. They were bunched together and tied at each side with a heavy cord. The room was dark, too dark. Lots of expensive old furniture—shiny, lacquered three-legged tables, a big marble-topped table with claw-foot legs, doilies everywhere, two authentic-looking Tiffany lamps, not the cheesy ones you see in the stores. An old gooseneck grandpa lamp with a gray cloth shade and long, glistening tassels gawked from the corner. Much of the light was blocked out by heavy curtains that covered the tall windows, or was sucked up by the dark rosewood furniture. What could have been a bright and airy space was sad and gloomy. A teak bookcase, devoid of books, was filled with magazines—*National Geographic*, old *Life* magazines, others I didn't recognize. On the lower shelf was a big crystal ball all of eight inches across. Expensive, if it were indeed crystal. We sat in a pair of wingback chairs on either side of the marble-top table. A brown-and-black cat entered the room, nonchalantly in charge of the place. It leaped onto the window ledge, poked its head between the curtains, looked out for a while, and jumped down and moseyed off.

"So, what is it you want to know about the house...your house? That's why you came, isn't it?"

"Not necessarily."

"Tea, then?" she asked.

I laughed. "I do have a few questions."

"Well, I expected you'd be by sooner or later. And here we are."

Ruth was right. No point in being evasive. "Tell me, what do you know about the inside of the house?"

"The inside? Nothing. I've never been in it. Very few people ever have."

"I keep hearing that."

"The Ostermanns had no friends out here. None that I know of, anyway."

"Well, there are some odd things, shall we say, about the house. Stuff has happened that we can't explain." I gave a couple of examples. "Moreover, someone managed to get inside without setting off the alarm while we were gone."

This brought little reaction from Ruth. I said, "I figured maybe Adam or Bud might have some information, could tell us what they know about the house. After all, they lived there a long time. They should know it well. But according to Louise, Adam is somewhere in California."

"That's what I heard."

"And Bud's gone. Louise doesn't know where he is. All she said was he's gone."

A sudden, surprised look spread over Ruth's face. She leaned back and shook her head several times. "Bud? Bud's here in Krivac." She held her hand out as if Bud himself were standing right in front of us. "I see him in town from time to time."

"In Krivac? Are you sure?"

"Sure? I'm certain."

"But when we met in town, you told me both Bud and Adam had left."

"Did I?" Ruth then veered off and described Bud, saying he was in his fifties, brown thinning hair, mustache, about five feet ten inches tall, a little overweight maybe. "He usually wears a baseball cap. One of those camouflage things hunters wear."

"Do you ever talk to him?

She shrugged and shook her head. "No, of course not."

"Why not?"

'Because I have nothing to say to him. I don't know him."

"Not even hello? Or how's your mother? Something like that?"

"Well, hello, maybe. But that's about all."

"What does he say?"

"Nothing. He nods and goes on."

"Where does he live?" I asked.

"He doesn't live anywhere, far as I know."

"Well, he has to live *some*where. Do you mean he's homeless?"

"No, I just mean I've never heard of him living anywhere in particular. As I said, I know most of what goes on in Krivac, but I don't know where Bud lives."

"How often do you see him?"

"I never really kept track," she replied. "Once a week, maybe once every two weeks. I've seen him at the supermarket, the C&J Grocery. And I know I've seen him at least once going into Tommy's Place. You know, that dumpy bar over on South Austin Street. If you wanted to find him, I suppose you could try those places. Beyond that, I'm not sure."

I glanced around the room. The house was certainly magnificent. But Ruth had turned it into a bleak and eerie place. The cat came by for a second visit. It stopped and gave me a demanding look, as if it knew me or wanted me to scratch its ears or something. Or maybe it was telling me to get the hell out of the room. Cats! It hopped up onto a divan, curled up, and went fast asleep.

"The real reason I came here is to find out about the house, the Ostermann house," I said. "When we talked by the courthouse, it seemed you wanted to tell me something."

"Yes, what I was getting at is that the house has a history, a reputation going back many years. Things have happened there."

"Such as?"

"The neighbors claimed to see glowing colors, bright lights of some kind, coming from the house and out on the property. People have been seen coming and going. Herman Ostermann met with them in the fields."

"I thought you said the Ostermanns had no friends."

"That's right...none from town, anyway. They were complete loners when it came to Krivac and the area around here. But people were seen out there at night."

"What kind of people?"

"I never saw them myself, but I heard they were...well, different from us."

"In what way?"

"Some were supposed to be small while others were tall, extremely tall. That's what Jesse Gonzales told me some years ago. Unfortunately, Jesse's gone now. He died a while back. He lived down the road from the Ostermanns. He told me that one night he was out looking for one of his sheep when he noticed lights in the Ostermanns' field. He walked toward the field and watched for a couple of minutes. Jesse said Herman was out there with a bunch of people or whatever. Then as Jesse started moving closer, one of them noticed him and held out his hand and pointed it at him. Jesse was suddenly struck to the ground, unable to move, unable even to get up. He was on the ground for ten minutes or so and when he was finally able to move, he ran off the property. When he got home, his wife asked where he'd been, but he couldn't remember. He didn't realize what had happened for several days, as if his memory had been wiped clean. Little by little, it all came back."

"You really believe that?"

"I certainly do. Jesse was as straight as could be. I knew him his whole life. He was not the kind of person who'd make up a story. He had nothing to gain from it. But it wasn't just Jesse. My understanding is that others have witnessed those things, too."

"Well, we've never seen anything like that—strange lights or whatever. For that matter, Herman's long gone. Buried in the graveyard out on the property."

"But odd things are continuing to happen, right?" Ruth said. "You already mentioned some of them." She leaned forward in the chair. Speaking in little more than a whisper as though letting me in on some well-kept secret, she said, "*Mister Felton, this...stuff...doesn't...surprise...me.* If it were happening somewhere else, I'd question it. But it all has to do with the Ostermann house. The *Ostermann* house. Don't you see? *That's* what makes it different. *That's* what I'm trying to tell you."

Ruth's drama wasn't all that convincing. "You make it sound like something truly sinister is happening," I said.

"From what you described, some pretty darn strange things are going on right now, aren't there? They're not happening over on the Clausens' farm next to you, or here in town. Only out where you are."

"There still could be perfectly rational explanations for it all," I said.

"Oh? Like what?"

"These lights you talked about could have to do with... I don't know, a magnetic field, something in the ground. Things we don't know anything about. A malfunction in the alarm system could account for the break-ins. There's also the possibility—"

"But it doesn't explain why someone wants to get into your house, now, does it?"

"We're looking into that," I replied, not giving any details.

"In truth, Mr. Felton, I can't imagine someone actually wanting to get inside that place. Most people I know would prefer to stay as far away as possible."

"Well, we're there. And still *alive*," I said, holding my arms out. I waited, giving Ruth a chance to respond, but she said nothing. "True, we don't know who's getting in. Maybe, for some reason, it's one of those people who used to visit Herman. Who knows?"

"There you have it," Ruth declared, as if she had made her point. "See what you're up against, you and your wife… um—"

"Audrey."

"Yes, Audrey. You got your hands full. You're wrestling with the gods."

"Wrestling with the gods?"

"You get the point."

"Not really. What exactly are you saying?"

"Just that it will get worse."

"And how do you know that?"

"Call it a strong hunch. Now and then I get these feelings and they're almost always right. I have a knack for that, you know. I can't nail it down but the feeling is there."

That did it. These vague premonitions of Ruth's were beginning to annoy me, gigantic crystal ball notwithstanding. The afternoon light—what little there was of it, what little came in through the shrouded windows—was quickly abandoning the room. I felt like turning on the Tiffany next to me or pushing open the curtain a trace just to cut through some of the ashen gloom that hung around us. It was pointless, though. There didn't seem to be much more I could learn from Ruth. I was more than ready to leave. I thanked her for her time and left.

Walking to my car, I thought it unusual that Bud was still around and yet no one had said a word about it until now. Ted Zelinski, the real estate agent who had sold us the house, hadn't mentioned him. I realized he didn't need to be at the closing; however, even if Louise couldn't make it, Bud might want to go, assuming he was here in town. Maybe he refused to participate for some reason. Perhaps he wanted nothing to do with the house or the estate. But it was Louise herself who'd told me Bud was gone. Of all people, you'd think *she* would know.

Truth is, I had no particular interest in finding Bud except perhaps to talk to him, to get information that was not embellished by Ruth's rather vivid imagination. But finding him would be a challenge. I had never seen him, had no picture of him, and had little information to go by except for the description Ruth gave me, which could apply to about 70 percent of the town's male residents.

I stopped at the C&J Grocery. I asked the girl at the check-out if she knew Bud. "Never heard of him," she said. By itself, that was perhaps not surprising given that she appeared to be barely sixteen and had worked at the store for only a couple of months. Far more confusing, however, was the fact that the store manager, a person who had lived most of his life in Krivac and had spent upward of twenty years working at the store, also had no knowledge of Bud. He was aware that the Ostermanns had lived out on the edge of town, but he knew nothing more about them.

"If he's from around here and comes into Krivac to shop, I'd pretty much know him," Mr. Larson, the manager, said. "Sooner or later everyone in Krivac comes in here for food. You get to know folks."

How was it that Ruth had seen Bud Ostermann frequently in the C&J Grocery, yet the long-time store manager knew nothing of him?

I visited Tommy's Place on Austin Street and also several other bars in and around town. No one had any knowledge of Bud. No one had seen him. It was clear that finding Bud this way was going to be time consuming and chancy.

On the way home, I stopped for gas at Rudy's Shell station on the edge of town. I asked the attendant, a kid in his teens, if he'd heard of Bud Ostermann. One last try couldn't hurt.

"Sure. He comes in here a lot," he said. "Drives a pickup truck, old gray thing, kinda faded-out GMC...fifteen years old, prob'ly."

"What's he look like?" I asked.

"I dunno. Maybe six one, thin, clean shaved."

"Are you sure?"

"Am I sure? Yeah, I see him all the time."

"Does he have a mustache?"

"Not long as I've known him."

"What about a baseball cap? You know, one of those camouflage-type caps that hunters wear?"

"Nope. Never seen Bud in one of them. Does tout a cowboy hat sometimes. Baseball hat? Nope, never."

"You're sure."

"Sure I'm sure."

"Where does he live?" I inquired.

"Don't know. Never asked."

"Did he ever leave an address here? You know, an account for gas or something?"

"Nope. Just comes in, fills up, pays, leaves."

"Really?"

"Yep. That's Bud."

"How do you know this?" I asked. "I mean, what makes you think it's Bud Ostermann?"

"If someone says they's Bud Ostermann, that's good enough for me. I ain't no FBI or nothin'. Far as I'm concerned, that's who he is."

I paid for the gas and drove home. The day was nice, the type of cool but warm midautumn day I remembered growing up in Chicago. I went into the house and opened windows all about. A wistful breeze came and went.

CHAPTER 16

I worked on my book for a while but accomplished little. My thoughts bounced around between my conversations with Ruth McDonald, the confusing information about the house, and the story about the Broding boy disappearing on the property. From the back porch, I looked out across the property at the distant trees, the old school bus, the barn, the pond, the small graveyard behind the row of bushes, and the Waumtauk burial mound I knew to be a stone's throw farther on.

Walking across the field, I stood by the bus. It listed to its side like some forgotten wreck in an automobile junk yard—rusted, faded, flat and decayed tires, broken windows. An old Texas license tag from 1962, as worn out as the bus itself, hung from the back. It must have been from the last time, the last year, the bus had been used. Over fifty years ago now. There was something uncanny about it. Why keep this piece of trash, this God-awful eyesore, for decades, I wondered.

Had Broding and his buddies been playing around out here? Had they gone to the graveyard, to the Waumtauk mound?

Back at the house, I put in another hour on the book but, fully disgusted with what little I had accomplished, I tucked the computer away and drove into Krivac, stopping at the drugstore. As I walked through the aisles, my attention was pulled to the checker, who was talking to someone named Bud. I listened but could make out only bits and pieces of the conversation. From down the aisle, I saw the features of a man about fifty or so with brown thinning hair. No hat. As I moved in closer, he angled away, making it difficult to see much of his face. He spoke in a low voice, saying little, then grabbed his purchase and left. I abandoned my basket and walked toward the front of the store and watched as he crossed the parking lot and climbed into a car—not a pickup truck as the gas station attendant had described but a late-model dark-blue car in good condition. I knew I had seen the car before in Krivac.

Head tilted down, I walked to my car, glancing occasionally toward him. As he pulled onto the road, I drew in behind him trying to keep a safe distance. Not too close, not too far. With so few vehicles, tailing him like this was going to be tough. Another car swung in between us. Yes, I thought. Now I'll be able to follow with less chance of being noticed.

His car stopped in front of the hardware store. He got out and went inside. I drove half a block up the street, parked along the curb, and watched through the rearview mirror. Time passed. I checked my watch: 2:05 p.m.; 2:14 p.m.; 2:22 p.m. I began to wonder if he would be coming out at all. He finally emerged carrying a small bag. He got into his car and drove past, glancing over at me. I turned away and waited until he pulled ahead, this time leaving plenty of room between us. If I could find out where he lived, I would be able to approach him at the right time perhaps. That was all I wanted.

He proceeded slowly, making several unnecessary and redundant turns, once circling around the courthouse for no apparent reason before heading off to the west. Now I had no choice but to slow down and let him get far ahead. Then he looped back through town again. Ah, Christ…now I'll be noticed for sure, I thought.

Then, a second car angled in behind me. I watched it in my mirror, realizing that now *I* was the one being followed. The interloper was close on my tail. Each time I turned, it turned. Time to stop this. I made a sharp left, then a right, and pulled out onto the highway, but the car was with me, holding a steady fifty or sixty yards. When I accelerated, it accelerated. When I slowed down, it slowed down. Finally, thank you, it turned and sped off in the opposite direction.

Feeling foolish and juvenile, I headed back to the house. What in Sam Hill was I doing? Here I was, a new resident in a small town, following people around. How would that look? If nothing else, I had come to know that towns like this have their own natural level of suspicion. I knew that was the case just from talking with a snoop like Ruth McDonald. This could only make matters worse. Back in the city, one as large as Houston, it was possible to be invisible, to blend in with millions of other people. In a small town, one's personal information soon became everyone's business. And I was fueling that attitude. It was the last thing I wanted to do.

I turned onto the dirt road that led to our house. Up ahead, a car was parked in front of the driveway almost blocking it. It was the same car that had been following me minutes before. I coasted onto the shoulder and came to a halt, contemplating what to do. It was obvious that whoever was driving the car knew a much faster way to get to our place. There must be shortcuts I knew nothing about. Worse yet, they knew where I lived.

Perhaps the person just wanted to speak to me. If I could get in close enough, I would be able to see the license plate. I started up again. When I got within distance of the reading the tag, just close enough to make out one or two letters but not all of them, the car accelerated, sending a plume of dust behind it.

I pulled into the driveway, entered the house through the back door, and disarmed the security alarm. The kitchen was warm from the sun glowing in through the windows. I pushed up a window. A gust of autumn air bounded inside.

All I wanted to do now was dislodge my thoughts from the events of the morning. I stood in the dining room doorway and stared at the table. My papers and books were laid out just as I had left them. The chair, too, was exactly as before. But there was an empty space where the computer had been. Dammit! Some bastard had stolen my laptop. It had been in plain sight from the dining-room window, an easy target for a burglar. I searched the house top to bottom and then went outside and walked the edge of it, hoping to find evidence of forced entry, perhaps even the laptop itself.

There were no signs of intrusion. All at once, I realized the obvious. I had set the security alarm before I had left that morning and had disarmed it when I returned. It would have been impossible for someone to enter the house without tripping the alarm and activating a siren so loud it would have been intolerable for more than a couple seconds, and it would have sent an instant message to the central security office.

At the barn, I reached into my pocket, retrieved the barn key, and opened the door. There it was. The computer was sitting on an old table near the far wall, the screen facing away from me. I crept through the barn and looked at the front of the computer, not believing what I saw. In large, red, italic letters was the word

LOCUS

Backing slowly away as though witnessing something alive and dangerous, I stared at the word. The computer was running off the battery; no power cord had been plugged in. Suddenly, the word began to flash on and off. I moved farther away, watching the flashing word in disbelief. There was a pattern—three flashes followed by a small pause, four flashes, another pause, and two more flashes. This went on for several minutes, then stopped. The word *LOCUS* remained on the screen. I glanced around the barn. The floor was a mosaic of footprints, most from myself and Audrey, no doubt. It would be difficult to associate any of them with how the computer had ended up in the barn.

Time to call the police.

Chapter 17

The response from the local police was quick. Within minutes, a Krivac patrol car turned into the driveway. As I walked toward the car, a tall heavyset man who looked every bit the image of a small-town cop stepped out. He had gray-brown hair that crossed his head in a slight comb-over. His face, tanned and ruddy, gave evidence of long hours in the blistering Texas sun. He wore a white well-pressed shirt that held closely to his gut, brown trousers with a black stripe on the side, and a wide black-leather belt to which the usual assortment of police devices and paraphernalia were attached: handcuffs, mace, an automatic pistol, a small flashlight, and a key ring with what appeared to be enough keys to open every door in Krivac. A walkie-talkie was strapped to his shoulder. He retrieved a cowboy hat from the patrol car and nestled it on his head. No cowboy boots on this cop, though—just simple black shoes. Even being the city kid I was, I knew that cowboy boots, the perfect creation for riding a horse, were useless for running or climbing stairs.

"Jack Rainey," he said, giving a good strong handshake. "What can I do for you?"

"Well, I think someone broke into the house."

He glanced about the grounds and then at the house. "Huh. This is the old Ostermann place, isn't it?"

"That's right," I said. "We bought it a couple months ago."

"Hmm. Didn't know it was for sale."

"Really? I thought it had been listed for some time."

"Ah, maybe. I don't keep up with that stuff. You're probably right. So, what's going on?"

I led him to the barn and showed him the computer, telling him that it was in the house on the dining-room table before I went into town, and that when I returned it was out in the barn, turned on, with the word *LOCUS* on the screen as it appeared now.

He looked at the word. "So…who is Locus?" he asked.

"I don't know," I replied. "I don't think it's a person. I'm not sure what it is or what it means, but that's what was on the screen when I found it out here."

"Could mean *locust*. You know, them bugs that come out late in the summer. It could be a misspelling or something. Some people out here ain't so well educated. Maybe they was trying to write *locust*, and it came out *locus*. And we do have a lot of locusts out here, especially this time of year. Kids doing pranks might do something like this… use a word for no reason at all. You wouldn't believe all the stuff I see. Just take a look at the graffiti scribbled on the sides of buildings and boxcars. Huh, try to make sense out of that!"

He had a point.

"But I guess the real question is, how did your computer get from the house to the barn, right?"

"That's right."

He inspected the area around the table and the ground below it. "I don't think we'll learn much from all these footprints," he remarked. "Unless they match up exclusively with some on the outside, perhaps. But we'd have a lot of matching to do. The better thing to do might be to get the computer dusted for fingerprints." He called the station from the radio attached to his shoulder and requested a fingerprint unit. "Let's let things sit here and take a look inside the house."

I showed him the dining room where I had been using the computer earlier in the morning. We went through the whole house, the upstairs and the attic, and went down into the basement.

"Geez, quite a place," he said. "You never see basements in the new houses out in these parts. No point in having 'em. Just collect spiders," he added and chuckled.

Rainey inspected the entrance to the wine cellar. "Looks like someone put a door on here fairly recently."

"I did," I replied. I explained how we had discovered the room and opened the entrance to it.

"Odd," Rainey said, looking at the other basement walls. "Could be more like this down here."

"Other rooms, you mean?"

"Sure. Why not?"

"I suppose. I haven't really looked very hard."

Rainey shrugged and said, "I remember about six or seven years ago there was a house just south of Krivac. The old lady's husband had disappeared. Nobody knew where he'd gone. She said he ran off on her. Well, first thing you do is suspect the spouse. That's Basic Detective Work 101. But she checked out pretty good, even passed a polygraph. But me, I couldn't let it go. Sure enough, down in the basement was a little room, sort of like this one here. She had buried him inside and covered up the entrance. Real spooky—kinda like one of those stories by...what was his name? Edgar Allan Poe, I think." Rainey looked at me, his face half-illuminated by the dull basement lighting, appearing strangely surreal.

"The Cask of Amontillado," I said.

"Is that what it was called? In any event, I had a similar situation a couple of years back. One of your neighbors, actually. Charlie Blacek. Know him?"

"Charlie Blacek? Who doesn't know Charlie?" I said, parroting the response of Ted Zelinski when I'd asked him the same thing. "He was poking around out here the first time I came to take a look at the house."

"That's my boy, Charlie. Well, a couple of two, three years ago, no one had seen Charlie's wife Emma, everyone called her Em. No one had seen her in a while. I paid Charlie a visit. Turns out Em had died at home. Heart attack. Collapsed and fell dead in the kitchen, according to Charlie. He got a pine-box coffin and buried her in the backyard. It's not all that uncommon in these rural areas, even today. I did a little snooping around inside the house; he's got an old root cellar just like this one here. There was a grave outside with Em's name on it. I was in no mood to have her dug up…exhumed, so I let the whole thing go. In fact, I felt sort of sorry for old Charlie." Rainey turned to the wine-cellar door. "Anyhow, you put up a hell of a strong door. Don't get yourself locked in here. You may never get out."

We walked inside.

"I see you like wine. Now that's what I call a hefty supply. Could open your own liquor store. Me, I'm sort of a beer guy, myself." He picked up a bottle from the shelf. "Got a fancy label. Must've cost a pretty penny."

By the time we emerged from the basement, the finger-print unit had arrived. They proceeded to take samples from the laptop.

"Lots of prints here," the technician said, "but we'll see what we get."

"You'll need to do the doorway entrances and the lower windows also," Rainey said, pointing to the house and barn.

We walked around the outside of the house, moving along the perimeter in search of evidence of a break-in. All in all, it proved fruitless.

"So, what do you think happened here?" I asked.

"Well, as I see it there are only two possibilities. The first is a direct break-in through an unlocked window or something like that. But there is no indication of it, and anyway, I assume it would have set off your security alarm. The second, then, is that someone knows how to get into your house. If so, they would need a house key, a barn key, and since you have an alarm system, they would need knowledge of that as well. How to turn it off and how to turn it on, that sort of thing. The second possibility is the only one I consider likely at this time."

"It's a brand new security system," I said. "And all the locks were changed when we moved in a few months ago."

Rainey was unimpressed. "Somehow, *that* computer," pointing to the barn, "got out of *that* house," pointing to the house. "I don't think it walked out. Someone had to move it. And I know what you're probably thinking. If someone went in and took the laptop from the house, why didn't they steal it?"

"Why didn't they?"

"Can't say. I'm a good cop, but I'm not very good at abnormal psychology. The longer I do this, the worse I get at predicting human behavior." Rainey digressed for quite a while, explaining all the types of people he confronted on a regular basis. He pulled a pair of shiny reflective sunglasses from his pocket and put them on, making him a virtual caricature of the typical country cop. He looked around the grounds as though trying to find something he might have overlooked.

"Fact is, someone is messing with you," he continued. "That's how I see it. They ain't trying to steal nothin'. They're sending you a *nice little message* that this place ain't as secure as you think."

My mind flashed to the car that was parked in front of the house when I returned from town this morning. I considered mentioning it to Rainey, but realized it might lead to an explanation of what I was doing in town following Bud's car around and all. That was not something I wanted to share with the local cop.

"You can stop all this pretty quick," Rainey declared.

"Oh? How?"

"Simple. Change the locks…and get the security people out to check the alarm system. Change the alarm code, too."

"We're planning to do that."

"Ah-yeah, well, you do all those things and your house problems will stop. That's my bet." Rainey wiped small beads of perspiration from his brow. He looked out across the property. "Say, what's that out there?"

"Where?"

"There." He pointed to the far end of the pasture.

"That? Just an old school bus. It was here when we bought the place. I was out there this morning. Not much to it, really. Grass has grown up around it. I'm planning to have it hauled off. Great big eyesore."

"Let's have a look," Rainey said and plodded into the pasture.

Walking across the field was slow in the open sun with grass up to our ankles. "Got enough land here for a couple head of cattle, you know, maybe more," Rainey stated, almost with envy. "Good, healthy grass. Get yourself a few steer…do that and you can put beef on the table for a year from just one."

I agreed but told him this was just a retreat for us, our jobs in Houston being time consuming and demanding. I seemed to be explaining this to everyone I met.

When we got to the bus, Rainey circled it several times, making casual comments as he went, suggesting that we might get lucky and find some footprints we could tie in with the intruder. He searched the ground with the eyes of a hawk.

"This here's an old bus," he said. "We haven't used these for years. Cripes, I probably rode on this very bus when I was a kid. I wonder why the Ostermanns had this thing on their property."

He climbed into the bus. Every inch of it had a layer of brown dust across it that had blown in through the open windows. He ran his finger over one of the seats. "Nobody's been here in a long time," he said. "Far as I can tell, just a junky old bus." He looked around, inspecting each part as he moved toward the rear of the bus. On the floor behind one of the seats was an old tin box—some kind of cheap toolbox or fishing-tackle box. It was open, empty of contents. He kicked it aside and looked down, bending over and picking up something under the box. "Huh. Take a look at this, will you," he said.

"At what?"

He rubbed a round piece of metal between his fingers and thumb. "Ever see anything like this?" He handed the object to me.

"Yeah, I know exactly what it is," I replied. "We found it in the house just after we moved in. In the basement, in fact. In the wine cellar. I don't know how it got out here, though. I'm sure it's still back in the house." I examined each side. "You know, now that I look at it, I think it's different from the other one. Yeah, I'm certain of it. The markings here, these glyph-like inscriptions, they aren't the same."

I handed it to Rainey. "Looks like some kind of Indian ornament. All these weird things carved onto it. What'd you call them?"

"Glyphs."

"Uh-huh...well, I don't know. This thing's in good condition. Shiny. Almost like a brand new coin. I'd expect something from Indian times to be old and tarnished. Odd-looking thing," he remarked, rubbing his fingers over it.

"I had someone back in Houston examine the other one, the one at the house. He couldn't make sense of it, so we've just pretty much ignored it."

Rainey tossed it to me. "Well, now you have two." We climbed out of the bus and circled it again. "I don't think we'll get much from here," he declared.

Back at the barn, the fingerprint unit was finishing its work. "You can take the computer if you want," the technician told Rainey. "We're finished with it."

"I guess that's it," Rainey said. "If we find anything, I'll let you know." He started toward his car.

"Uh...Officer Rainey?" I said.

He stopped and turned.

"Let me ask you something. How well did you know the Ostermanns?"

"The Ostermanns? Not very well. All I know is that they lived here a long time."

"Did you know Herman Ostermann? Or Louise?"

"Not really. They were a bit reclusive. But then, so are a lot of people who live out here. They like their privacy. That's why they're here."

"What did Herman do? For a living, I mean."

"I'm not sure. He was retired, I think. They must've had money of some kind, though. Anyway, I don't think I ever made a call out here in all my time on the force. Not until now, that is."

"What about Adam and Bud, their sons? Did you know them?"

"Sure, I knew both of them. I went to school with Bud. Adam was two years older than Bud and me."

"Are you still in touch with them?"

"Boy, this is a change. You're making me feel like *I'm* the one being interrogated," Rainey said, repositioning his cowboy hat, turning it left and right and then up and down until he had it exactly where he wanted it. "Naw, I have no contact with either of them. Anyway, they're not around anymore."

"Not even Bud?"

"Nope. Left years ago."

I looked away and then back at Rainey. "We were told by a couple of people that Bud's still here."

"Here? Here where?"

"Here in Krivac."

Rainey shook his head. "That's not possible. I'd know it if he was. Who told you that?"

"A couple of people," I said.

"Well, they're trying to mess with you, that's what I say. Look, I can tell you something about almost every person in and around this area. Bud Ostermann isn't one of them."

"Uh-huh. Just wondering."

Rainey raised his shoulders as if to say, "That's it, that's all I know."

"Officer, one last thing," I said.

Rainey gave me one of those "Now what?" looks.

"Did you ever hear of someone named Jeffrey Broding? He was a teenager, I think. Apparently he—"

"You don't mean that old rumor about the Broding kid disappearing somewhere out here, do you?"

"I don't know. Yeah, I guess so. What makes you think it's a rumor?"

"Cuz it never happened, *that's* why," Rainey said.

"Really."

"That's right. Total hocus. It never happened. It's a Krivac rumor that's been floating around for decades. Every now and then someone out here dreams up something like this. I don't know why that is, but this isn't the first time. Some folks out here got a real wild imagination, I guess you could say. And I get stuck looking into it all. Doesn't matter, though. They all got it dead wrong because there never was a Jeffrey Broding. Couldn't have been cuz there never was a Broding family. Not in Krivac. Not anywhere *around* Krivac. Nowhere. So that's how it is, Mr. Felton. Case closed. Now, about that computer of yours, if we learn something, I'll let you know." Rainey nodded, got into his car, and drove off.

I removed the computer from the barn. It felt strange picking up and carrying something that had been transported out of a locked house. I returned it to its place on the dining-room table. The word *LOCUS* didn't exist in any of the files on the computer. Whoever put it on the screen must have typed it in and left it there.

I walked to the living room and picked up the first nonagram from the mantle. Examining the new one and the one we had found in the cellar, it was clear they were different in subtle ways. Although both had the same sunlike image trailed by three shooting stars on one side, the inscriptions on the other side were different. I sat in a chair and looked at both nonagrams side by side. Each was in perfect condition. Neither was scuffed or worn, not even the one Rainey had picked up from the floor of the school bus. I pulled a key from my pocket and made a small mark on the edge of one of the nonagrams. The metal, solid as it was, was easy to scratch. I took a quarter from my pocket and did the same thing to it. The faded quarter was far more resistant to scarring. I rolled the nonagrams in my hand the way you do with a couple of coins, wondering what they were, then clicked a picture of them using my cell phone, both sides of each, and loaded the images onto the computer with a description of when and where I had found them. I returned them to the fireplace mantle.

CHAPTER 18

Later that day, I called the security company. The earliest they could come by was the following day. I scheduled an appointment for the morning.

At first planning to return to my book again, I changed my mind, feeling the need to occupy myself with other things—anything that would take my thoughts away from the morning. The comment Rainey had made about not getting locked in the wine cellar stayed with me. Of course, when I put the door up, my intention had been to make the room so secure no one could break in. The wine cellar already contained hundreds of bottles of wine, and we were continuing to add to it all the time. Some were ready to be enjoyed now; most were waiting to mature. The last thing I wanted was for some he-ass to get in and clean us out. Thousands of dollars of wine gone without so much as a sip on our part. When we were away from the house for any length of time, I kept the door bolted. I saw little real chance of locking myself inside.

But Rainey had a point. Communication with the outside world from the wine cellar would be difficult at best. It made sense to have a way to get out in the event we were trapped inside. I took a spade and a crowbar from the barn and placed them behind the wine rack. If nothing else, I figured we could pry open the door.

Later, I talked to Audrey on the phone. It was always good to hear her voice, but especially now in the face of the latest break-in and the latest computer incident. I decided against going over everything that had happened. She would come out to the house on the weekend. I would fill her in on all the sucky details then.

The rest of the day was uneventful. In the evening around ten o'clock, I went out onto the back porch. High, loose, vaporous clouds spread across the dark sky like thin sheets of Belgian lace. The emptiness of the night settled around me. This kind of pure, natural serenity was something we rarely experienced in the city. The feeling of being shut off from the rest of the world. I watched the sliver of a moon as it slipped across the sky.

In the morning, Jennifer Walker, the technician from the security company, arrived as scheduled. She inspected each part of the alarm system throughout the house and opened the control box on the wall next to the door and checked the wiring. "Everything's fine here," she said, closing the box.

"So now what?"

"Let me show you something," Walker replied. We went to her truck, a plain-white van parked in the driveway. She opened the side door. The inside was filled with tools, rolls of wire, and stacks of equipment and diagnostic gear for installing and testing alarm systems. On a small bench sat a computer console with a couple of stools in front of it.

"Are you aware, Mr. Felton, that your system has been deactivated several times in the past couple of months?"

"Well, yes, of course. We turn it off when we come into the house after it's been activated," I said. "If that's what you mean."

"No. What I mean is, someone has managed to turn the system off in order to gain entry to the house. Here, I'll show you." We climbed into the van. Walker turned on the computer and opened a file. The screen flashed through a long list of dated entries that ran down the page, ending with today's date.

"That's the entire record of when your alarm system was activated and deactivated using the control panel in your house. You know how it works. When you leave the house, after you set the alarm, you have thirty seconds to go out the door...front or back, it doesn't matter. When you return, the process is reversed. But here's the problem." She pointed to a specific entry on the screen. "The record indicates that someone—you or your wife, we'll assume—set the alarm and left the house. Then the system was deactivated using the control panel. A short time after that it was reactivated again. But there's no evidence from what I can tell that any of the doors were opened or closed. It's as if someone did this from *inside* the house. This happened several times." She pointed to at least a half-dozen similar entries. "I've never seen anything like it, and I've worked for the company for a long time. I know a lot about how security systems work. I could tell you every little trick used to get around one, but this is a first."

I took out a pencil and piece of paper and scribbled down some of the dates of when the alarm had been deactivated. We climbed out of the van. I said, "So, whoever did this, how'd they get into the house to turn off the alarm?"

Walker closed the doors of the van. "That I don't know. But they did, of course."

"Let me get this straight. You're saying whoever got into the house did it without opening the door."

"That's right. Once they were inside the house, they turned off the alarm and *then* opened the door."

It was unfathomable, yet it made perfect sense considering everything that had happened.

"How many entrances are there?" Walker said.

"The ones you already saw—the front door, the back door, the windows around the house. That's pretty much it."

"Right. And they're all fine."

"Now what?" I asked.

"Reprogram in a new code. Whoever got into the house must know the code because they managed to turn off the alarm. The record confirms that much. Besides yourself, who else has the code?"

"My wife."

"You didn't give it to a neighbor or the police or someone, did you?"

"Absolutely not."

"Well, set up a new code. That's important," Walker said. "We'll see if it makes a difference. If the problem continues, give me a call and I'll come and take another look." She handed me a business card, got into the truck, and backed out of the driveway.

I went into the house and put on shorts, a T-shirt, and running shoes. I needed to process this new information, running would help. I headed down the road in front of the house, going for a long while, then turned onto a small dirt farm road, thinking about what Walker had shown me. If the alarm had been deactivated from inside the house, whoever did it must have been inside at the time we set the alarm. That, I considered impossible. Alternatively, someone knew of a way to get in that didn't involve a door or window. There had to be another access route. Entry through the attic and second floor windows was out of the question. We had ruled these out as being too high, too inaccessible. The only other possibility was the basement. But how? From where? By now, I pretty much knew every inch of it.

I circled back onto the two-lane road and returned to the house. When I arrived, Officer Rainey was leaning against his patrol car in the driveway. "Thought you came out here to relax," he said.

Looking at Rainey, I doubted he had ever so much as run around the courthouse in his entire life. The healthiest horse in the glue factory, as it were. He was eating french fries from a white paper bag. "Waldo's Burger Barn over on Highway 35," he said. "Best fries in the world. Heart attack in a sack is what I call 'em." He held the bag toward me.

I thanked him and declined.

"Well, we didn't get anything from the fingerprints," Rainey said, munching away. "Or perhaps I should say we got too much. Fingerprints everywhere, but nothing of any significance. Just the same, I thought I'd come out and let you know. Too nice a day to be writing parking tickets in town."

"I hope we can get to the bottom of this. I don't like it one bit. I'd like to know who the SOB is and get his ass thrown in jail," I told Rainey. I didn't bring up the security issue Walker had described. I had no intention at this point of sharing it with him. I wiped my face across the sleeve of my shirt.

"We might eventually find out who the perp is. If kids are involved, we'll know sooner or later. They're not good at keeping secrets, that's been my experience. You start asking questions and they fold like a cheap suit. But actually, that's not why I came by. What I want to say is…well, I want to clarify something we talked about yesterday."

"Oh? Clarify what?"

"You see, I do in fact remember responding to a call that had to do with this place about eight or nine years ago."

"But yesterday you told me—"

"Uh-huh, yeah, I know. I said I had never been out here. Well, that's actually not true," he said, making it sound like a trivial oversight. "See, there was this one time. It was in the summer. It had been one of those blistering hot days, hotter than hell's shingles. It was around dusk or a little later. I got a call to go to the Ostermann place. Apparently the neighbors, the folks who lived on the farm down the road, had seen peculiar light coming from the property, but they weren't sure. They said the pond was all lit up...maybe even on fire."

"On *fire*?"

"These things can happen if oil gets onto the water and starts burning. It can start a brush fire. Real dangerous."

I thought about Ruth McDonald's comment about the glowing lights on the property.

"But the pond wasn't on fire," Rainey said.

"What was it, then?"

"I'm not sure."

"Did you see it, the pond?"

Rainey hesitated as though unsure of whether or not to continue. "Okay...I've thought about this for a long time, many years. I never wrote up a report. It had been a busy weekend and I figured if I didn't write a report, no one would know. I'm a real level-headed guy. I didn't want the captain or someone thinking I was losing my marbles."

"What did you see?"

"You ain't gonna tell no one, are you?"

"Of course not."

Rainey took a deep breath and said, "Okay. I remember turning the patrol car into the driveway here. Back then we had these simple black-and-white cars. You know, gumball machine on top and all. I guess I parked about there." He pointed to a spot a few feet from us. "I looked out and sure enough the pond was all lit up in orange and red and green light, sort of glowing, almost shimmering." Rainey shook his hand back and forth, imitating the motion of the lights. "I could see how from a half mile away it might look like fire. So I got out of the car. I remember that the Ostermann house was mostly dark inside, maybe one little light on. As I started walking to the pond, I saw people standing around it. I didn't recognize them—only Herman Ostermann—and I think I saw Charlie Blacek."

"Blacek?" I considered telling Rainey that Blacek claimed he had never been on the property, but I held back.

"That's right, Blacek. And there were others—quite a few, in fact. But no one I recognized."

Rainey's eyes wandered about, occasionally looking at me, sometimes glancing to his left and right.

"And you walked out to the pond?" I said.

"Not exactly. I mean, I *started* walking and then it happened. I got about halfway there when suddenly I was unable to move, as though I was paralyzed standing straight up on my own two legs. I didn't move, didn't fall over. Just stood there. I could see everything…for a little while, at least. I saw the people out by the pond and the lights, then I blacked out. I guess that's what you'd call it. My mind went totally blank. Odd thing is, I could still hear. It was strange. I remember hearing a mockingbird singing all the way throughout the whole thing. It never stopped. Anyway, after a short while, I'm not sure how long, I snapped out of it and was standing exactly where I had been before it all happened. The pond was out in front of me, but it was no longer lit up, just a little glow from the evening sky. Nothing unusual. The people were gone, too. Oddest of all, Herman Ostermann was standing right there beside me. He looked at me and said, 'Are you all right? What are you doing out here?' It was probably the only time he'd ever said two words to me. Ever. And I'm not sure he even knew who I was. Anyway, I was dazed, to say the least...sort of out of it. Herman walked me out of the field and over to my car. I remember feeling tired. Very, very, very tired. The way you feel when you wake up after a lousy night's sleep. You know how it is."

"Then what?"

"Well, in spite of it all, I remember everything that had happened, except maybe while I had blacked out. I'm not real sure about that. But otherwise I knew exactly why I had come out here, and I remembered the glowing pond and the people and all that. Whatever happened, it didn't screw up my memory or nothing."

"When Herman came by, did you tell him what you'd seen? The pond lights or whatever?"

"Okay, that part I'm not so sure of, either. I don't remember if I asked him about it or not. You'd think so, since that was why I had come out here in the first place, but I don't remember for certain. I only remember getting into my car and driving off. Sure as I'm standing here now, that's what happened." Rainey looked at me with a loose stare and said, "Well, I guess that's it." He did his hat thing—side to side, up, down. It seemed to be something he did when he was buying time. Or maybe it was just a quirky habit people develop. I don't know. "You're not going to spread this around now, are you?" he said. It came out more like a warning than a question.

"Why would I?" I replied.

He nodded, shook my hand as though we had sealed a deal of some kind, and started toward his car. He stopped about halfway there, turned, and said, "Incidentally, while we're at it, I suppose I should tell you. Bud Ostermann is here in Krivac. I know I said yesterday he's not, but he is. I see him now and then."

"*What*? Why didn't you tell me yesterday when I asked?"

Rainey looked as if he was about to say something, but merely shrugged and left.

I sat on the back doorstep and watched Rainey drive off. Now I had two descriptions of strange things happening on the property, both involving lights and Herman Ostermann and other people. One story had come from Ruth McDonald. I had dismissed most of it as too far-fetched. But now, Rainey had a story with similarities to Ruth's, the difference being that it had happened to him personally. Oddly, both Ruth

McDonald and Rainey had claimed that Bud Ostermann had left the Krivac area years ago. Then both recanted and claimed he'd been here all along. Part of me didn't give a shit whether Bud Ostermann was in Krivac or California or Timbuktu, but why had I been given such conflicting reports of his whereabouts, most recently coming from an officer of the law whom I would expect to provide straight answers from the very beginning?

I wondered about Krivac. Could it be that the whole town was full of people like Ruth McDonald and Rainey? That it was a town with a strange, screwed-up history? A place as tilted as a lopsided craps table? What if...what if? Fine, go about your business, but leave us out of it. The real question was, could we ignore the things that were happening right under our nose— the troubling situation with the house's security system, for example? To what extent was everything connected—the town, the people, the house? I went inside and reprogrammed the alarm system with a new code and went to the basement and inspected every inch, every millimeter, of it—rubbing the cold old stones, scraping the mortar, looking for evidence of an entrance or hidden portal. I did this back and forth across each wall until I was convinced that whoever got into the house couldn't have done it from the basement.

Later that day, I called Audrey and told her that the security tech had been to the house and that everything checked out fine, which was partly true. I said I had reprogrammed a new code into the system. I didn't mention anything about the alarm being deactivated as Walker had described. It wasn't like me to withhold information from Audrey, but I just couldn't bring myself to tell her at this point. I would give her the details when I saw her. That's how I rationalized it at the moment.

I walked across the pasture and out to the pond. I wanted to see this place, the spot where the "mysterious things" that Rainey and Ruth McDonald had described to me, had taken place. It was a small body of water, about big enough for a few cattle, as Rainey had wistfully said. Looking around, I could barely see the house where the Clausens lived; a line of trees on the distant edge of the property blocked much of the view. Yet, it would have been possible to see what might appear to be flames coming from somewhere far off even if you couldn't see the pond itself.

Nothing about the pond seemed unusual. Ankle-deep grass grew up to a narrow dirt rim that traced the perimeter of the muddy, probably shallow, water. I walked around the edge, kicking over rocks and branches as I went. On the far side, I noticed a cluster of stones arranged in the grass. It was obvious someone had stacked them into a small pile. I knocked them apart with my shoe. They had been there for a long time, the ones on the bottom having settled down into the soil. Underneath one of the stones was something I had come to know well: a nonagram. I picked it up and examined it. Like the other nonagrams, this one was clean, shiny, and unmarked. Now we had three of these strange little buggers—two of which we'd found in just two days.

I wondered how many more there were and how many we would find. I looked at the property, across the pasture, back to the barn, out to the school bus surrounded by grass and weeds. A lot of land for someone used to measuring it in square feet rather than acres. To find two nonagrams by chance, the one Rainey had discovered in the bus and this one, seemed next to impossible unless there were scads of them all over the place.

If I were to find more, what were my chances? I ambled across a swath of land, turning over everything I came across. There were several rock clusters that bore similarities to the one by the pond, but none had nonagrams. I turned over dozens of rocks, even poking down into the soil. I looked under logs, branches, and remnants of old fence posts. From the pond, I viewed the school bus and the graveyard and then headed back to the house, where I photographed the new nonagram and set it on the mantle with the other two.

CHAPTER 19

The next day, I went into Krivac to talk to Rainey. The desk clerk at the small police station said he was down the street at Carter's Lunchbox Café. I later learned that Rainey ate at Carter's almost every day and that he always had the same thing: chicken fried steak with mashed potatoes and cream gravy.

Carter's was a simple place located on the corner of Main and Wellington. It had a lunch counter with a few stools, a half-dozen tables in the center, and a row of booths along the windows. The menu was written on a large blackboard on the wall. The food was basic—all homemade—including the apple, cherry, and pecan pies as well as the bread pudding. Grilled cheese was the special of the day. The waitresses, clad in white uniforms, hair tall on their heads, looked homemade too. Custom designed for a small southern diner.

Rainey was sitting with another man in one of the booths. They had finished their lunch. Rainey took a sip of coffee and looked up. "Mr. Felton," he said. "How are you?"

"Fine," I replied.

"This is Wayne Martin...Colonel Wayne Martin, US Army, retired," Rainey said in a dutiful voice.

A lean middle-aged man with close-cropped salt-and-pepper hair, tanned skin, and steel-blue eyes shook my hand. He mentioned that he had settled into the area after leaving the military. "Nice meeting you," he said. He set some money on the table and left.

I looked at Rainey. "Got a minute?"

He nodded.

I sat at the booth. "You know, yesterday you told me you knew Bud was living somewhere around here. I was wondering, if I could talk to him, I might be able to get some information about the house."

"Like what?"

"You said some interesting stuff yesterday. In fact, Ruth McDonald told me almost the exact same thing had happened to someone named Jesse Gonzalez. Did you know him?"

"Sure, I knew Jesse. Lived here most of his life. Had a small piece of land just down the road from the Ostermann place."

"Raised sheep, I was told," I said.

"I think so. Jesse died sorta strange, though."

"Oh?"

"Yeah. About nine or ten years ago."

"What happened?"

"'Lectercuted hisself. He was trying to rewire part of his house. Ended up rewiring hisself. Too bad. Nice guy. A few people thought there was something suspicious about his death, even speculated that he'd been murdered somehow. I looked into it. Didn't find anything."

"Did you ever tell Ruth McDonald what happened to you out on the Ostermann place?"

"Hell, no! Like I said, I never told anyone. Besides, she's the last person on the planet I'd say something like that to. Not unless you want the whole freaking world to know, to have it spread all over town. That's what Ruth's good at," Rainey said, slightly rattled. "Ruth used to be the town fortune-teller. You know, crystal ball, all that stuff. I don't think she got much business. In a place like this, no one wants to be seen going to a fortune-teller. She eventually gave it up...far as I know, anyway. Ruth's dabbled in a lot of things. For a while, she was the village artist, I guess you could say." He made a pair of air quotes with his fingers as he said the word *artist*. "If that's what you can call it, that is. You'd see her painting in the park. Don't think she ever sold much. These days she mostly dabbles in knowing what other people are doing. She finally found something she's good at."

Rainey's eyes moved about the café, then sharpened on me. "You want me to tell you where Bud is, is that it?"

I nodded.

He sighed and in a low voice said, "Look, I really don't care if you know where Bud is, but just leave me out of it. I don't want anything to do with him."

"What's the deal with Bud?"

Rainey paused and thought. I waited him out, figuring soon enough he'd have to speak. He drew a loud breath and said, "All right. You see, some people think Bud is...well... how should I put it? Not normal."

"Meaning what? That he's, you know, slow or something?"

"No, nothing like that. Just not normal like you and me."

I wasn't sure how much I liked being classified as "normal" with the likes of Rainey. "I don't understand. You mean he's weird or screwed up? Or has some kind of mysterious power?" I said, mostly joking.

"Something like that."

"Something like what?"

"Has a type of power," Rainey said.

"You're serious."

"Yeah. Remember yesterday when I told you what happened out in the field when the Ostermanns lived there? Well, there was more to it than that. I remember a lot more about it. First thing is, it wasn't Herman Ostermann who was standing next to me after I went into the daze. It was *Bud*. I'd seen Bud out in the field by the glowing lights with the other people. I knew it was him right away. Herman and Bud don't look much alike; Herman was older, of course. So anyway, there was Bud suddenly next to me. But he didn't walk over to me or nothing like that. He just *appeared*."

"If you were paralyzed, how can you be sure? Maybe you didn't see him coming up to you. Yesterday you told me you had blacked out. I don't see how you could see him if you had blacked out."

"I did black out. But then there was this time—a short time, not long—when I could see but couldn't move. That's when the thing with Bud happened. One second he was a hundred yards away; a second later, he was right next to me." Rainey reached across the table and clutched my arm with his thick hand, and said, "I'm telling you, there was something real eerie about it." Rainey let go of my arm. "I damn near had a heart attack. Probably would have, but my whole body was stiff as a stone."

Now Rainey seemed to want to get everything out, as if I were a psychiatrist and he were a patient in desperate need of relieving himself of a great burden. "But there's more," he said. "Bud was standing in front of me as close as you are now. I looked straight at him. Everything about him looked like Bud except for his eyes. They were bright red. Fiery red. They glowed like the eyes of an animal at night when you shine a light on them. Fierce looking."

Rainey's story was getting more and more bizarre the further he went, as if he was trying to come up with something big and spectacular, or was testing me to see how I would react to a far-out story he had concocted.

"How can you be sure it was Bud?" I asked.

"Ah, it was *Bud*, all right. I know Bud too well to make a mistake. The hair, the face, everything but those eyes. Then, as soon as he started to talk, the eyes changed back to Bud's. He was completely normal again."

"What do you make of all this?" I asked, turning the issue back on Rainey.

"You mean what do I make of Bud?"

"Yeah, Bud and everything you just said. What's your take on it?"

"I don't have a take on it, that's what happened. I can't explain it, if that's what you mean. All I know is something was going on by the pond. The people out there weren't from these parts. I'd have recognized them if they were. And there were a lot of them, too. Fifteen or twenty. Could've been more."

"Doing what?"

Rainey shook his head. "Holding a meeting of some kind. They were all gathered together. Some held their arms out in front of them; some stood motionless. One of them—I'm not sure who, but I think it was Herman—held his arms up to the sky."

The waitress came by, filled Rainey's coffee cup, and shot a quick glance at me. After she left, he said, "Anyway, what I'm saying is that I want nothing to do with Bud. Dude's way too strange."

"But you're sure he's still here?"

"Absolutely. I see him around town quite a bit."

"And he's never caused you any trouble?"

"No, but that time out on the property was pretty damn spooky, to say the least." Rainey rested his hand on the table and pointed it at me like a pistol. "I hate to tell you this, but what you should do is sell the place—the house, everything. Fast as you can! There's something not right about it."

"We just bought it," I replied.

"Doesn't matter. Get rid of it. Bad juju, Tarzan. Let it be someone else's trouble. Everyone knows the Ostermann place is different, but you'll never get them to talk about it."

"Well, Ruth MacDonald was eager to talk."

"I already told you about Ruth. She's an old windbag. You can't know what to believe with her. I know more about this town than anyone. The reason the Ostermann property was so cheap was because no one from Krivac would ever buy it. They had to knock the price way down, and even then, not a thing until you folks came along. Know how long that place was on the market?"

"Couple of weeks, according to Ted Zelinski."

Rainey threw his head back and guffawed long and deep and hard. He leaned forward and looked at me with sharp eyes. "Couple of weeks? Couple of weeks, my ass. Let's try three years. That's how long Louise Ostermann has been away, too. At least three years. Zelinski tried selling that place, all right. He'll sell anything he can slap a sign in front of, or stick a picture of in that real estate window of his. Zelinski's sold more houses, ranches, *and* trailers out here than a hound dog has fleas. The guy could sell dentures to sharks. But he had that baby listed for three years and couldn't move it to save his soul. It was as though there was some weird barrier surrounding it. He once told me he was so sick of it, all he wanted to do was unload it any way he could. It had become a royal pain in the ass. Every time he located a serious buyer, something happened. Once he had this couple…soon as they pulled into the driveway, the guy's wife got a call on her cell phone saying their daughter was about to have her baby. They had to leave right away. That kind of stuff happened over and over. Zelinski all but gave up showing it. That was fine with the town folks. They'd just as soon pretend it doesn't exist."

"It was no problem for us. We drove up, checked the place out, bought it. That was it. Pretty normal really."

"Normal, ha! Let me tell you what's really normal. You didn't buy the Ostermann house. The Ostermann house bought *you*. Don't ask me why," he said, holding a palm toward me. "But it did. Place has a mind of its own."

"Well, regardless, that's not what I came here for," I said. "I got this in the mail." I pulled an envelope from my shirt pocket and tossed it on the table. "Go ahead, take a look."

Rainey picked up the envelope and removed a sheet of paper. On it, the words *TIME TO LEAVE!* were typed in tall letters. He read it and turned his eyes to me. "*Hey, now wait just a minute, hermano! You think I sent this?*" he said emphatically, pressing himself against the back of the booth.

"It came today. That's all I know. It's postmarked from Krivac."

"Well, it didn't come from me!"

"Fine," I said. In fact, I never considered that it had come from Rainey despite what he had just said about selling the house. "But it seems as though there's more than one person

171

who thinks we should leave. Ruth said it. You said it. Now this letter. Is there some way you can find out where this thing came from? Find out who sent it?"

Rainey shifted back into cop mode. He shook his head and said, "Next to impossible. That thing was printed from a computer. Standard font. Every computer would have that font. And you can be pretty damn sure whoever did it wore gloves or something...no fingerprints. You won't get any juice outta that orange." He handed the letter back to me.

"I mentioned this to Audrey when I called her today. I can assure you she's not at all happy about it."

"No, of course not." He leaned forward, resting both arms on the table. "Tell me, Mr. Felton. What exactly do you know about this town?"

I remembered Charlie Blacek asking almost the exact same question the first time I was at the house. "Krivac, you mean?"

"Yeah, Krivac."

"Nothing. We've only been here a couple of months. We didn't exactly conduct a detailed historical evaluation of it, if that's what you mean. Why would we?"

"Well, this is not your ordinary small country town," Rainey affirmed. "Not by a long shot. We don't have many people moving in. Not very often. Hardly ever, in fact. People here don't take well to it, if you want the truth."

"Oh?"

"You're telling me you hadn't noticed this?" Rainey said.

"Not really."

"Everyone's been fine, then."

"Why wouldn't they be?"

"That's the reason you got the letter in the mail. Look around the café here. Any one of these people could have sent it. Any one of them. I hear the stuff they say among themselves, talking about the city folks who moved in."

"What are they going to do, tar and feather us and run us out of town on a rail or something?"

"Nah, they won't do *that*. Besides, I wouldn't let them," Rainey said.

"That's comforting."

"My job here is to keep the peace, pure and simple. But they have their ways. That letter of yours," he said, pointing to the envelope, "is as good an example as any. That's more their style. You see, the people in this town hated the Ostermanns. Hated them! Say what you want, these folks here have a long memory. What they might lack in this stuff," tapping the side of his head with the tip of his finger, "they make up for in memory. You could say they operate on a very basic set of instincts."

"You make it sound like they're all a bunch of goons."

"Do I?"

"Well, listen to what you just said."

"What I said is, it's a small town with its own way of doing things. That's all. People here aren't accustomed to outsiders. For example, a couple of years back we had some Gypsies come through here. Every summer they move across the south from Arizona to Florida hitting the state fairs and whatnot. Gypsies are easy to spot because they always travel in small caravans of three or four campers. They set up shop outside the fair, do a few palm readings, Tarot cards, that kind of junk. For me, I couldn't give a hoot so long as they don't break the law while they're here. But the locals don't like them. We got a lot of people in this region whose ancestors came from parts of Europe where Gypsies were common. They heard bad stories from their grandparents and great-grandparents. Well, the people here didn't like the Gypsies staying out on the edge of town. It's all you heard anyone talk about when you were in here." Rainey held his hand out toward the café. "In the middle of the night, someone spray-painted the side of one of the Gypsy vans with the word *EVIL!* Risky business, but somehow they managed to pull it off. I don't exactly know who did it or how they got away with it. The Gypsies usually have dogs and plenty of guns."

"Come on, now, you're not saying these folks think Audrey and I are a couple of Gypsies."

"Probably not, no. I'm just saying beware."

"*Look*, we came out here to relax. We really don't care what goes on in town. We don't pay much attention to it, if you need to know. All we do is drive in now and then, get what we want, and go back to the house."

"Let's put it this way," Rainey said. "You folks already have two strikes against you. See…first, you're from Houston. That might as well be Cairo or Calcutta or somewhere. Second, you live in the old Ostermann house."

"Well, we're not the Ostermanns, okay? These people need to get it straight. Whatever those folks did has nothing to do with us. For that matter, what exactly did they *do* to piss everyone off so much?"

"For one thing, the government, the feds or whatever you want to call them, did a lot of poking around out here. It all had to do with the Ostermanns. Herman Ostermann was up to something and the feds wanted to know what it was… wanted to know real bad. The G-men always tried to blend in when they were here, but it was obvious as hell who they were. You could spot them a mile away. It was like the Pope walking through town or something. So, what were the feds doing here? Can't say. They never really let on about what they were up to. And as I said before, no one knew the Ostermanns very well. I knew Bud when I was a kid, like I just mentioned. Louise tried to give him and Adam a normal life. It wasn't easy, though. Not with Herman there. It was because of Herman that the government was here at all. That's all I know. But back to the townspeople. As far as they were concerned, whenever something strange happened, it was always because of the Ostermanns. If we had a drought, it was the Ostermanns' fault. If we had floods or heavy rains, it was their fault. The year the old Smith Department Store on Main Street burned down, same thing. If someone's steer got sick or a heifer died, it was because of the Ostermanns. Now, you folks own the house…and if anything bad happens—get ready."

I looked around. "No one here seems particularly hostile toward me. No one's even paying attention."

"They are, mark my word. You just don't see it. The cook, there—Bernie. Every time he slides an order up and rings the bell for the waitress, he takes a quick look over here. I see it. You're just not tuned in, that's all."

"Louise Ostermann said people from town had been trying to break into the house for years."

"Did she?"

"All the time they lived there. That's what she said."

"Ah-yeah, I wouldn't know about that. I never talked to Louise. They were total recluses—Herman and Louise. Never left the property. Almost never, anyway. Maybe into town, once, twice, in all the years. That's about it. Wanna know when the last time was someone moved into Krivac?"

"We playing twenty questions now?"

"Nobody's *ever* moved into Krivac. You folks, that's it."

"What about the colonel dude?"

"He doesn't count."

"Why not?"

"Long story."

I told Rainey about the third nonagram I'd found out by the pond. It drew little reaction.

"How many of these things do you have now?" he asked.

"Three. But I'm beginning to think the property's loaded with them," I said, half-serious. I gave him the details of where I found the new nonagram.

Rainey listened, sipping coffee, saying nothing. His face portrayed casual interest. The "no-surprise" cop look was all

I got, though I could tell he was following every word. That lack of reaction made me wonder if I had hit on something he already knew or if he was just letting the information filter through himself. "Got a minute?" he asked.

"Uh-huh. For what?"

"Come with me."

Rainey tossed a few bills on the table. He told me to follow him in my car.

CHAPTER 20

We drove through Krivac to the edge of town. For some reason, I thought we might be going to meet up with Bud, but that's not what happened. Rainey pulled to the side of the road near a bridge that crossed over a small stream I knew to be Bell's Creek. Getting out of my car, I followed him under the bridge to the creek.

"Wait here," he said. "I'll be back in a minute."

Even at midday, it felt strange standing in the dark shadows, not knowing what to expect. Soon Rainey returned carrying a small strongbox. He set it on the ground and dusted it off; it was evident it had been buried. He took a key from his key ring, unlocked the box, and removed a clean cloth bag that had been placed inside. He laid a second cloth on the ground with great care, as if he was about to spread out a packet of precious jewels. He deposited the contents of the bag: a collection of nonagrams, eleven in all.

"Where'd you get these?"

"From Bud. He gave them to me a long time ago."

"When? Before the incident happened on the property, the one you described at the café?"

"Way before that."

"What'd he want you to do with them?"

"Keep 'em. That's all he said. Just keep 'em safe. And here they are."

"They're nonagrams, just like the one you picked up out in the school bus. But you acted as though you'd never seen one before."

"I had no plans to tell you about these…or about anything else that has to do with the house. It wasn't my business to do that. Not until you started asking. Then I figured, okay, if you want to know, I'll tell you."

"You must have some idea what they are."

"They're connected to the house and to the land, that much I know. It's why Bud wanted them away from the property."

"But he could have done that himself. He didn't need to give them to you."

"That's the whole point," Rainey said. "He *did* need to give them to me…or to someone. You see, he couldn't keep them. Everything's connected—the house, the Ostermanns, these. As long as he had them or knew where they were, the connection existed. Exactly in what way, I have no idea. Bud knows but he'll never say, that's what I reckon. He knows stuff no one should ever know. Everything that happened out at the pond, the things we talked about yesterday—that's just the tip of the iceberg." Eyebrow raised, staring straight at me, Rainey said, "Let me tell you, a lot of crap happened out at the house. Bud told me bits and pieces when we were kids. Not all of it by any means, but enough."

"What was it?"

"Dangerous stuff, experimental stuff."

"Such as."

"The most he ever said was that his father, Herman, was messing around with mind experiments of some kind. That's where the feds, the G-men, fit into this. And all the weird stuff I told you about back at the café. It was all related to what Herman knew, or had figured out, or whatever. He had a lot of connections with strange people. The feds, they wanted to know what Herman knew. That's what Bud claimed. They could control you, these people could. Control what you think, control what you do. Just like what happened to me in the field. A lot of folks in Krivac know about this. That's why they're scared as hell to go near the place. Bud said Herman had special ties with the, you know, with the strange people. The feds knew about all this, but they let Herman do his thing. The government could have stopped it, but they didn't. In the end, Krivac became a human laboratory of sorts—a bunch of human lab rats. The government watched it happen. Benign neglect on their part is what it was."

"Sounds like a lot of conspiracy hooey to me. I don't see what the Ostermanns or the government had to gain from this."

"What they had to gain was simple. Could they control people or not? That was the question. Ostermann was trying to see if his method, his system, worked. He had to test it out on someone. He couldn't exactly stick a sign on the bulletin board at the café saying: 'Need volunteers who want to have their heads twisted. Stop by the Ostermann place if interested.' I know it's true because people out here have changed a lot. A hell of a lot," Rainey declared. "It's a different kinda place, different sorta people, from when I was a kid. It all started about the time the feds began hanging around."

"Everything's different from when we were kids. The whole world has changed. You haven't noticed?"

"Not that. What I'm saying is, something was done to screw with people's heads, the way they think."

"Cut it out."

Rainey shrugged. "Have it your way. I know what I know. It was sporadic, though. Something strange would happen one minute and then everything would be back to normal the next. And it never affected everyone. A few here, a few there, off and on."

"You?"

He shook his head but didn't answer.

"What makes you think it was something Herman did?" I said. "Could be all those pesticides they've been dumping on the land out here for the past fifty years. Ever consider that? That stuff will screw your head up pretty bad, you know. No way to rule that out."

"Then why not Shiner? Or Yoakum…or Gonzales, or any other small town nearby? They drink the same water, eat the same food. You don't think a couple of miles this way or that makes a difference, do you? No, it was the feds…*and* something about that place of yours."

"You *think* so or do you know it for a fact?"

"I have it on good background," Rainey said, giving no details. "Look, when people start acting weird for no reason, do something crazy one minute, then they're perfectly normal the next, it *ain't* from pesticides. For example, one time I was sitting in Carter's—right in that very same booth we were sitting at a few minutes ago. George Ballard comes over and sits right there where you were. I've known old George for years. Guy's regular as cornflakes. Has an insurance office up the street. He starts talking. Nothing unusual at first, but then his eyes crossed and he went into this weird stare for a few second, ten or twenty maybe; not long, but he doesn't move a muscle. Then he looks at me and suddenly starts talking backwards. Says, 'breakfast some me get I'll think.' He went on for a good five minutes like that. Some of it was just plain gibberish. And there were these funny sounds mixed in. Clicking sounds. Real strange. I thought it was a stupid joke at first, but he even tried ordering from Evelyn, the waitress, that way. And out of the blue, *bam*—he stares straight ahead just like before and starts talking normal again. It was like someone was flipping switches on and off in his head. When he came out of it, I said, 'George, what the hell's going on?' I was thinking we might have to cart him off to the clinic down the street. Thought he might have had a seizure or something. I told him what had happened. He remembered nothing...he thought *I* was the one joking."

"And you believe the government's involved in this? Is that it?" I said.

"They had their hand in it. Of course, it was Herman Ostermann who actually did it. *That*, I'm convinced of. He was the one popping the switches on and off." Rainey read my skepticism. "You don't believe me? Try this one out. There had been a push on the part of some of the locals here in Krivac to get rid of the Ostermanns—make them leave. No one knew exactly how they would do this. Buy up the house somehow, who knows. But there were lots of meetings about it. Molly Graham led the whole affair. Did all the organizing. Called all the meetings. What happens to Molly? Right there during one of the meetings, she has a heart attack. Right while the whole bunch is listening to her talk about the Ostermanns and all. Fell down dead and not a soul could get her back, try as they might. That was the end of old Molly Graham. And the end of any attempt to chase the Ostermanns out of town." Rainey looked around as if making sure no one was lurking nearby. "It gets even stranger," he said. "Everything was pretty much normal for a while until—" He abruptly stopped talking.

"Until what?"

"Okay. Suddenly people started having visions of the future. Not everyone, of course, but enough did. And it wasn't pretty, either. I mean, it wasn't never about winning a few million in the lottery. Nothing like that. Take Frank Stenko, for example. One day, he tells me he's been having these visions that he's falling off a building. He said they weren't dreams but were vivid images that flashed into his head in the middle of the day. Then, he's working up there on the top of one of the stores over on Timmons Street just around the corner from Main. And what happens? Off he goes. Lost his balance. Tripped, according to the people who were up there with him. I've got a dozen stories like that, all having to do with elaborate visions of the future. Now, you're not going to tell me *that's* normal or that it's due to pesticides or something. It was old man Ostermann. Exactly like what Bud told me when we were kids. Mind experiments. What's more, it all stopped about the time Herman died. I wouldn't say everything is exactly normal now, but it ain't as screwed up as it had been."

"These nonagrams—does Bud know where they are?"

"No. It's why he gave them to me in the first place. I'm always careful when I come out here—you know, making sure no one's following me or anything."

"Who else knows they're here?"

"Just me...and now you."

"That's it?"

"Just you and me," Rainey said, as if I should be proud of the fact.

A little odd, I thought. "Why me?"

"Because you found the other ones."

It wasn't very convincing. Rainey picked up on this. "Okay, the reason I showed you these is because I think you need to give me the ones you have. Give me those and any others you find out there on the property. I can keep 'em safe. It's the best thing to do."

I didn't answer.

Rainey tried again. "If they're away from the house, your problems will let up. The break-ins, for example. Then you and Audrey can get on with your life the way you planned."

"Whoever is messing around with the house isn't after nonagrams. They were sitting right there on the mantle for everyone to see." I reminded Rainey that he had made a similar prediction when he told us to change the security alarm code and the door locks.

"That was different," he claimed.

"Different how?"

"Just like you said. The people messing with the house are not after nonagrams. For that matter, hardly anyone knows about them."

"This doesn't add up," I told him. "If townspeople are breaking in, why would they do that if they're so uptight about the house?"

"Maybe it's not townspeople. Did you ever consider that?"

"Who else would it be?"

"Hey, you're looking at the local cop, not Einstein."

"I don't know, you seem to have figured out a lot of other stuff," I said, acerbically.

"It could be anybody. But if you put two and two together, here's what you come up with. Someone gets into the house. You don't know who or how, but they do. They leave the nonagrams alone, right? And they move the computer around and write something weird on it."

"*Locus.*"

"Yeah, *locus.* Personally, I don't think that *locus* word means beans. It's just another way to mess with your head. Doing a right good job, aren't they? There you have it, two and two equals four. They're messing with your head, pure and simple. But whoever is doing it—who knows, maybe it's the same person that sent you the letter you got—whoever is doing it is telling you to get the hell out of there."

Rainey was putting a lot of pieces into a puzzle that didn't fit well. On the one hand, he claimed the nonagrams were connected to the break-ins, said that if they were away from the house, the break-ins would stop. Then he stated that the intruders weren't after nonagrams at all, which was correct. I knew that as well. I put it to Rainey.

He shrugged, collected the nonagrams, and wrapped them. "While we're out here, I might as well tell you something else," he said, setting the bag in the box. "It's about the Broding kid. Yeah, he was from Krivac, and yeah, he did disappear out there on your property."

I was stunned. Another bombshell from Rainey. What was going on? Why not just level with me the first time around?

He took in a long slow breath, and said, "It's a complicated mess. People out here are real sensitive about the

Broding situation. As they see it, it's one more bit of bad news tied to the Ostermanns. And *that* they don't need. But he disappeared all right, the Broding boy. I was the one given the job of looking into it. And look I did. Talked to all his school buddies. Turns out Broding had found something on the Ostermann property when he was out there once by himself. Found something or learned something, not sure which. But whatever it was, he shared it with his pals Schneider and Lefty Robinson. They wouldn't tell me what they knew. Wouldn't say a word. Believe me, I tried to find out. Pressed those kids hard but got nothing. You can't force someone to speak. Even so, I'm pretty good at getting information out of people. Know how to work people. I have good cop psychology, you might say. Not this time, though. Whatever it was those kids knew, they were keeping it to themselves. All I know is that all three of them went back to the Ostermann place on that day in December. It really had nothing to do with the school bus like they'd originally claimed, that much I did learn. It had to do with the old graveyard out on the back of the property. That's it. That's all they'd say. I tried again several times over the years but got nowhere. Then, when they turned eighteen, both of them—Schneider and Robinson—left. Left real quick. Haven't heard from them since. Don't even know where they are. And the Broding family, they took off right away after young Jeffrey disappeared. Packed up and left."

"That's what I heard. But about the kid—correct me if I'm wrong—wouldn't you guys get a search warrant for the property and maybe the Ostermann house too, just to check things out?"

"Not necessarily," Rainey replied. "You need a good reason to go poking around in someone's house…on someone's property."

"*Good reason!*"

"Yeah, good reason. We weren't even sure it happened out there at all. What can you believe from a couple of thirteen-year-olds? Tell me, how'd you find out about this?"

"From the library."

"I thought all that stuff was gone," Rainey said. He looked quickly at me as if wanting to retract his words.

"Well, people don't just vanish," I said.

"Broding did."

"There must be something more, because if that's all it was, why would Schneider and Robinson be so reluctant to talk?"

"Because they were scared as hell, that's why."

"Do *you* know what happened to Broding?" I watched Rainey's reaction closely.

"Me? Do *I* know?"

"Do you?"

"How would I know? I was trying to find out what happened."

"Did you, eventually?"

"I just got done saying I tried like hell to find out."

"And?"

Rainey was uncomfortable with this.

I said, "Even if Schneider and Robinson never told you, you could piece things together. Cops do that…on television, anyway."

Rainey tried to laugh. He said, "I have my suspicions."

"Foul play on the part of the two boys?"

"Nah, not those two. When you've been in this business as long I have, you can read people. Those boys wanted to tell me—both of them did—but they were scared out of their pants to say a word. That's not the behavior of kids wanting to get something off their chest. Kids crack easy."

"Nonagrams?"

"Nah."

"These suspicions of yours."

Rainey glanced up at the trees and then down at the box at our feet. "The Ostermann grave," he reluctantly said, sounding as if he now regretted bringing the whole matter up. "Something to do with the Ostermann grave."

"I learned that someone removed newspaper articles from the library about the Ostermann house," I said. "Know anything about that?"

Rainey shook his head. He picked up the box. "Better just give me whatever nonagrams you have…for safekeeping."

I didn't know what Rainey was up to, but I didn't like it.

Chapter 21

O nce a night owl, always a night owl. I sat in the living room until late. The lights were off. There was nothing but darkness—soft, tranquil, quiet darkness. The stillness of the night seeped into me and perfused my body like a vapor, tempering my thoughts. I went to the window and gazed at the black and tarry sky, at the pasture and the pond, now a blur in the distance except for the reflection of the moon off the water. The air was motionless; all movement of the trees had been aborted. For a moment, I thought I saw a flash of light from the pond but decided it was only a trick played on my brain by my eyes.

I returned to the chair and sank deep into thought, toying with the idea of finding other nonagrams. I wondered if they were truly valuable in some way. Why would Rainey have buried them if they weren't? But what was the chance of finding something the size of a coin on sixty-three acres of soil, grass, leaves, and stones—not to mention stacks of wood, a rusted old school bus, a pond of muddy water sitting on top of a layer of thick Texas mud? This was the proverbial needle in the proverbial haystack. I would need a strategy. Trying to search the entire property would be futile; the chances of success were minuscule. I needed a way to zero in on the nonagrams, sort of a strong electromagnet to pull that needle out of the haystack. Of course, I had no electromagnet of that sort. A metal detector perhaps. One of those things old guffers use to hunt for coins on the beaches in Florida.

Yet the limitations of this were obvious. First, it would require scanning the vast surface of the property foot by foot, inch by inch. Second, what if the nonagrams were buried deep in the soil? That would preclude finding them with a simple metal detector. Perhaps my odds would be enhanced by selecting only areas where I had found the other nonagrams or where human contact was most frequent—in and around the house, the school bus, the pond, plus places like the barn and maybe even the graveyard. The flaw in that assumption did not escape me, however. Just because three nonagrams had been there didn't mean others were nearby. They could be anywhere on the property—tossed around like beads at Mardi Gras.

As I thought about this, I both accepted and rejected my own arguments. And yet one thing kept coming back: Rainey wanted them. They must have *some* value. Okay, so why had he not hunted for them? The Ostermann property had been vacant for some time before we purchased it. It would have been easy for him in his position as a cop to stop by and snoop around anywhere he wanted to. I went upstairs and climbed into bed.

The morning was clear and cool. I had coffee on the back porch. The pale gray-blue sky was dotted with fluffy, slow-moving clouds that had tattered diffuse ends, making them look like pieces of teased cotton stuffed high overhead. The misty fog that had settled onto the pasture was now gone, burned off by the sun that filtered through the clouds.

In the afternoon, I went to the hardware store in Krivac to buy a handheld metal detector. The old codger who ran the store told me they don't carry "widgets." I should try the Walmart on the south side of town. I drove over to Walmart. They had a stack of metal detectors—right there in the "Widgets and Doodads" aisle. As I was leaving the store, I crossed paths with Rainey who was on his way in.

"Ah, Michael. Doing some shopping, I see," he said.

Carrying the well-marked package with the description of its contents written in big letters across the side, it was clear what I had bought.

"A metal detector," Rainey said, glowing like a butcher's dog. I felt like a sixteen-year-old caught with a six-pack of beer. "Looking for nonagrams out on the property?"

"Looking for metal."

"And nonagrams?"

"And whatever I find. The property is old. The house has been there a long time. No telling what's there."

"True," Rainey conceded.

"Have a good day," I said and walked away.

"Ah-yup. You too," Rainey replied. "Incidentally," he called. "You didn't tell me you and your wife are university professors."

I turned and glared at Rainey. "How do you know that?"

"I know lots of things. It's part of my job."

"Oh really. Is this what you were telling me the other day at Carter's? About keeping track of the city folks who move here? Or do you look into people's lives for no reason at all?"

"Not for no reason," he said. "The reason is maybe I can help people better if I know something about them."

I didn't like his answer, and I didn't like what seemed to be Rainey's frivolous invasion of our privacy. He wasn't trying to protect us; he was feeding information to the townspeople. Stoking the fire. That pissed me off in spades. As I walked away, I heard him call, "By the way, Michael...you're wasting your time if you plan to use that thing out by the school bus. The metal will light that gizmo up like a carnival ride. And another thing..."

I stopped and looked at Rainey. "What?"

"About the other day out at the creek. Not a word to anyone, huh? Nothing about the Broding kid."

Back at the house I drew up a map that I would use for searching the property, one for each section to be explored. If I found anything, regardless what it was, I would mark it with a number on the map that would correspond to a detailed description I would record in a journal. I reasoned that at the very least, this would permit me to identify places where human activity had been greatest. I would start at the most distant locations—the school bus and graveyard—and work toward the house.

I spent several days scanning the property. A large cache of assorted metallic objects turned up: nuts, bolts, screws, old tin cans, part of an old crankshaft, bottle caps and the remains of picnics, a metal dinner plate of some sort, more metal can parts, and an assortment of interesting old coins, including one dating from 1914, suggesting there had been a lot of activity on the property going back many years.

The best source of metal came from around the pond. I had the feeling a lot had happened out there over the years. In contrast, I found little out by the graveyard. Rainey had been right about the school bus. It sent the metal detector into a tailspin. The barn, however, yielded predictable pieces of farm junk: lug nuts, screws, bolts, nails, cotter pins, you name it. I kept going back to the pond; the amount of metal continued to pile up.

Then one day I got a break. The dial snapped to the right. There it was—the tip of a nonagram sticking out of the soil. I picked it up, cleaned it off, studied it for a moment, and went to the house. I took a picture and put it in the computer with the images of the other nonagrams. So far, none of the four nonagrams were identical. Each was slightly different. What set them apart was the number of symbols they had, the glyphs that were carved onto the back. The first one had four, the second had eight, the third had seven, and the new one had twelve.

I returned to my search. Along the east edge of the property close to the road, I found a stone marker about four inches across. It was almost flush with the ground and nearly covered in a patch of grass and weeds. I stooped down, dusted it off, pulled grass away, and gripped it with both hands, trying to move it. It didn't budge an inch. Whatever it was, it went deep into the ground.

A nine-pointed star was cut onto its surface. I stood up and gazed around the field. On the north end was the old school bus. The graveyard was up near the northwest corner. I walked along the east side heading south, where I came upon a second marker. Then, just around the edge of the northeast side, I found a third one. All three were flat to the ground and all had the same nine-pointed star. I retrieved a tape measure from the house. The distance between two markers was a 198 feet. I cut a piece of rope to that length, staked one end next to the marker, and trudged across the pasture with the other end of the rope. When I got to the end, I walked up and down in an arc, kicking away grass and weeds until I came face-to-face with the old school bus.

I looked under the bus. Even with its flattened and rotted tires, the bus's underside was above the ground by eighteen inches or so. The grass had grown almost to the bottom of the bus in some places; in other places it was sparse.

With a long stick in hand, I started under the bus. I hadn't gone far when I encountered a large spiderweb a foot or so across. At its center was a mean-looking black-and-yellow spider as big as my palm. Not at all one of my favorite things!

I took the stick and encouraged it to take a stroll. I thrashed across the ground several more times in case other members of the spider's "family" remained.

From where the rope ended next to the bus, it was easy to predict the probable location of a marker underneath. Sure enough, there it was. I climbed out from below the bus and dusted myself off.

I found a fifth marker in the northwest corner behind the graveyard. A sixth and a seventh marker were positioned along the west end of the property. Two additional markers, an eighth and a ninth, were on the south end—one between the house and the road, the other between the barn and the road. So, there were nine of these in all, assuming they were equally spaced and assuming I hadn't missed any. Big assumptions. I sat at the picnic table and made a sketch in my log book of the location of the markers. Funny, but they more or less formed a giant nonagram, each marker designating the end of a spoke with the pond making up the center. A peculiar but odd arrangement that would not make sense until much later.

Chapter 22

Strange how it goes sometimes—once the ball gets rolling, it's hard to stop it. Momentum takes over and you find yourself going headlong in a direction you could never have predicted.

The day was cool and overcast but not cold—a typical November day in east-central Texas. I went to town for charcoal. Audrey would be out in a couple of days. Weather permitting, we would toss something on the grill and procure a good bottle of Bordeaux or a Rhône from the cellar. The peace and quiet of the house was good, but it was beginning to get to me. I was in need of conversation...not to mention someone whose bones I could jump.

Walking down Main Street, I heard the screech of tires on pavement and a wallop. Turning, I saw a young boy about eight or nine or so lying in the street. People rushed to his side. Someone checked his pulse. Someone listened to his heart. He might have been alive, I couldn't tell from where I stood. A crowd gathered on the curb, mouths covered in horror.

The response of the fire department ambulance was quick—they were there in minutes. They placed the boy on a stretcher. Even from a distance, I could see his chest rise and sink—he was still breathing. The doors of the ambulance were closed. In seconds it was racing down the street for the hospital in Hallettsville. Hallettsville or somewhere else, Krivac not having a hospital.

Seeing that took the wind out of my sails. I abandoned my thoughts of buying anything. Turning to go to my car, I heard a loud and shrill shout.

"It's all *his* fault!"

I assumed the person was screaming at the driver that hit the kid, but not so. I saw an outstretched arm and a finger pointing at me. Me! Why *me*?

Someone else yelled, "Yes, it's him! Get him!"

Soon a half-dozen people of all ages joined in. I felt trapped as I watched the display of anger directed toward me. Never in all my years had I been accused so blatantly of something I had not done, something I'd had no hand in. As I began to back away, Rainey came rushing down the street, chugging and puffing. He called to several people by name. "Wilbur! Jonas! Scottie! Stop it! Get control of yourself!" he ordered, as if talking to a pack of angry guard dogs.

"It's because of *him*!" came a voice from the crowd.

Rainey's voice boomed. "That's it, everybody! Enough! On your way. Hear me? All of you, get moving. Go!"

More invectives flew from the crowd. As Rainey started in their direction, they cowered and slunk off. Rainey came over to where I stood. He looked uncomfortable, as if he had succeeded in controlling the mob, but not by very much. He removed a handkerchief from his pocket, swept it across his face, and said, "There are some people out here that have a real short fuse. Told you that in Carter's the other day. Best thing to do is go back home. Maybe do your errands some-place else for a while."

To this, I willingly agreed.

When I arrived back at the house, I considered telling Audrey what had happened. Although deciding against it at first, I decided she needed to know. I called and gave her the details of my encounter in Krivac, telling her how quickly the people had turned on me for no reason at all. She was flum-moxed and hugely concerned.

For the rest of the day, I thought about it almost all the time. The incident itself was disturbing, but perhaps worse was the way it fulfilled Rainey's prediction of the town's per-ception of us. A prediction that Ruth McDonald herself had warned about without providing any details. Did I believe them now? One thing for sure, we would be staying out of Krivac for a long time, probably for good.

The thought occurred to me that we might need some-thing to protect ourselves, something besides a thirty-two-inch Louisville Slugger. There was nothing inside the house that would be of much use. From the barn, I retrieved a hand ax and stashed it under the kitchen sink for easy access.

All evening I sat nervously in the living room, keeping the lights low and the shutters mostly closed. I had a strange feeling that I might be getting a visit from the Krivac Kiwanis Club or some other jovial bunch of Krivac do-gooders like the ones who had descended on me in town after the accident. It was making me edgy. Though I wanted to remain clear-headed and calm, I gave in and resorted to taking an Ambien, something I rarely do. Out I went with barely a nod.

I had a troubling dream. There I was—all alone in the house. The night was late and colder than usual. The sky was inky black. I heard people outside and went to the window. Far down the road, I saw a wall of white glittering light—flames.

The next thing I knew I was on the front porch watching a cluster of people march in my direction, holding torches. They were chanting, but I couldn't make out the words. Soon, the road in front of me was clogged with people—townspeople, Krivac people.

One of them said they had come to burn down the house, that it was filled with demons, and that whether we were in it or not, it was going up in flames. I tried to reason with them but got nowhere. They started toward me across the lawn, the flames of their burning torches dancing against the black sky.

I heard a noise. Off in the distance, a police car came racing toward the house, streaming a row of red and blue lights as its shrill siren blared. Screeching and spinning to a halt, Officer Rainey leaped from the car. He called out names just as he had done in Krivac, ordering people to leave. The mob grabbed Rainey and held his hands behind his back. Out of the morass of vague and diffuse faces, I saw Blacek, Charlie

Blacek...the unmistakable Charlie Blacek. He took a rope from Rainey's patrol car, made a noose, and slung it over a high tree branch as Rainey fought helplessly, giving torrid orders to stop.

I burst awake, wide-eyed and in a cold sweat.

In the morning, I detected the smell of burned kerosene. Out in the front of the house were a dozen torches, three feet long and wrapped at the top with cloth that was scorched from fire. I picked one up. It had the smell of ignited distilled petroleum. I gathered the torches, doused them with water, and crammed them into the trash. I had no earthly idea how they had ended up on our lawn.

For the next two days, I did little but pace around inside the house until Friday when Audrey came out from Houston. We'd discussed over the phone most of what had happened. I filled her in on the details of Jennifer Walker's visit from the security company and told her I had changed the alarm code. I told her about Rainey, saying he'd been the one who broke up the trouble in Krivac.

"Rainey did?"

"That's right, Rainey. The same guy who came out when the computer was in the barn."

"What's his game?"

"Local Krivac flatfoot. You can tell he's been at it for a while; he knows a lot about what goes on in Krivac. But there's something about the guy I don't trust, and the more I know him, the less I trust. When we were sitting in Carter's, for example, he tried telling me the town was spooked about us being here. It just didn't click with me, though. Nobody in Carter's seemed the least bit concerned. Then recently, the blowup in town when the kid got hit by the car. Something about that was strange as hell, real peculiar. Rainey shows up as if on cue, stomps out the fuse, and tells everyone to go away."

"Geesh."

"He described some wild things that happened to him on our property." I told her of Rainey's tale about his purported encounter with Bud years ago out in the field. "And he claims the town's uptight about us being here in Krivac, saying they don't like outsiders. And he starts talking about Gypsies, as if the town thinks we're a couple of Gypsies or something."

"Gypsies! Where'd he get that?"

"It's not worth getting into. But he says that's why everyone's got their shorts in a wad over us being here. That and the house in general. The whole town hated the Ostermanns, according to Rainey. Probably best we just avoid Krivac totally."

"Suits me just fine," Audrey said.

"Anyway, Rainey says that for years the government, the feds, had been coming out to Krivac, snooping around." I described the box of nonagrams Rainey had buried by Bell's Creek. "It was totally surreal. There I was standing under this bridge. He opens a box with a bunch of nonagrams in it. I'm thinking, what's going on? The local cop with a treasure chest hidden in the ground like Blackbeard the Pirate or something.

He said he got the nonagrams from Bud Ostermann a long time ago, and that Herman Ostermann was involved in some kind of weird mind experiments. It was all a bunch of horse-shit as far as I'm concerned. Strangest thing, though—for no reason, he starts pouring out info about the Broding boy, a kid who disappeared somewhere out here. But at first, he pretended the kid never even existed."

Audrey rested her forehead on her hands. "That's it, Michael. Time we get out once and for all. Peddle the place and leave. It's not worth the trouble. Let them have their screwy little town. While I was driving out I-10, I kept think-ing about this. Now I'm more convinced than ever. And when you come down to it, we're not 'country'—as they say. Are we? We thought it would be relaxing to be out of the city, but look at us now."

"All hat and no cattle?" I said.

"Try no hat and no cattle. Maybe buying this place was a bigger mistake than we thought. It's starting to wear me out."

Funny, she was the one who looked calm and rested, hav-ing spent a week working hard back in Houston. I was the one who looked like I'd been dragged through a knothole.

"Think about it," Audrey said. "People breaking into the house, the word *locus* and the creepy light you saw in the window, Rainey and Ruth McDonald and their convoluted stories, someone putting the computer in the barn, some-one putting the key and the camera in the barn, a letter telling us to leave, a broken windows that gets fixed all by itself. Then you find out that some kid from Krivac disappeared on the property. Rainey claims it's a bunch of BS, but changes his story, right? And the nonagrams, whatever they are. Now this Rainey dude wants you to give him the ones you found. And the hostile folks in Krivac. Did I leave anything out?"

"Charlie Blacek."

Audrey groaned. "It never ends. What I'm getting at is that all this crazy stuff doesn't happen to us anywhere else. Why is that? Remember back when you met Ruth McDonald the first time in town and afterwards you wondered about the property, if there was something strange about it? What do you think now?"

"Wish I knew. If you believe Rainey, and that's a big stretch all by itself, everything is tied together—the nonagrams, Herman, Bud, the property—although he never said how or why or in what way. That's the thing with him...he's a little short on details sometimes. Good old mushroom management is what it is. Keep 'em in the dark and feed 'em shit. But there is one thing about what Rainey said that made me wonder. When I was with him at Carter's and then at Bell's Creek, he talked about a lot of screwy stuff that happened in town, in Krivac. He tried to say it was part of Herman's mind experiments. Normally I wouldn't believe a word of that, except for the situation at the hardware store. Remember? I told you the old guy who runs the place knew all about the key getting locked in the barn, as if he was reading my mind or something. Was that part of the mind-control crap that Rainey alluded to? I don't know. Makes you wonder."

"Not me, not by a long shot. Maybe the guy just made a lucky guess," Audrey said. "Let's not let these people mess with our thinking."

"Well, I'm not quite ready to abandon this place just yet," I told Audrey. "That would be caving in to what the town wants, and that bugs the shit out of me. We own this place whether they like it or not. What we do is stay away from Krivac and that whole crowd as much as possible."

The following week was Thanksgiving. The university would be closed down. We talked it over. We could stay at the house at least that long and decide what to do after that.

In the afternoon, we climbed into the old claw-foot bathtub and filled it so high with water it came up to my chest. Audrey dumped in a scoop of bubble bath, something most men would never be caught dead in alone. I told her about the metal detector I bought and my nonagram-hunting plans.

Audrey slumped back in the suds, only her head above the water. "You're not serious! Do you realize what it will take to find nonagrams out there with a metal detector? How do you know that thing even works on them?"

"I tested it out with the ones I have. It works fine," I said.

"Okay, but there could be tons of them," she said, waving in the direction of the pasture. "Surely you can't expect to find them all."

"Every last one. What have I got to lose?"

"And what if Herman Ostermann was hammering them out in the basement for no reason at all like some loony north-pole elf?"

"What if he was?"

"Maybe what Rainey told you about them is total nonsense."

"Probably is. Then we'll have thousands of pieces of worthless junk...think how rich we'll be." I scooped up a handful of bubbles. I felt the soft soapy water pull the tension from my body. "On another subject, let me ask you something, Aud. Yes, this was the week from hell, all right, but I did a lot of thinking, and...well, do you believe in the supernatural, the *supra*natural? You know, the paranormal?"

"In what sense?"

"In the sense that things might occur that aren't from this world. Let's say there are two, maybe more than two, maybe a dozen world orders. There's the one we see all the time. That's the predictable one, for better or for worse. Then there's the other one, the supernatural one where everything operates by a different set of rules. This has been flitting around in my head for a couple of days now."

Audrey sat up and said, "Boy, you *did* have a bad week." She slumped back in the tub again.

"Is it possible that that's what's going on here at the house? Something supernatural? Can a house be possessed the way people become possessed and go crazy? A poltergeist, for example, like in that Steven Spielberg movie. They say those things really happen. And what about a town? Can a whole town go crazy, if they all drank the Kool-Aid, let's say?"

"I don't know. Anything's possible, I guess," Audrey said in a rather unconvinced voice.

Of course, I knew she was far too practical to buy into a half-baked notion about the supernatural or poltergeists. We were ordinary people. We lived in a logical world where things occurred predictably. But what do you do when logical explanations fail? You look for other interpretations, I suppose. On my own, I could probably slide further and further away from logic. It was Audrey, the scientist, who kept everything on an even keel. I had seen how she dealt with off-the-wall experimental results in the laboratory. Research in molecular biology of the kind she conducted involved complex, elaborate, sophisticated experiments. Experiments that challenged one's thinking, one's ability to integrate vast amounts of information. There are always hundreds, probably thousands, of reasons why experiments fail to produce the expected results. When something doesn't work in the laboratory, you didn't say, 'Well, there you go, poltergeists again.' But logic works great when you know events and outcomes are logic driven, as in the case of biologic experiments. There's no reason to dredge up illogical, convoluted explanations for those.

I said, "I guess what I'm getting at is this—let's just assume for a second that Herman Ostermann is not really gone. Not just out there in the graveyard on the back of the property, but that he's still around. He's the one messing with us.

Sure as hell wish I knew what he looked like." I thought back to the night when I had been confronted by the mirage-like apparition in the hallway as I came out of the bathroom.

"Nah, I don't believe it. Why would Osterman do that, hang around the house?" Audrey asked.

"Just because he's still here, I guess. Who knows?"

"Please, not ghosts. Or maybe he's Casper the Friendly Ghost, and he's the one who fixed the window for you."

"Cute, real cute," I replied. "I'm not talking about ghosts, though. I'm talking about something more organic. That he's in a different reality plane and can move back and forth into ours. Alternative universes, if you will. Rainey tried to get me to believe that Herman could control people, that he had some extraordinary way of doing that. Maybe he learned it from the people he gathered with out in the fields, the strange people that Ruth McDonald told me about."

Audrey gave a short blast of hot water from the faucet. I was beginning to like this bubble-bath thing.

"In any case, there's something else that's been chewing at me, something a bit more sinister" I said. "What if the disappearance of the Broding kid had nothing to do with him being out on the property with his two buddies, Schneider and Robinson? What if Broding was out here on the property all by himself, without them, and he came across a bunch of nonagrams. Maybe out by Ostermann's grave or wherever...or by the school bus. Rainey finds out about this and—"

"I thought you said Rainey questioned the other two boys and they wouldn't talk. They were scared as hell."

"Of course, because Rainey had put the fear of God in them after they found out what he had done to Broding. *That's* why they wouldn't talk."

"You're saying Rainey had something to do with Broding's disappearance?"

"Maybe."

"For one thing, I don't think he'd resurrect the whole matter and talk about it with you if he were somehow involved. I think he'd want to keep it as quiet as possible."

"Okay. Then why did he tell me he'd never been out at the Ostermann house and later admitted he had? And why did he say the Broding incident never happened, and then tell me all about it, all the while standing next to a box of nonagrams buried in the ground? Don't try to figure out that work of art, cuz you won't get far."

CHAPTER 23

We had dinner at a small restaurant over by Shiner. Restaurant choices in the area were limited and usually not great. Menus with lots of beef, hamburgers, enchiladas, tacos, chicken-fried steak, chicken-fried chicken, chicken-fried everything.

But sometimes it was possible to hit on a good place. Rico's was one of those. We had a good meal and headed back to the house down small roads past empty farmland dotted here and there with an occasional house trailer, that annoying blight that contaminates the American countryside.

The evening was spent on the big front porch that faces the farm road. Few cars ever passed down there, rarely more than a half dozen all day. We sat with our feet propped on a table. The ceiling fan sent soft currents of air twirling around us. An old pickup truck rumbled down the road, one of those half-dozen or so vehicles that pass by. I leaned back and watched the slow movement of the fan.

The night was dark and still with not so much as a whisper of wind. The trees were motionless. The sky, black as cast iron. A dog barked far off in the distance. We spent the rest of the evening in the bedroom having fun. Later, I opened the window a trace. A slight chill crept in; I pulled an extra blanket across the bed and fell asleep.

Little by little, life slipped into a routine of doing only what we wanted when we wanted to do it, and little by little, I was able to push the unsettling incident that had happened in Krivac from my thoughts. Having avoided Krivac altogether helped immensely.

Every morning we went for a run down the empty country roads. For the time being, we put aside our discussions about giving up the house. I was once again making good progress on my book. I had negotiated a light teaching load from Dean Busey in order to have the book to the publisher by January. Time was closing in. The project was growing whiskers. I needed to crank it out as fast as I could. My efforts throughout autumn, when I'd hoped to make significant headway, had been an on-again, off-again event. Some days I accomplished a lot, other days almost nothing. It frustrated me at times, being the persistent critter that I was.

For now, we were still committed to the house. Once you make a decision, don't make it half-assed. That was my rule of life. I continued building a workbench in the barn, a casual project I had started months ago. What a gem, big and solid. Tools of all sorts hung above it. Best of all, the drier inland air away from the coast did not threaten them with rust. I had made a bench like this once in the garage of our house back in Houston, not knowing that the soggy near-tropical climate would turn everything into crusty oxidized implements.

Just being out in the barn made me feel better. I loved its open space, its roominess, the light that filled it when the large doors were opened. Whenever I was there, I felt connected to the land. Audrey worked on several paintings, read on the porch, and wandered out on the property, collecting an assortment of fascinating small rocks that ended up in an ever-growing pile next to the back steps.

I resumed my search for nonagrams, concentrating this time on the pond, going again and again around the perimeter. I thought I had found everything, but metal of all types and sizes continued to show up.

Audrey was out by the barn working on a painting. The day had turned out to be warmer than usual for November. In the afternoon, I abandoned my quest for nonagrams, popped open a beer, and sat on the back porch.

Audrey made her way from the barn over toward me. She had that look—that impish look I'd come to recognize. She stood there in a painter's smock that wrapped around her and tied in the back. I watched as she loosened it and let it fall to the porch. There she was, naked, a natural blonde. She went inside the house and came back with a soft old quilt. I followed her to a patch of grass under a tree behind the house.

Afterwards, we sat naked on the back porch drinking beer, talking, laughing. We had just walked into the house when a car pulled into the driveway. I peered out the kitchen window. "Ah, don't tell me. Krivac police. Looks like you're going to meet Rainey. I thought we were done with that cat. What in the name of Sam Houston does he want?"

Audrey went upstairs to get dressed. I slipped into a pair of jeans and put on a shirt. I probably smelled like sex, but there wasn't much I could do about it now. Rainey walked up to the house, looking as he always did: the spitting image of a country cop. Every stitch of clothing in perfect order, if perhaps a little snug around the middle.

I opened the door, not thrilled to see him but curious about his visit. "Officer Rainey, what brings you here? No more parking tickets in town?"

"Yeah, well, you know…gets to wearing thin…all day long." Rainey invited himself in and sat at the kitchen table.

"Don't the teenagers in Krivac get drunk in the park like teenagers usually do?" I asked, sitting down.

"Now and then." He removed his cowboy hat, swiped his hand across the table to make sure it was clean, and set his hat upside down on it like a true cowboy.

Audrey walked into the kitchen. I gave her a wink and introduced her to Rainey.

"I got to thinking," Rainey said. "Thought I should come out and see how you're doing after that not-so-pleasant affair in Krivac the other day. No matter what you might think, I do try to keep order as best I can."

"I survived. I've put most of it out of my mind, if you need to know. I figure if we don't make any more appearances in Krivac, they won't bother us."

Rainey nodded a couple of two times. He seemed pleased with the compromise. "But there's something else I wanted to go over. I guess it wouldn't hurt if I told you where Bud lives. I mean, I know I'm not supposed to do that. Part of my job is to protect people's privacy. But you were sort of annoyed when I said I know what you do back in Houston—"

"Sorta still am."

"Like I said, I was only trying to help. So, what's this professor thing like, anyway?"

"We teach and do some research, just like any other university professor."

I could tell this was of no interest to him. I suspect all the snooping around he had done frustrated him. Too many things he didn't understand.

"Uh-huh. Yeah, well...whatever." He retrieved a small piece of paper from his shirt pocket and handed it to me. On it was written 8532 CR 72. "That's his address." He pulled a pen from his shirt pocket, sketched a map, and took us through the details of getting to County Road 72. "We need a few ground rules here, though. If you do go see Bud, you can't tell him how you got his address. You'll have to come up with something. Tell him whatever you want, I don't care. That's your problem. And no mentioning anything about the nonagrams buried out by the creek. What I mean is, don't tell him they're there, and don't tell him you know where they are. For that matter, don't even bring them up. Got it? Otherwise, you can do whatever you want."

Rainey's rationale for letting us know where Bud lived seemed like pretty weak tea. As I saw it, he wasn't the kind of guy who would do this to make up for prying into our lives. He was too much of a cop to worry about such small indiscretions. And besides, while sitting in Carter's, he told me he wanted nothing to do with Bud. Why the turnaround now? There had to be another reason for passing this information along to us, for making a special trip out—his desire to check on me and to avoid writing tickets in Krivac notwithstanding. The thought hadn't escaped me that maybe it was *Bud* who wanted to talk to *us* and that Rainey was just the messenger.

I could see Rainey wasn't planning to leave anytime soon, so I offered him a beer. "A cup of coffee might be better," he replied. I made a pot. He settled back in his chair. His conversation veered off for a while into the mundane, commenting on the bright colors we had used on the kitchen walls—a rather unusual remark coming from a hard-boiled guy like him. After a while, he looked at me and said, "How are things going here at the house? All the crazy stuff stop? The break-ins, I mean? The walking computer?" He let out a small chuckle, tickled by his little joke.

"Fine. Perfect as can be," I said.

Audrey gave me a quick glance. Rainey's reaction revealed little. He was either a very good poker player or he believed what I was saying. He pursed his lips and nodded as if taking credit for the good news, then began talking about baseball—the Rangers and the Astros. The afternoon wore on. He eventually got up, stretched, and picked his hat up from the table. "Well, back to town for me," he said. "So, are you planning to pay Bud a visit?"

I looked at Audrey and then at Rainey. "Not sure," I said.

He positioned his hat on his head—left, right, up, down—and gave a nod and left.

I toyed with the sheet of paper with Bud's address on it. My first reaction was to roll it into a tight ball and flick it into the trash can. But I didn't. "I guess we know where Bud is," I said with little enthusiasm.

Although I still retained a touch of interest in talking to Bud, Audrey could find no good reason for that. What did we expect to learn from him that was so important? What did we think Bud was going to say? "Oh, by the way, you folks are living in a really screwed-up house in a really screwed-up town, and you need to get your ass out of there as soon as possible"? Then what?

Audrey was much more suspicious of Rainey's motives. Meeting him in the flesh did little of anything to inflate her opinion of him. Why had he come all the way out just to give us Bud's address?

I took the paper with the address and stuck it on the refrigerator. Returning to the pasture, I continued my nonagram search and right away hit the jackpot. Within the span of ten minutes, I located three. I inspected them. Two were virtually identical; one had different markings. I photographed each and placed them on the mantle with the others.

CHAPTER 24

Thursday arrived. We made a grand Thanksgiving meal. The house brimmed with glorious smells of roast turkey, dressing, potatoes, green beans, cranberries, gravy—all the usual suspects. The temperature had dropped a good thirty degrees. The day was cool and overcast, almost gloomy. I didn't mind. It was the kind of Thanksgiving Day I remembered growing up in Chicago.

After dinner, Audrey sat in the living room reading. I waded through a stack of New York Times crossword puzzles she had brought with her from Houston. I got up, walked over to the fireplace, and tossed another log on the fire. As I glanced at the nonagrams on the mantle, it hit me. There should be seven, but there were only six. One was missing.

I looked closely at the six remaining nonagrams, turning them over, examining them, comparing them, trying to determine which one was missing. There was a much easier way. In the dining room, I turned on the computer and hunted through it for the nonagram pictures. I scrolled up and down the page. The file was gone.

"You're not going to believe this, but the pictures of the nonagrams are missing," I said, calling to Audrey in the living room. "The file is gone."

"What do you mean gone?" she called back.

"Just what I said. Gone. It's not in the computer."

"You must have deleted it, then."

"I didn't delete it. I *know* I didn't." I leaned back in the chair, befuddled.

Audrey came into the dining room. "They're still on your cell phone, aren't they?"

I pulled the phone from my pocket and paged through the photo album. Every picture I had taken over the past several months was there, including the one I had snapped that afternoon in the barn and the ones I had taken of Audrey earlier in the week—every picture *but* the ones of the nonagrams. Whoever had stolen the nonagram had also gone into the computer and deleted the picture file.

It would have been no challenge, of course, but first they would have to know I had photographed them. And they would have to know I had put the pictures in the computer. The cell phone was a different matter altogether. I had it with me the whole time. And there was also the issue of why someone had stolen only one nonagram. Were it a random act of burglary, I would expect all seven to be gone.

"Son of a bitch," I muttered.

"Michael, just forget about the nonagrams, okay? I thought you weren't going to spend the week screwing around with them. Isn't that what you said? Give them all to Rainey and be done with it. *Who cares?* Maybe then he'll quit creeping around out here. Cripes, you're becoming like a kid who sticks a screwdriver into an electrical outlet. If you don't mess with it, you won't get shocked. Let the whole bloody thing go."

"Kid sticking a screwdriver into electrical outlet?"

"Okay, bad analogy. But do what Louise told you, just get rid of them. Maybe that was the real take-home message from your visit with her. Then, everything might go back to normal. Wouldn't that be nice? Wouldn't it? No more Krivac crap, no more Rainey crap. No more nonagram crap. Anyway, suppose there were only *six* nonagrams, not seven."

"No way. There were seven. I know there were seven."

"If that's true, we're back to where we started, aren't we?" Audrey said. "It means someone broke into the house again. Face it, if this was happening back in Houston, we'd be going nuts. The security system here flat-out sucks. I thought you changed the alarm code."

"I did change the alarm code."

"Then how are people getting in?"

"I don't know, Audrey!"

The next day, I wrapped the nonagrams in paper and placed them in a cloth sack and went to the wine cellar. I took a trowel and began digging into the dirt floor. I hadn't gone far before I hit a hard surface.

"Jesus Christ, now what?" I muttered, as I pushed dirt away. I took the spade I had placed behind the wine rack and began removing dirt. Not more than a half-dozen inches down, I came to a large smooth piece of slate roughly three feet wide and seven feet long. It could have been the top of a tomb, but it bore no name and no dates. The edges were carved with images of woven branches with sprouted leaves. A sunlike object had been skillfully carved on the left corner; a crescent moon was on the right corner. In delicate ornate letters were the words

Here I lay
Some say gone
But will be back
Before the dawn

"Will be back before the dawn." I repeated the phrase several times. Other than those few words, the slate itself revealed little. It could have been relatively new or scores of years old—there was no way to tell. If it was a grave, it was the second one that lacked complete identification. Herman's grave had no date of birth and no definitive first name.

How did this massive thing get down here, and what the hell was it? Perhaps it had been relocated from the graveyard to the cellar. The rings on the walls could have been used to lower it into the ground. But moving what appeared to be an enormous casket down the narrow rickety cellar stairs would have been next to impossible.

The better explanation was that it had been in the basement for a long time, possibly built with the house itself, possibly even before the house. Now it became clear that the room, as we had found it, had been left that way—empty, free of debris—because of the tomb. The room was nothing more than a sarcophagus. And the nonagram that had been lying on the dirt floor may have been placed there because of the grave, may have been connected to the grave.

I spread the dirt back over the slate and sat on the floor and leaned against the stone wall, thinking about what Audrey had said the night before. What if she was right? Suppose there were only six nonagrams, not seven? I had no way of being sure now that my record of them on the computer had been obliterated.

But my overall memory wasn't *that* bad, was it? Consider that I had hunted for these for days and could recite verse and chapter of where I had found each one. Yet I was beginning to wonder…was I really forgetting things, or did it just seem like I was? That possibility had been seeping into my thoughts for quite a while now.

Could it be that I had never photographed the nonagrams, had never put the images on the computer? Good God, was that possible? I wasn't senile, for Pete's sake! For a fleeting second I wondered if I was flipping out. There were times when even Audrey looked at me as if I were…well, getting a little flaky on her. I'd catch the look now and then. It was an empty and suspicious glance she'd slip in my direction as though she had been watching me, checking me out.

Yeah, I saw her doing it. It didn't matter because I knew I wasn't going crazy. People who go crazy don't know it. They think they're sane and everyone *else* is nuts. So if I even considered the possibility that I was getting a little dusty up top, then I must be fine. Right? That's all I needed to hear. I got up, cleaned myself off, and went upstairs.

We had made a decision that morning to wrap up our holiday a couple of days early and return to Houston. It just seemed like a good idea. Audrey was outside putting things in the barn—flower pots, planting soil, rakes, wheelbarrow. I gave her a hand. We closed and locked the barn doors and headed back to the kitchen. There on the wall in large hand-written letters were the words

LOCUS LOC—US *LOCUS!*

We stood motionless in the doorway, eyes locked on the words. I took a step forward, stopped, moved a couple more slow steps, stopped again, and took a last cautious step. Audrey backed up against the sink, hand over her mouth.

I touched the letters, swiping my fingers across them. "My God," I groaned. "Whatever it is, it's totally dry." This was the first time we had seen the word separated into two parts, and it was the first time it had appeared on anything other than the computer.

"That's it! I'm out of here," Audrey snapped and walked to the dining room.

"Audrey...Audrey, honey, wait," I said. "Come here... please."

She turned and looked at me. "*Michael*, whoever did this walked right past us. *While we were out in the barn.* They were probably watching us all the time, watching us right at this very moment. We need to get the hell out of here! *Now!* We shouldn't be here one more minute!"

I walked over to her. "I understand. I understand. But hold on a second. I don't know who did this, but I have a way to find out. I've been thinking about it for quite a while now. I know how to find out who this asshole is."

Audrey threw her head back. "*Michael!*"

"What I'm saying is I have an idea, a plan."

"*A plan!* A plan to do what? To find out who's doing crazy things to us? And what if we find out? Then what? Suppose someone like Rainey is involved? What do we do then? Get the local cop arrested? Hah! Fat chance! Someone wants us out of here. I don't care who and I don't care why. If they want us gone, that's good enough for me. Let's do them a favor and *leave.*"

"It could be there's something important here, Audrey. Who knows? Something extremely valuable, and I don't mean nonagrams. I mean a...a treasure of some kind that they don't want us to find. There's no telling what's here."

"Jesus Christ, Michael, you can't be serious! Now you're talking about *treasures*! This stuff's going to your head. It's starting to make both of us crazy. Don't you see?"

I looked at her. I could tell she'd had enough. There was no point in pushing it. "All right. Tomorrow, you return to Houston. I'll stay a few more days."

"Why?"

I stepped back into the kitchen and looked at the freaky, immutable words stretched out on the wall across from me. I leaned on the sink for a second, head down, then looked at Audrey and said, "There's something I need to tell you. I should have mentioned it before, but didn't know how to. Now I feel shitty about it." I went into the details of my conversation with Jennifer Walker, the security company technician, and about the alarm being shut off prior to someone entering the house. I told Audrey I had checked the dates and they matched the break-in dates perfectly.

Audrey stood wide-eyed. She started to say something but then just stared at me for what seemed like an eternity. At long last, she said, "How could you not tell me? *How?*"

I couldn't think of a single time she had kept important information from me. Not once in seventeen years. I could imagine the betrayal she must have been feeling.

"I don't know how they're getting in, but I'm going to find out who these bastards are," I said, hoping to mollify the situation. "I'm going to install surveillance cameras in the house, in every room. I know where to get them and I know how to install them. A couple of days at the most, that's all it will take. Then I'll go back to Houston."

Audrey said nothing. She turned, marched into the living room, and sat in a chair. Wow, she was pissed. Later in the afternoon, she said she would stay at the house long enough for me to install the cameras. After that we'd leave.

I took two pictures of the writing on the wall—one with my phone, one with my camera—and went to the barn and opened a can of paint and obliterated the words. The next morning, I drove to a store about twenty miles outside of Krivac that specialized in surveillance systems. The manager showed me how to rig the cameras to motion detectors that would start recording as soon as someone entered the room. They would record for an additional ten minutes after the motion ceased.

It took longer than I expected to set up the cameras and get them to work, two full days from morning until evening. When I was done, there were eleven cameras in all: one in the kitchen, the front hall, the living room, the dining room, each of the three bedrooms, the upstairs hallway, the attic, the basement room, and the wine cellar.

The entire house was covered. I set up a video display panel on a table in one of the unused bedrooms. I tested the system; everything worked fine. I could see almost every inch of the entire house. Moreover, because the cameras recorded the time someone entered a room, it was possible to track an intruder's movements.

"I feel like we're living in a bank," Audrey groaned, shaking her head. "It's all a waste of time, Michael. We're just rearranging the deck chairs on a sinking ship." She got up and went down to the kitchen.

We headed back to Houston. On the way out, I stopped at 8532 CR 72, Bud's address that Rainey had given us. Several lights were on in the house. A pickup truck and a car were parked in the driveway. I pulled off the road and walked to the front door. Audrey waited in the car, staring straight out the window, not wanting to participate. All I wanted to do was see the place.

The number 8532 was printed next to the door in faded blue letters. As I turned to leave, I glanced into one of the narrow windows that flanked the door. A man walked across the room. Bud, I assumed. I saw a woman. I squinted, trying to make out her face. "Damn," I muttered. "Damn." It was Ruth McDonald. I was certain. Two men were seated on the sofa with their backs to me. I couldn't make a definitive identification without seeing their faces, but I had a good idea who they were. Both appeared to be tall, likely over six feet. One was thinner. He wore a red cap; I could see the straps of overalls on top of an old blue shirt. No question, it had to be Charlie Blacek. The second man, based on the thick rumpled skin on the back of his neck, was heavier. He had thinning hair. I wasn't certain, but my best guess said it was Rainey.

So, there was this "Bud-looking" guy, Ruth McDonald, Charlie Blacek, and Rainey gathered at the exact place, the exact address, that Rainey had scribbled on the piece of paper he had given me. I returned to the car but didn't mention what I had seen to Audrey. She didn't ask.

Back in Houston, Audrey's classes and the work on my book took up most of our time. It was a distraction we desperately needed. There was no talk about the house or about

Rainey or about Ruth McDonald or about Bud...or about words on walls and computer screens. Nothing about Krivac or buried strongboxes. For the time being, we managed to push those things out of our lives.

Chapter 25

It was two full weeks before we returned to the house. The time away had been good. We immediately went to the second floor and examined the surveillance records. Just as I suspected, someone had entered while we were gone. Now at last we would find out who these bastards were, and learn how they were getting in. We would have solid evidence, enough to get them arrested. This would wrap up the whole sordid episode and we'd be done with it forever.

Nothing was further from the truth.

Entry occurred through the kitchen door on Tuesday, the fourth day after we'd left, at 6:03 p.m. It was bizarre and frightening. The recording started when the back door opened. We expected to see an intruder, but there was only a gaping open doorway. The key was in the lock on the inside of the house. The drawer in the kitchen where we had left the key was open several inches.

The mere presence of whomever had taken the key from the drawer should have caused the recording to start, but there was no one in the room—not a soul. It was the movement of the door itself that had activated the recording. And no matter how you sliced it, the door had been opened from inside the house using the key from the drawer.

Suddenly, the buttons on the alarm panel were being pushed one after another in the exact sequence needed to deactivate the alarm. But again, there was not a person to be seen. I zoomed in and reran the recording. Sure enough, each button was entered in the correct order to turn off the alarm.

Seconds later, a book I had left in the kitchen floated three feet into the air. It was opened briefly, something was placed in it, and it was closed again. The book moved out of the kitchen, through the dining room, and into the living room where it was set in the bookshelf. As it made its way through each room, its presence activated the motion sensors, allowing us to follow it along the way.

Next, the camera in the hallway on the second floor came on when the attic door swung open. This occurred forty-seven seconds after the camera in the living room had been activated, about the time it would take to climb the stairs, walk down the hall, and open the attic door. Yet none of the cameras along the way had been triggered, not the ones in the upstairs bedrooms, or the one in the hallway itself. It was the movement of the attic door that started the recording.

Moments later, the camera in the attic began recording when a box was moved from one end of the room to the other. Then, a second box was transported across the attic. All floated through the air. As soon as the camera in the attic came on, the basement door opened and the camera in the basement was activated, followed by the camera in the wine cellar when its door swung open. This was startling because I had placed a strong padlock on the heavy metal hasp of the wine-cellar door before we'd left for Houston. But the door was open with no evidence of forced entry. Something had managed to unlock it without effort.

The small trowel I kept in the wine cellar began to scrape dirt off the floor, digging down three inches or so. A few seconds later, the dirt was replaced in the hole and the trowel floated across the room to its original place against the wall.

Now, in both places—the attic and the cellar—nine small flames began to flicker, each about six feet in the air, each positioned in what appeared to be the exact places I had seen charred spots on the ceilings.

"What's going on?" I said.

"Flames, I think."

"Yes, but just flames. No candles, no matches…nothing. Just flames hovering in the air all by themselves."

We watched the flames quiver. Nine perfect glowing spots in the darkened rooms. They oscillated synchronously through weak and bright phases in both the attic and cellar, as though regulated in unison.

Each flame emitted a wisp of thin smoke that rose to the ceiling like incense at a requiem mass. A harmonic sound came from all the rooms, gradually getting louder. It undulated in deep low pitches followed by short high pitches. Over and over this continued.

Within seconds, the images from the videos throughout the house began to blur as if the whole place had begun to vibrate, causing the cameras to shake with it. All in all, this went on for no more than a minute. The sound ended; the flames faded away. The attic and wine-cellar doors were closed. The buttons on the security alarm panel were reset in the kitchen. The door was locked from *inside* the house *after* it had been closed. The key came out of the lock and floated through the air into the drawer, and the drawer was shut.

We sat in total silence for a desperately long while. All I could think to say was, "Holy shit. It's damn hard to believe, but I guess we know why everyone's been telling us to leave and why everyone in Krivac is spooked about the house. And why they threatened to burn it down like Louise had said."

"And why Ted Zelinski said he could sell the place for a lot more without the house," Audrey added.

I was more flummoxed than ever. This was hardly what I expected. We had fewer answers than before. I was sure we would find out who the intruders were and have the necessary evidence to get their asses thrown in the slammer, thus ending months of aggravation. But not so.

"Whatever...whatever it is, it can get into the house even when it's locked up tight," Audrey said, almost out of breath. "That's how they unlocked the back door, got the barn key from the kitchen, and used it to open the barn—how they locked the key inside the barn and left. And how they got in and moved the computer around and typed the word *LOCUS* on it when we were gone. It explains everything."

"Want to see it again?" I asked.

Audrey shook her head. She offered an alternative explanation for what we had seen. "Maybe it's not someone getting into the house from outside. Maybe it's someone opening the door from inside. This thing…person, whatever it is, was already inside. Is here all the time. Right now."

We went down to the living room. I pulled a book off the shelf. I had a good idea which one had been moved from the kitchen to the bookshelf. It was *A People's History of the United States*, by Howard Zinn. I had been reading it and had left it on the kitchen table before we returned to Houston. I opened it. Inside was a scrap of paper with the words:

> *Imminent it is, there shall be war*
> *LOCUS alone can open the door*
> *Look to LOCUS and wait no more.*

The words were as enigmatic as the recordings we had just seen. Now what? I sure as hell wasn't going to show this to Rainey and watch him titter in amusement over the whole thing. I was sick of his pissy little games. And Jennifer Walker from the security company—show her? My ass!

Louise Ostermann had claimed people from town were trying to break into the house, but she never said a word about what we had just seen. Perhaps it was just too much to say something like that to a total stranger. It's pretty tough to start talking about invisible intruders coming and going in and out of the house; pretty tough to suggest that if you're eighty-some years old, I guess. Not without everyone looking at you out of the corner of their eye, winking and saying, "Poor Louise, she's lost it." But I wanted answers.

That left only one person. Bud. He had lived in the house a long time, just like Louise had. He would know a lot about it. How could he not? Maybe he'd say something, maybe he wouldn't. Thanks to Rainey, we knew where he lived. We had even been there briefly once. The worst that could happen would be for the elusive Bud Ostermann to shut the door in our face. So the fuck what?

We drove over to 8532 CR 72. The house was dark. There were no cars in the driveway. From all appearances, no one was home. But what we learned was far stranger.

Someone had painted over the house number next to the door. We walked around the side of the house. I looked into one curtainless window after another. There was not a stick of furniture anywhere inside.

The back porch had uncut weeds growing up to the steps. The grass in the yard was calf high. This place had been vacant for a long, long time. Yet, when we came by just two weeks ago on our way back to Houston, the house was furnished and occupied.

I opened the rusty screen door and gave the inner door a shove. Cupping my hands, I called inside. "Anyone here?" We waited and listened. Not a sound.

"Come on. Let's go, Michael," Audrey said. "There's no reason for us to be here."

I stepped into the kitchen and flipped the light switch. The electricity was off. Into the dark living room I went. The very place I had seen Bud and Ruth McDonald and Rainey and Charlie Blacek was now empty and quiet as a cave. It had that smell...that same musty fragrance the Ostermann house had the first time I set foot in it. A smell of dry oldness.

"We're trespassing, you know," Audrey said, a step behind me.

"The place is empty."

"It belongs to someone."

I crossed the living room and entered a bedroom. Audrey waited behind. Something flew from one of the dark closets and dipped just above my head. I pulled back. "Goddamn bat," I said, fluffing my hair.

Little more than a trickle of light came in through the two small windows. Once again, I felt an uncomfortable presence in the room. The same presence I had detected back at the house moments ago. As though something had lifted itself from the video recording and was now following me, pissed and mean. I turned quickly, scanned the room but saw nothing—mere darkness. Everything about the house suggested it had been long ago abandoned. The windows were nailed shut. The closets were empty and dusty. But more than that, they held a rancid smell. The same rancid smell I briefly encountered the very first time I ventured into the cellar of the Ostermann house while Charlie Blacek clomped across the kitchen.

Farther on, I stumbled over a book on the floor. I picked it up and looked at the spine. *A People's History of the United States.* Flipping it open, I found a small piece of paper with the exact three-line verse about *LOCUS*, exactly as in the book back at the house. On the inside of the cover were the words *Michael Felton, PhD, Department of Philosophy, Monclair University.* This was my book, and I owned only one copy. I made no mention of it to Audrey.

We drove up and down CR72 several times thinking I must have gone to the wrong house. But based on the numbers on the mailboxes, there was little doubt it was the correct one. The same place where I had seen Bud and Ruth McDonald and the others talking in the living room just weeks ago.

"Let's go," Audrey said, her voice weary. "We're wasting our time."

We headed back to the house under a dark and sinister sky. A big storm was on its way.

CHAPTER 26

By the time we returned to the house, rain was coming down in sheets. A wall of water rolled off the roof and gathered in ever-growing puddles in the yard. We made a dash for the door, getting drenched in the process.

"Hard rain," I said, standing in the kitchen, hair stuck to my forehead.

Audrey peeled off clothes. "If those weirdos, whoever they are, want to watch, so be it."

We left everything in a pile on the floor and went upstairs to dry off.

"You really want to stay here tonight?" I asked. "After what we saw on the video?"

"It's that or drive in this storm. And I don't know where we'd go."

"Some dumpy motel in Krivac."

"That's a scary thought. I'm in no mood for an encounter with Norman Bates," Audrey said, without a trace of humor. That was pretty much it. Stay in the house or spend the night out in the car parked in the driveway until morning. How safe would that be, sitting in a tin-and-glass bubble pounded by rain on a black night?

Audrey opened the closet door in search of a dress. "What in the world is this?" she said, retrieving a solid-black men's suit that hung inside.

"I have no idea, but it sure as hell isn't mine," I said, holding it in front of me. "This thing's made for someone five-seven or eight…no more than that." I looked at the label on the inside of the collar. All it said was *Dubbins Brothers, London and New York*. It had the look of something an undertaker would wear—fine threading and well made. It looked old and smelled old, as though it had been stored in a box in an attic somewhere, yet it had not a single wrinkle. I turned it around. The elbows, cuffs, and hems were smooth and untattered. "Some fucker must have put it here while we were over at Bud's."

"Or while we were back in Houston," Audrey groaned, as she slipped into a soft cotton dress.

"I can tell you where this thing is going now." I got dressed and started for the stairs. On my way, I grabbed the baseball bat from the hall closet.

In the living room, the rain lashed at the windows, the sky was dark and fast. Stuffing paper and logs into the fireplace, I built a roaring blaze. When the flames were streaming up strong and high, I wadded the suit into a ball and dropped it onto the fire. "Take that, you bastard," I uttered as I watched fire burn into the cloth.

All at once, the room was filled the most foul smell. An odor of rotten flesh—something akin to a week-old dead opossum you discover out behind the barn, something maggots had sumptuously dined on.

Audrey cracked open a window a couple of inches. Moist air came gushing in, but it had little effect on the abominable smell that surrounded us. The cloth of the suit in the fireplace seemed to crackle as it folded into lumps and collapsed and burned. Audrey tried to fan air from outside into the room, holding her hand over her nose all the while in an effort to block the odor that was now so bad you could taste it. "Quick, burn that thing! Kill it!" she ordered.

I poked the embers and tried to force the cloth down inside, but it refused to go. A slow defiant death is what it wanted. I had every plan to give it that if need be. From upstairs came the sound of footsteps moving down the hallway. We looked at each other simultaneously and then climbed the stairs, stopping at the top. The door to the bedroom where I had set up the recording equipment was half open. I remembered all too well closing it, hoping to leave inside the memory of what we had seen. But now the door was again open. I couldn't see how the storm could account for that, thrash as it might outside. Okay, perhaps when Audrey lifted the window a sudden vacuum of air had sucked the door open...possibly.

I flipped the light switch and peered inside the room. Nothing looked particularly out of order. Stepping into the room, I stood in front of the display monitor when all at once the glass shattered from side to side and top to bottom.

I flinched and stepped back and stared at the thousand fragments that once had been the screen. Then I noticed that the web of wires that had been connected to the various components and sensors had been ripped out. Each thin copper wire was bare and frayed. It would take a near miracle to get this thing working again—my eight hundred dollar investment was gone forever along with any future use of it. Audrey gawked wide-eyed from the doorway.

We climbed the creaky stairs to the attic. From what I could tell, the dozens of boxes we had stored there hadn't been tampered with. All nine of the small black spots on the ceiling were much the same as they had been before the storm. We went to the first floor and down into the cellar.

The storm raging above us made the subterranean room more mysterious than ever. The door to the wine cellar was locked, just as it had been when we left for Houston. I opened it, turned on the light, and inspected the dirt floor. There was no evidence that anyone other than us had been in the room. Or if so, they had done a good job of obliterating any signs of it. I took the trowel and dug into the soil exactly as we had seen on the recording, sifting dirt through my fingers and poking into the ground where the nonagrams were buried. There they were, seemingly undisturbed.

Stepping out of the cellar into the kitchen, the sky let loose with a huge lightning bolt followed by a bomb of deafening thunder. The house lights blinked once and snapped off. We crept back to the living room, now lit only by the small neurons of light sent out from the fireplace mixed with stark-white flashes of lightning, eight or ten in succession one after another. A massive burst of thunder exploded and rolled across the sky like the bang of a kettledrum in an echo chamber.

The bad odor that filled the room was worse than ever. Then, in one grand burst, the last of the black suit in the fireplace broke into flames and sank into the hot embers. With that, the foul and hideous smell was instantly gone.

Did this mean everything was finally over? Not in my book. I retrieved the hammer and the hand ax from under the sink in the kitchen and set them next to the coffee table. I didn't know who or what we were sharing the house with, but if we were planning to stay—and by all accounts that was still the decision at least until the end of the storm—I was going to be prepared.

On the bookshelf as though calling me over to it, I saw the Howard Zinn volume, the one we had seen floating in midair on the recording, the one I had stumbled over in Bud's house on 8532 CR72. I took it from the shelf and opened it. Sure enough, there it was: my name and university address stamped inside. This was indeed my book, yet how did it get to 8532 CR72 before we did? How did it get back before we returned? Just the same, how did they—they, whoever had done this—know we were going to Bud's house at all? I decided not to bring this up with Audrey. Enough was enough for now.

"Bad storm," I mumbled, trying to turn my attention to nature even if in one of her more capricious moods. Audrey said nothing. I picked up the baseball bat and gripped the handle with both hands as if getting ready to swing for the fences and looked out the window, wondering what was yet in store for us. I watched the angry sky for a long time, again trying to piece together everything that had happened.

From the Kitchen, I recovered a bottle of Jack Daniel's and brought it to the living room and poured a stout shot and downed it. The effects of the whiskey spread through me. Audrey motioned for a shot. She was in one of her no-speak moods—the I'm pissed as hell mood. I had seen it before, not often but enough to know it.

Was everything that had happened all these months really due to something invisible, I wondered? Was that possible? Do the spirits of the dead exist, really exist? Was this dead Herman Ostermann refusing to leave the old house? It was a hard prospect for me to buy into—me, being a person who puts little stock in such crap.

Eventually Audrey said, "As soon as the storm is over, we're getting our ass out of here. For good! Gone! We're dumping this creep-pot ASAP…like fast!" She sat on the edge of the sofa for a few minutes, got up and paced through the living room, then sat nervously down again. "What was that?" she said.

"What was what?"

"Clicking. That damn clicking stuff."

This time, at least, I didn't hear it. I told her so.

On an antique secretary we had in the corner of the living room, I noticed a pad of paper with versions of the word

LOCUS scribbled across it, written by Audrey weeks earlier during the Thanksgiving break. The word was written backwards. The letters were jumbled and mixed up, their order changed. Next to *LOCUS* she had written *USCOL*. "What's this *USCOL* thing?" I asked.

"That? Some gibberish I was messing with a while back. I was trying to figure out what *LOCUS* is. Now I don't give a hoot anymore, if you care to know."

I thought about it, then it hit me. US Col: United States Colonel? Who would that be? That pal of Rainey's I had met at the diner? I tried to remember his name. Wayne something. Wayne Martin...yeah, Wayne Martin, that was it. But so what? I never actually met him—he just shook my hand and left.

Audrey had two more entries, two numbers, scribbled on the paper. 1899 and 2016. They meant nothing to me other than that 1899 was the year the house had been built, and 2016 was the present year. I recalled Philip Pollard telling me about the number nine back at the university. I added 1899 and came up with 27, which when added was 9. Likewise, 2016 added up to 9. I subtracted 1899 from 2016 and got 117. "Lord," I muttered. "One, plus one, plus seven, is...is nine." I tossed the tablet on the desk and sat on the sofa next to Audrey and watched the sputtering and crackling fire.

The storm continued to wage war above us. Rain came down in torrents. The sky lit up with flashes of light as though sent out from a huge strobe. Eerie and mean, the weather thrashed on. We talked about what to do now. Maybe the motel in Krivac wasn't such a bad idea after all—Norman Bates or no Norman Bates.

Audrey grabbed a comforter from the closet and spread it over us. I set the baseball bat, hammer, ax, and a flashlight next to the sofa. As time wore on, the pelting of the rain began to let up until it became a firm but subdued downpour, eventually weakening into a constant drizzle against the windows. We pulled the blanket to our chins. Exhausted and fighting to stay awake, we both slipped into an unworthy sleep.

Hours later, Audrey was awakened by an odd noise. She reached over and nudged me. "Michael...Michael, listen. Do you hear that?" she whispered.

"What...what? Hear what?" I said, rustling from sleep.

"I don't know. Some kind of humming sound, I think."

"It's coming from the basement."

We lay motionless, listening, then got up and started slowly down the basement steps. By the time we arrived at the bottom, the humming consisted of high and low pitches. We moved toward the wine-cellar door. I gave it a nudge with my foot.

"*Good God!*" Audrey blurted.

The room was bathed in a deep-blue light coming from a spot on the floor. A brilliant iridescence covered the entire room. I stepped inside.

"Michael, what are you doing? Stay away!"

As I moved closer to the glowing spot, I could feel heat emanating from it. I picked up the trowel and stooped down.

The heat became warmer. Suddenly, a tremendous force slammed my arm over my shoulder so hard my entire body was thrown back several feet, plastering me against the stone wall. For a second I thought my arm had been dislocated from my shoulder.

Audrey screamed and rushed toward me.

I looked up from the floor. "What the hell was that?"

"Are you okay?" Audrey asked frantically.

I got to my knees and rotated my shoulder. "You wouldn't believe the force it had. I thought my arm was broken."

The rhythmic humming continued, at times loud, at times soft. As the sounds changed, the colors began to cycle through shades of red and then into purple. The shifting colors cast a sickly hue across the room.

"What in the hell is going on here?" I said, standing next to Audrey. "It must be the nonagrams I buried there."

"Let them go. Just get away." Audrey pulled me back to the doorway.

We went up to the kitchen. Bright light was coming in through the window. The pond was shimmering in shades of blue and green and yellow and red. The rain had stopped. From the porch, the field seemed to be engulfed in radiant neon light. It had the appearance of being on fire, just as Rainey had described, but it was clear there was no fire, no flames.

I said, "You want to know what's happening? Come on, get dressed, we're going out."

"*Out?*"

"You'll see. Get your coat."

I drove down the road in front of the house and turned onto a two lane highway under a black sky, passing through dark and gloomy Krivac, continuing down a small deserted road. I pulled to the shoulder by a bridge, the same spot Rainey had taken me to in the middle of the afternoon. I turned the car off and picked up a shovel from behind the seat.

We went under the bridge and down to Bell's Creek. The water was as black as the sky. "Careful...don't trip," I said. "Stay close."

"Michael, wait up."

We walked along the edge of the storm-bloated creek. I had no idea where we were going—I just knew that Rainey had buried the strongbox with the nonagrams somewhere nearby. Moving along was difficult. The dull beam from the flashlight was of little help except to keep us from walking straight into a tree, or go sailing down the slippery bank into the water.

We inched forward. The night was empty and still. Up ahead, I saw a faint glimmer of light. "There, that's it." We went another ten or twelve feet. "Huh...odd," I said, stopping and looking around. "It's on the other side of the creek. We need to cross over."

"We can't do that. We have no idea how deep it is. We can't even see what's right in front of us."

"It's all right, we can get across, go slow." I wondered how Rainey had done this the other day and still managed to stay dry.

We rolled up our pants and waded through the water, holding onto each other and moving one small step at a time, using the shovel to check the depth as we went along. Even with the rain, the creek was shallow, just above my knees at its deepest part. The current, what there was of it, offered little resistance. Once across, we walked along the bank until we arrived at the light. I put my arm around Audrey's shoulder as we stood in silence, staring at the ground. Pulsing colors exactly like those on the pond were coming from the ground.

"This is where Rainey brought me," I said in barely a whisper. "He had me wait back by the bridge while he got the box filled with nonagrams. That's all I really know. This must be where he buried them."

The light from the ground began to fade out. I took the shovel, held it out at arm's length, and tapped on the surface of the soil, once, twice, pulling it quickly back each time as though provoking a rattlesnake.

"Crazy. It's like rock. You can't penetrate it." I pushed the shovel into the earth next to where the ground had been glowing. It went in without resistance. I tried again in both places, where the ground had been glowing and next to it, and got the same results.

All at once, I sensed someone was nearby. That feeling you get when you think you're being followed but don't know who's doing it or from where. I turned and looked around, but could see nothing in the coal-black night, a night so dark I was barely able to make out Audrey standing next to me. I heard a twig crack. Someone moved toward us. I saw the shape of a large hulking person and momentarily heard a voice.

"Michael…Audrey."

In the bleak light I saw the profile of a face and a set of sloping shoulders. "Officer Rainey," I said. "What are you doing here?"

He flipped on a bright flashlight. It was the middle of the night, yet he was dressed in a spiffy police uniform. "Checking out the nonagrams?"

"How'd you know we were here?"

"Saw your car parked along the road. It was pretty easy to conclude—"

"Keeping tabs on us?"

"Like I said, just passing by."

"What's going on?" Audrey asked.

"Strange things are happening at your house, right?" He looked at us one at a time. "You want to know what's going on, do you? These are things I can't tell you."

"Can't or won't?" I said.

"Can't." With that, Rainey reached back, his right hand moved over his gun. A chill ran through me as we stood in the blackness staring at a person about whom we knew little. I pulled Audrey close to me. Rainey's hand fumbling for a second. From his back pocket he retrieved a handkerchief and swiped it across his brow. "I can't tell you what's going on because I don't know. Sure, I know some of—" He stopped speaking, then presently said, "Well..."

"But you knew this was happening here or you wouldn't be here," I said, not believing Rainey's claim that he had come down to the creek because he saw our car along the road.

"It's the night of the new moon. That's how I knew. It happens when the sky is darkest. Sometimes it lasts five minutes, sometimes five hours. The light show, I mean. I don't know why, but that's how it is. When it ends, it won't happen again until the next new moon."

"We've never seen this before, and we've owned the house for months," I said.

"Have you been there during a new moon?"

"I don't know."

"If you had, you would know."

"And the pond. It's going crazy, too," I said.

"Same thing," Rainey replied. He waved the beam of his flashlight across the ground. "It all happens together."

I said, "Then the pond must be *full* of nonagrams, the way it was lit up."

"Doesn't take many. Look at what happened in your house. I'll bet the whole room was glowing and you have... what, just a couple of them."

Rainey pegged that one right. He wiped his forehead again and slapped a mosquito hard against the back of his neck. "And anyway, they're not in the pond, they're *under* the pond," he said.

"How do you know that?"

"It's what I suspect, that's all."

"When I got close to where the light was coming from in the cellar, I got knocked across the room."

Rainey's face was hidden by the night. He was nothing more than a tall frame and round shoulders. "If you think *that* was bad, you're lucky you didn't try to pay a visit to the pond. Doesn't matter, though. You'd never get within fifty feet of it. Believe me, I know. It's as if a wall of some kind surrounds it. I already told you to get your ass out of that house, remember? Well, now you know why. As for all the crap that's going on *inside* the house, don't look to me to help you out. You guys are on your own, okay? And while we're at it, you're wasting your time trying to dig those things up here." He swung light over the ground. "That soil is like concrete. You'll never penetrate it. It's so no one can just stumble onto this and start digging. Find the box and cart it off."

"Apparently you were able to get it the other day," I said.

"There are ways."

"No need to be specific."

"Sort of a code, let's call it. Without it you'll never get anywhere down there. But don't believe me. Dig away."

"Who has the code?" I said. "Uh, hold on, let me guess. Harry Potter."

"Nice," Rainey snorted. "I do. I have the code."

"And who else?"

"Bud might…well, I know he does. He's the one who gave it to me years ago when we were teenagers, the same time he gave me the box with the nonagrams. He learned about it from Herman, his father. I don't know if Herman ever knew Bud had the code."

"Then Bud could get the nonagrams if he wanted to, couldn't he?" I said.

"Sure he could, if he knew where they were. But like I told you before, he doesn't know. They're right here below the soil not more than six inches." Rainey rattled on for several minutes, for the first time providing some specifics about the nonagrams, tying them directly to the weirdness at the house. "The deal is, these things hold tremendous power, enormous power. And not just the power to knock your ass across the room. Not that. What I'm talking about is unbelievable power of the kind that exists nowhere else on the planet, probably not in the entire universe. Energy that can be used any way you want. For good. For evil. The power itself is neutral. It depends on how it's channeled. If it's used in the wrong way, the whole planet, probably the entire crutchin' solar system, would be vaporized. One order of total destruction, please— hold the mayo. Or it could be used to cure every disease in the world. But you need the whole set of nonagrams, and they have to be together at the same time under exactly the right conditions. Right now, the set is incomplete. There are thirteen in the full set. I have eleven. Two nonagrams are missing. Just two, that's all. If they get put with the eleven buried here, the power would be fulfilled. Trouble. Big trouble."

I reminded him that I have several back at the house.

"Those are different. They're not part of the set," Rainey said.

I wondered how he could say that if he hadn't examined them all. As far as I knew, he had only seen the one he found in the school bus. "Someone must know where the rest are," I said.

"Herman knew. And possibly Louise, too. But you won't get anything from her. She's gone. Croaked last week."

"Who told you that? I thought she was in a home in Austin."

"Ruth MacDonald mentioned it. You know Ruthie—she's a first-class busybody. She may be a pest, but she's up on everything that goes on."

"Regardless, the rest of the nonagrams are out on the property somewhere. You already know that, don't you?" I said.

"No, I don't know that," Rainey replied.

"Well, you may not know exactly where they are, but you know they're out there."

Rainey shrugged, in essence conceding my point.

"So why haven't you gone looking for them?" Audrey said.

Rainey took a half step forward, waited a bit, and said, "Maybe I don't want them to be found. Think about it. What would I do with all that power? Rule the world? You've got to be kidding," he said and laughed sardonically. "I'm just a small-town cop. That's all I am and all I want to be. I know something that other people don't know only because Bud gave me a bunch of those things years ago. That's about the only way I am different in this whole matter, I guess." He stopped talking, as if reflecting on that for a couple of seconds, then said, "Anyway, I've been a cop for a long time. I've seen what power does to people...even a little power. And a part of me hopes no one will ever get these things."

He slapped a mosquito on his arm. "We need to get the hell out of here. I'm being eaten alive." He shined the light on the ground near us.

"How did you manage to cross the creek and stay dry?" I asked.

"Took the bridge—the little footbridge someone put together upstream a ways." He pointed with the light. "It's not much really, but if you're lucky, you can keep your ass out of the water."

We followed Rainey across the bridge and returned to the road. Rainey's patrol car was parked behind ours, yet we hadn't heard him pull up even though we were little more than a few hundred feet away.

We headed back to the house.

"I don't like this Rainey dude one bit," Audrey said.

CHAPTER 27

The morning sky was clear and clean, as if scrubbed by the storm. Amber light gleamed into the living room, filling it with warmth. I got up and pushed open a window an inch. The air had that effervescent smell it takes on after a hard storm. In spite of it all, I felt as though I had a bad hangover even though I hadn't had much to drink the night before—a couple of shots of whiskey. My head throbbed and my throat was dry. I went upstairs and climbed into bed for an hour. By mid-morning, I began feeling better.

Just as Audrey had declared in the midst of the storm and the bizarre goings-on in the house, we stuck with our decision to leave, to get out for good, to go. ASAP, as Audrey had put it. Now, only the details of doing that remained.

I drove to Shiner to run a few errands. Afterward, I stopped at Tommy's Place on Austin Street, figuring it was just far enough outside Krivac to be safe. Judy, the barmaid, took one look at me and concocted a Virgin Bloody Mary that she claimed would fix me right up. I lingered in the tavern for a while. People came and went, the usual rural bunch one finds in a country bar, the cartel of paunchy men drinking light beer of one kind or another.

My thoughts returned to Rainey's comments about the energy held by the nonagrams. Was I really supposed to believe that garbage? Energy of a kind never before known, stashed away in a small pit along a country road in east-central Texas? The entire energy of the universe waiting for someone to release its entrapped power like the energy of inert atoms inside a nuclear bomb ready to spin, go to critical mass, and split apart? That such power, even more, can be held in nothing but a speck of matter is well known, of course. The energy that gave rise to all the matter of the universe originated that way. But what Rainey described was way too far-fetched. Yet if I hadn't been slammed against the wall of the wine cellar, I wouldn't have believed a word of it.

As I was leaving Tommy's, I ran into Rainey in the parking lot, spoke to him briefly, and returned home.

Audrey was out by the barn. Sitting at the picnic table, I told her about my encounter with Rainey. "I talked to him for a few minutes, not very long—but it was strange. He yakked about the weather, how dry it's been up till last night, crap like that. When I mentioned meeting him at Bell's Creek, he said he wasn't in Krivac. Said he had gone to Lyckesville. You know, that town about an hour south of here on Highway 59 near Victoria. He claimed he spent the night at his brother's place and drove back early this morning to work the day shift.

All I can say is if it wasn't Rainey last night, it sure as hell seemed like him. Even in the dark, there was that voice, that gruff Rainey voice. And I got a good look at him when we were out by the road. But when I mentioned seeing him at Bell's Creek, he stared at me like I was nuts. He has a way of doing that. He tilts his head down, arms crossed, looks over his glasses and frowns, saying nothing. He lets you blab on and on until you're out of words. Some cop trick he's picked up over the years, no doubt."

"I don't care what he says. There was a Krivac police car out at Bell's Creek last night and Rainey was driving it," Audrey said.

"Yeah, I know hon, but hold on a sec. There's more. Finally I beat old Rainey at his own game. After I ran my mouth for a couple of minutes, it came to me what he was up to. So, I did an end run on him and told him we found out that the nonagrams are total junk, some kind of stupid little toy. I claimed I searched the Internet and sure enough, there they were. You could buy all you wanted. It was a lot of BS, of course, but it threw him for a loop, tied him in knots. You could see it in that thick face of his right away. He became real defensive, insisting the nonagrams *are* big stuff. You should have seen him. He said the nonagrams are the whole enchilada, salsa and all, and we were the only other people who knew it. Then he slipped up. Mr. Cool Cop tripped over his own words and said, 'Like I told you last night out by the creek—'. In a split second he corrected himself and said, 'The other day,

I mean. When I told you the other day.' But I knew what he meant, and he knew I knew what he meant."

Audrey had been waiting a long time to hear this, and now there it was. "He's a wacko, Michael, just like I suspected. A first-class nutcase," she said.

"Ah yeah, he is, but let me tell you, the guy's smooth. Damn smooth. You have to wonder how many people he's snookered. He's the provocateur who's been spreading the stories about the Ostermann house all these years. It's Rainey who has this whole town believing it. He uses his position as the local cop to lend credence to it. I've got a strong feeling he set the townspeople up to go after me that time when the kid was hit by the car in Krivac. He didn't have anything to do with the kid getting hit, I don't believe that. But the moment was perfect for him to turn loose his pack of hyenas. It fulfilled the prediction he had warned me of when we were sitting at Carter's. He parks that big ass of his in a booth over at Carter's most of the day. It's a little Peyton Place. Droves of people coming and going, lots of chances to stir the pot. I'm beginning to wonder if the guy is really all there." I tapped my finger on the side of my head. "Anyway, I haven't quite figured out how he pulled off the light show in the basement and out on the pond...or at Bell's Creek. Or how he managed to get the word *locus* on the kitchen wall. There are ways to do it though, *that* I'm sure of. Yet, all the junk with the videos is still a big mystery. Coming up with a hoax that sophisticated would be a bit beyond Rainey's pay grade. But there's always the possibility that Rainey had picked up a few tricks from Herman Ostermann despite claiming he hadn't known him. Herman was a pretty smart cookie, apparently. So we have to be careful. Rainey might not be as dumb as we might think, even though he got caught with his hand in the cookie jar this time."

"It's possible that what we saw on the recording was flat-out faked, a big forgery," Audrey said. "Done in bits and pieces and spliced together to make it look like the house was being invaded by something invisible."

"However you cut it, it's a Rainey work of art from top to bottom. And maybe Ruth McDonald is in on it, too. They're a pair, a team, even though Rainey talks her down all the time. And for all we know, the people from the security company could be in cahoots as well—Jennifer Walker. That'd wrap it together nicely, wouldn't it? She could have jiggered the recording pretty easy, judging by what I saw when she was here. She probably has everything she needs right there in that little van of hers."

It was a eureka moment, the first time we had good evidence that Rainey had been misleading us. Things were beginning to add up. All the times I had met with him, had talked to him—all the distorted stories, the changing stories—they had been invented in Rainey's dodgy mind and dished out to us on a silver platter. How he tried to put distance between himself and Ruth McDonald, how he made *her* out to be the flaky one. Now I was more pissed at Rainey than ever, yet it almost made me laugh. Like when you go to the doctor and find out the MRI he ordered showed that the nagging pain in your side is harmless, nothing bad going on with your kidney or liver or pancreas. Old age creeping in, that's all. Audrey's sense of relief was visible. For the first time in weeks, she seemed calmer. I could see it in her face.

"I'm convinced Rainey's the one who's been getting into the house," I said. "He's the perp, as he likes to say. That I believe. Or he has someone doing his perping for him. Either way, he's involved."

The plan was for Audrey to head back to Houston and for me to put the house up for sale. Let the whole damn thing be someone else's headache. That was our plan, anyhow.

CHAPTER 28

Audrey left in the afternoon. I spent some time fixing a gutter torn loose by the storm. When evening rolled in, I felt the need to go someplace and get a beer, to get away from the house for a while. I didn't particularly care where. Any place but Tommy's. They were getting to know me a little too well there. That left a couple of joints farther from town: the Last Shot, Frank's, and the Little Easy, so named because of its attempted New Orleans motif but known to most as the Little Sleazy. Truth be told, they all looked about the same from the outside. The inside was anyone's guess.

I picked the one farthest from Krivac, the Little Sleazy. A dark place with a couple of windows, a long bar, a dozen stools, some tables, some chairs, one pool table, and a worn-out dart board with a set of darts jammed into it as though they'd been blasted from a 16-gauge shotgun. A string of cheap Christmas lights drooped behind the bar. They'd probably been there since last Christmas.

Music—hard-core country—played now and then from an old jukebox. An attractive thirtyish waitress in tight jeans swiveled about the tavern, toying with the local crowd from which she was earning good tips and a couple pats on the butt. She didn't seem to mind as long as the tips kept coming.

I took a table safely over near the corner, where I sat drinking Budweiser, listening to the music. It was obvious I was an outsider—as foreign as a pint of Guinness in this place. Now and then I'd get a stare as if I were a Gypsy passing through Krivac, just as Rainey had described in Carter's Cafe. Or maybe they were thinking, ha, there's that stupid SOB who bought the Ostermann place. I didn't care. It felt good to be away from the house.

I hoped this wasn't one of Rainey's haunts, although it could well be. You knew Ruth McDonald wouldn't set foot in a place like this. I looked around—deer-hunting season, no doubt. Camouflage baseball hats and vests were the order of the day. Yet one look at these bubbas and you wondered how many of them could make it across the parking lot without sucking wind. Deer hunting in Texas had been reduced to going to a hunting lease where the deer have been all but tamed by months of feeding them corn. Then one day some dude with his fanny parked atop a four-wheel ATV drives up and blows Bambi's brains out when it stops by for lunch. Wild deer would get a whiff of these bumpkins from the other side of the county.

I went to the jukebox and scrolled through the list of songs, searching for one I knew. Just one would be enough. Not being big into country, it wasn't easy. But there it was. I had heard it in Tommy's once. I plunked a quarter into the box and played "Get Drunk and Be Somebody" by Toby Keith.

As I returned to the table, I recognized someone who entered the bar. There in the flesh was Colonel Martin. I got up, went over, and started to introduce myself as he was ordering a drink. He looked at me; before I could get a word out, he said, "Michael Felton. Right?"

"Geez, you have a good memory. We hardly met."

"Not a whole lot of new faces in Krivac. You come here often? The Sleazy…that's what the natives call it."

"First time," I said.

"It's one of my stomping grounds, I guess you could say. The choices out here are seriously limited," he said, with a sad but genuine laugh.

"Come on over." I pointed to the table in the corner.

He picked up his beer and glass. We went through the usual first-time small talk. Where are you from? What do you do? Martin, with a master's degree in particle physics, had a better appreciation of academia than Rainey, the military in the upper ranks being saturated with smart highly-educated people.

He no more looked like he belonged in this honky-tonk than I did, despite his claim to having a frequent-flyer card here. He wore chinos and a neat blue shirt, casual but almost executive in cut and style. His hair was trimmed and perfect. Every blade in place, not too long, not too short. His face had the countenance of Robert Oppenheimer: deep probing eyes, carved chin and jaw. There was something meaningful yet sad about it. His hands were the hands of a surgeon, neat and clean, fingernails filed and manicured and polished.

"So, I hear you own the old Ostermann farm up on the edge of town."

"How'd you know that?" I asked.

"I remember Jack Rainey telling me once."

You have to be kidding, I thought. If what Audrey and I had concluded about Rainey were true, Martin's head should be swimming with a thousand and one tall tales. "You know the place, huh?" I said.

"Who doesn't?" Martin replied.

"No one, as far as I can tell."

"Well, I'm no stranger to it." Martin poured beer into his glass and watched the foam creep up until it reached the top, where it came to a perfect stop as if on command. "I probably know more about that place of yours than anyone else out here."

When had I heard that before!

"I was a lifer in the army. Some of it in military intelligence, some in special ops. The military had a huge interest in the Ostermann property going back many years. It was all part of something called Operation Orion." Martin snickered and said, "Sounds sort of sci-fi, doesn't it? Well, don't put much stock in that. The military isn't particularly imaginative when it comes to naming things. This area—Krivac, I mean—was of great interest to them. They like a good mystery, especially when strange things are happening. Wonderful way to spend your tax dollars." He stopped speaking for a moment, then said, "You really want to hear this?"

It looked like I was going to get it no matter what. One thing for sure—I was in no mood for a Rainey-style tease from this guy or anyone else. Okay, humor the guy, I thought. It's that or watch bubba knock balls around the pool table for a couple of hours.

"Some of this was studied out of the Pentagon," Martin said. "Wright-Patterson Air Force Base in Ohio also had a keen interest in it. That's where most of the work on Roswell was done, the Roswell incident back in forty-seven. It's all stored neatly away at Wright-Patterson. The government would like you to believe they don't give a hoot about that kind of stuff. They try hard to project that image, but nothing could be further from the truth. They follow up on every lead, every thread. Anyway, various intelligence agencies got involved from time to time on the Ostermann thing. The CIA, the National Security Agency, the Defense Intelligence Agency, the FBI, the Office of Naval Intelligence, take your pick. Some of it even made its way to a covert group out at Area 51, the place in Nevada. But it was a big jumbled mess. Nobody talked to anyone; no one shared what they knew. Nothing was ever coordinated. It was frustrating if you were part of it. I worked on Orion for years, right up until the time I retired. By then, the military had pretty much beat the thing to a slow death. They'd gotten all they could, which in my opinion wasn't very much, so they let it go. *Adios, amigo.*"

Martin talked straight and to the point with none of the razzmatazz that peppered Rainey's conversations. Every now and then he would digress and then drift back on topic. One time, he talked about growing up as an army brat, the son of a lieutenant general, in Alexandria, Virginia, and about his years in Krivac. Somewhere along the way, he had picked up a touch of a Texas accent—a "you all" instead of the full-fledged southern "y'all" would slip out here and there.

"During the Cold War, the government had a keen interest in just about anything that might give the US an edge over the Ruskies. All sorts of things linked to the paranormal, ESP, photokinesis, mind control, stuff like that. They were especially interested in the use of energy fields, particularly in how to manipulate them. It had been known for decades that energy is concentrated in some places more than others, and it turned out that the Ostermann property was one of those places. *That's* why the military ended up snooping around out here. Your place isn't the only one, though. There are others like it in the area. There used to be a house not far from here that had its own version of weird." A smile passed across Martin's face. "The place is gone now. Leveled some years ago. Texas is teeming with strange things. In fact, more so than any other state in the US. Take the lights that glow in the desert out by the town of Marfa in west Texas, for example. It's been going on for a long time, first reported back in the eighteen hundreds. The lights appear as small orbs just above the ground. You can see them move about, hovering for a few minutes over here and then a few minutes over there. Nobody knows what causes them. Some think they're due to an electrical discharge from the earth. Or possibly caused by foxfire—methane gas that's released from rotting vegetation. If that were true, the desert would catch fire and burn, being as dry as it is out there, but it doesn't. And, of course, there are folks who think they're connected to UFOs somehow. The government studied this for years and came up dry. I was sent there twice. Didn't do much but eat a lot of Mexican food and put on a lot of weight."

Martin peered over the top of a pair of thin glasses as he spoke. His face was bathed in the murky shadows of the bar.

"Over at the other end of Texas out toward Louisiana near the town of Bragg there's a different light show that occurs on a regular basis. Unlike Marfa, Bragg is down at sea level and wet as hell, getting almost an inch of rain a week. The lights in Marfa and Bragg are very different. In Marfa they're yellow, sometimes white orange, sometimes red. In Bragg they're bluish white. You can see them from Bragg Road in Hardin County. The folks there call it Ghost Road."

"What are you getting at?" I asked, unclear what this had to do with anything.

"The lights that appear on your property. I'm sure you've seen them. They occur one night a month. That's all, just one night. On the night of the new moon when the sky is darkest. Why is that? It's hard to imagine them being tied to the cycle of the moon, don't you think? For a long time, the people in the military thought the Ostermann lights had to do with earth energy of the kind in the Bermuda Triangle. Everyone knows about the Bermuda Triangle, but to this day no one really knows what's going on out there. It could be as simple as a shift in the earth's magnetic field causing compasses and electronic equipment to malfunction. Planes and boats have disappeared. We've all heard the stories and seen the TV programs. The USS *Cyclops*, for example. March 1918 it vanished along with hundreds of men without a trace. No one's seen hide nor hair of it since. Planes, too. Flight 19, five Avenger torpedo bombers went missing in 1945. And I'm talking about people who know how to fly. Military jocks. Even today, there are parts of the triangle that some pilots—*me* for one—refuse to fly over. The Ostermann property is also energetically unique. The pond, for sure, and the area around it. The government figured that much out, and they figured out that the energy is linked to how reality is perceived when you're out there. Pretty much anywhere on the property. Hard to believe, but it's true. Strange stuff, huh? Some people think Herman Ostermann had developed this as a means of keeping people away."

Martin veered off again for a few minutes. He made a couple of comments about the storm and then got up. "Back in a second," he said and headed off to the men's room.

I sat at the table and looked around. Men waddled into the bar. A handful of couples whirligigged on a small dance floor. I hadn't come here for a diatribe about Krivac and the

Ostermann house. I already had too many of those. I had no idea whether to buy into Martin's story or not. He could be just as twisted as the rest of the crew I routinely encountered at Krivac. Or he could be nothing but a mole sent by Rainey. Sort of strange, I thought, that he showed up the one and only time I came here. He claimed to come to the Sleazy a lot, but one look at him said no way. The guy had never been in the Sleazy before, that was my calculation. No one in the place recognized him. Not so much as a nod or a wave or a hand shake. He was here because I was here.

I went over and pumped a few more quarters into the jukebox, playing a couple of random selections. By now, they all sounded about the same. When I returned, Martin was ordering a round of beer from Swivel.

"Come on now, Wayne," I said. "If the military was so damned interested in the property, all they had to do was con-fiscate it. Just take it. The government does it all the time, right? I'm sure they could have come up with some excuse. Then you guys could do all the nebbing around you wanted to."

"To a certain extent, the government did get what it want-ed. After Herman Ostermann left, it was easier to get onto the property even when Louise Ostermann was still there. But things changed once the Cold War ended and once Herman was gone. A lot of government programs were eliminated. Money dried up. Reports were written and filed away...forgotten. Operation Orion was one of them." Martin topped off his beer and said, "Anyhow, that's when I left the military—once they started screwing everything up, losing track of what they were trying to do, what they wanted to accomplish. And like I said, things changed after Herman left…died."

"Did you know him?"

"Herman?"

"Yes, Herman."

"No, not personally. No one did."

"In all those years, you didn't learn anything about him?"

"He was a hard nut to crack, even for us." There was something almost apologetic in Martin's tone. "Let's just say he was a tad strange," he added.

"In what way?"

"The old school bus. That's the bus Bud Ostermann died in."

"What? You're saying Bud died in that bus?"

"That's right. He was just a kid. The bus slid off the road on a bad rainy day. Morbid that Herman would keep the thing on his property. The locals, the people from around Krivac," Martin said, motioning with his hand as if referring to the very people in the tavern, "they all wanted him to get rid of it, but they never pushed him too hard about it."

"Why did you stay in Krivac?" I said.

Martin shrugged. "I don't know. Liked it, I guess. Gotta live somewhere, right? Things have been okay for you all at the house?"

"More or less…someone broke in a couple of times."

"You have an alarm system?"

"Yeah, yeah, yeah, we have all that," I replied. "But there are ways to get past those things. They're not foolproof." I told him about the video recordings, the key, the buttons being pushed on the security panel, the boxes being moved around in the attic. I really had no plan to get into that with a total stranger, but I was curious to see his reaction. I even went so far as to tell him about the word *locus* on the computer and wall. "As far as we're concerned, it's all a big hoax. We don't know who pulled it off, but—"

"What if I told you it wasn't a hoax?"

I laughed so loud a guy at the bar turned and looked. It didn't faze Martin. He said, "What I'm getting at is that it's not about what you see. It's about what you *perceive*, what you *think* you see. That much the military learned. It's not a trick."

"I can tell you, we get different versions of everything depending on who we talk to. People even contradict themselves sometimes. Take the situation with Bud, for example. *First* we were told he's living somewhere in California. *Then* we were told he's here in Krivac. *Now* you tell us he's been dead since he was a kid. We were even given his address here in Krivac."

"Did you go there?"

"Yeah, twice," I replied. I didn't tell him we ended up with different results each time. Martin's reaction, subtle as it was, suggested he somehow knew this.

"It's just a perception that he's alive or dead, that's all. Just like with the security-camera recordings you described."

Swivel came by and set a bowl of pretzels on the table, then spun away. After she left, Martin said, "There are two possibilities, two potential explanations. The first has to do with the altered perception of reality I mentioned. That possibility cannot be overlooked. In other words, the things you saw on the recording never happened at all. Don't forget, the video isn't real time. It's a recording. Maybe it happened, maybe it didn't. Who knows? So, it's possible that all the strange stuff you saw, whatever it was, never occurred. The second possibility—and there's a good case to be made for it—has to do with something called a time cloak. It's a process in which things can actually become invisible. In this case, whoever was in the house—or maybe I should say whoever *is* in the house—is invisible. You wouldn't see him if he were right here next to us, right now as we speak. It's a complex process that involves messing with the speed of light beams. Normally when you see something, what you see is the reflection of light off an object. In a time cloak, you split light so that some of it speeds up and some slows down. You can delete light in time, and when you do that— *bam*!" Martin snapped his fingers. "Things vanish. Let me tell you, the government was almost obsessed with this. Still is. To this day, a ton of research is being done in physics departments all over the place. And they're getting pretty damn close to making it happen. Think of the implications. Look how it would change warfare, for example. Or crime, for that matter, if you could wander around invisible." Martin's eyes glanced across the room. He toyed with the label on his beer bottle and, with absolute confidence, said, "Herman Ostermann knew all about time cloaks, we were *certain* of that. He had it down to a science...or maybe I should say he knew the science behind it. He could do it whenever he wanted."

"Yeah, but Herman's dead," I pointed out, "so I don't see—"

"So there's someone else out there who knows how to do it. And there's not a damn thing you or I or anyone can do about it."

I described the nonagrams to Martin. "Did the military find any?"

"Oh sure. But I don't know where they are. They could be sitting in some general's desk drawer in the Pentagon."

"Rainey thinks they hold the key to everything. He believes they have some sort of immense power. He also said that when you guys were out here, the military I mean, it caused a lot of commotion in town."

Martin leaned on the table and said. "Look, I like Jack Rainey. He's a hell of a good guy to have lunch or a cup of coffee with at the diner. Lots of great stories. But what's he got to do all day? Not a whole lot. Krivac is *Mayberry R.F.D.* all over again. He writes tickets, arrests drunks, and now and then gets called to pick up someone who got nailed shoplifting. He needs some excitement in his life. He enjoys stirring the pot a little."

"He tried to tell me that you guys, the feds, were in cahoots with Herman on some big mind-control experiment.

271

He claimed a few people in Krivac were pretty screwed up by it all, and that to some degree the whole town is still affected by it. He also said you folks knew about it and let it happen."

Martin didn't respond. He waited, as though wanting to find out how much I knew.

"Well?" I prompted.

"Sure, we wanted to know everything Herman knew. Especially about his ability to use time cloaks. But we weren't collaborating with him, that's for sure. Rainey knows that. He's a bit prone to exaggeration. He likes spinning webs."

"So I gather," I said. "But what's the relationship between the nonagrams and the Ostermann property?"

"Funny you call it the Ostermann property when in actuality it's yours now."

"In fact, we usually call it 'the house.'"

"Yeah, there could be a connection between the...um, the nonagrams, and all the rest," Martin said. "I really don't know. Those things are strange little contraptions, as you're probably aware. A few people in special ops thought they were real important, but most people just dismissed them. For me, there was always something stranger about the property itself. Especially the pond. You see, it was very hard to get onto the property while Herman was there. The army tried everything. High- and low-level reconnaissance, radar, photography, remote viewing, you name it. The pond was always a key target for remote viewing, but they could never ever get anything from it. Nothing. Nada. Zip. It was like the pond had some impenetrable covering over it."

"What's going on? Are we living on some kind of toxic waste dump or something? Is the soil full of radioactive material?"

"No, it's nothing like that. The soil's safe. The water's okay. That stuff's fine. It has to do with the mind-altering energy, like I said. Your perception of things gets twisted around." He fiddled with his thumb nail, and said, "It's not just out there on the old Ostermann property, however. That's what the military learned. It can have to do with other parts of Krivac as well, but the Ostermann property is the source. It radiates out from there. That's where Rainey and a lot of others in Krivac are off the mark. Sure, some of this was due to Herman himself, but some of it was always there, part of the Ostermann land long before it belonged to him and Louise. Before it belonged to anyone probably. If the Krivac crowd looked into their own history, they'd see plain as can be that you can't blame it all on the Ostermanns. But you know how it is...everyone wants a scapegoat."

Martin glanced left and right, as he had been doing periodically all evening, as if checking for enquiring ears. "See, the energy out on your place is unique. Nothing like it anywhere else. The concept is simple, but the application is complex. It so happens that the energy wavelengths match those of the human mind, similar to the brain's theta wavelength and sometimes delta wavelength, having an amplitude somewhere in the one- to four-hertz range. Delta and theta brain activity is typical of drowsiness and sleep. Any neurologist or neurosurgeon or anesthesiologist will tell you that. Out on the property, the energy comes and goes. It's not there all the time. That's what throws people off. So when it does happen, everything gets turned upside down. You see things that aren't there and you *don't* see things that *are* there. It goes both ways. It's like a dream where you think your flying, floating around. And then when you wake up, there you are, flat on your back in bed. But you still have that feeling, that sensation, and you think, 'I swear to God I *was* flying through the air.' Even though you know you weren't, it sure as hell felt like it in the dream. Out-of-body experiences are like this, too. The military identified it—the energy, I mean. Lock, stock, and barrel. It's there. It's out there, all right. Altered perception of reality. APR, is what we called it."

Up until now, I'd considered everything Martin said to be a lot of crap. Now, he was beginning to get my attention. As I saw it, this was either the biggest crock of horseshit in the history of the world, or…or I don't know what it was. I listened. Martin rolled on. It was starting to get corny, so I said, "Come on now, Wayne—level with me. You *really* don't believe this APR junk, do you?"

He took my challenge in stride. "Do I believe it? Yes, totally. And everyone who worked on Operation Orion did, too. We had strong, solid, tangible proof. You could measure the energy. There was no doubt about it. If you're asking whether it screws up people's thinking, if that's what you mean, you be the judge. What do *I* think? I guess I wouldn't have mentioned any of this if I didn't believe it."

Just then, a pair of jumbos over by the bar got into a tussle. I heard the bartender say they were heading for a game misconduct if they didn't stop. A couple of people managed to squeeze between them like the officials at a hockey scrum. Martin snatched a pretzel from the bowl and bit off a chunk and smirked. "That's what I like about these places. There's no cover for the entertainment."

Things settled down. Martin continued on. He talked about the nine poles on the property. This, of course, I knew to be true. I had found them, though I had no idea what they were.

"They're tied to the energy. They channel it," Martin said. "They may not look like much, but they go deep into the ground, possibly a half mile or so. It's a big deal, huge. We don't know who put them there, but as far as we can tell, they've been around for a long time. Inside each one is a precise mixture of metals—iron, zinc, titanium, some lithium, other stuff. They focus the energy in some way. Herman had something to do with the poles and the energy and how they worked. But, like I said, he was a total mystery. We had no idea who he was or where he came from or how he met Louise— none of that, even though Herman and Louise lived in the house for almost sixty years. As for the house itself, it's been around for a long time. There have been nine owners…well, eight plus you. You all are the ninth. I know the old place like it was a history lesson from grammar school, having studied it so long when I was in the military. The first owner was Jacob Weinlander. He was an immigrant from Germany who built the house in 1899, the same house you're in now. He kept it until 1908, then sold it to the Kuricek family. It turned over pretty quickly after that. The O'Malleys, an immigrant family from Ireland, owned it next. Then it was bought by Jorge Garza, a local resident originally from Mexico. Garza sold it to Hans Jilek, who sold it to a Russian immigrant named Ivan Stravonovich. Stravonovich came from Russia hoping to raise wheat but found the land better suited for a few head of cattle and not much else. He gave up, moved north to Kansas, bought a lot of land, and ended up a multimillionaire. The seventh owners were the Diefenbachs. They were Louise's parents. Her maiden name is Diefenbach. They bought the house in 1917. Louise was born there in 1926. She was the only child they had. The property was eventually deeded to Louise and Hermann after they married. They were the eighth owners."

I asked what Herman did for a living.

"He rarely left the property. That's about all we know. It's possible Louise had some money and Herman didn't need to work. We do know that Herman was somehow tied in with everything that happened on the property. There are several theories of this. Some think Herman himself was the source of the energy, that he *was* the power...or that the power came from him, through him. Others believed that he merely had knowledge of how to use the energy that existed on the property. Both groups believe that as long as Herman is buried on the property, the energy will remain there."

We talked for hours. Martin continued to fill in details about the house and the property. Some of it was old news, some new. I asked where Bud Ostermann was buried. "I didn't see a plot for him in the graveyard," I remarked.

Martin shook his head. "No idea. I'll tell you what. If you want, I can give you a copy of the military's report on Operation Orion. You can rummage through it yourself. This is the unclassified version, though. There's a classified version, too. I can't give you that one. It has some things the government doesn't want spread around. Not much I can do about it. That's the way it is. I'll bring it over to your place, to the *Ostermann* place," he said with a quick, light smile. "If you're not there, I'll leave it on the porch."

He glanced again around the bar and turned his attention back to the table, listening to the song on the jukebox. "You like Tim McGraw? This is one of his. It's called 'Living on Refried Dreams.' Kind of a moniker for my life, I think." Martin's face held an empty grin, as if confessing to a venial sin. "When you get sentenced to living in Krivac for a long time, you get used to this stuff. Funny how it changes you."

He took the last hit of his beer, set a couple of dollars on the table, started to get up, then sat down again. "Oh, yeah... there's another thing you might be interested in. During the time we kept track of the Ostermann place, eight members of the military died. More correctly, they disappeared, vanished. Remember what I said about the similarities between the Bermuda Triangle and the Ostermann property—the energy connection? The similarities are even more striking than that. An unusual feature of the Bermuda Triangle is that sometimes the boats and ships remain intact, perfectly fine, just floating around out in the sea without a single person on board. The passengers, the entire crew—*poof*, gone. Not a trace anywhere. As far as I'm concerned, that's what happened to the people who disappeared on the Ostermann property. We never heard from them again. All had managed to get onto the property. Something that was difficult to do, nearly impossible. They could have been killed and buried somewhere out there. We don't know. Or maybe they were taken off the property. We don't know that either. But right after Louise left, a while before you bought the place, we searched it from end to end and found nothing. No evidence of graves, nothing at all. Of course, it would be hard to find a grave on that much land if you didn't know where to look."

"Go get a search warrant. You could've done that long ago," I said.

"That's not the military's style. They didn't want to let on that the Ostermanns were being observed, even though Herman knew it all along. There had been a lot of discussion over the years to do exactly what you said. The concern was, if Herman controlled the energy, he might shut it down and leave us hanging. But right after Louise left, the few remaining people who had been part of Operation Orion searched the property and came up empty. No evidence of graves, nothing at all. Like I said, it's not really surprising; it would be damn hard to find an unmarked grave out there today."

I told him about the room we found in the basement and asked if he knew about it. He said they opened it when they searched the house and that they went inside but didn't see much, so they closed it off again. An odd comment, I thought. If you were looking for the remains of dead people, that's where you might start. I also wondered how they could have missed the nonagram I had found sticking out of the dirt floor. It was right there, evident even in the dull light from the flashlight when I'd first gone in. I started to wonder if Martin and his pals had planted it there. And what about the rings on the walls— how could they not notice and wonder about those? I explained to Martin that we had opened the room and had converted it into a wine cellar, and I explained that I had inadvertently found what appeared to be a tomb not far below the surface of the soil. Martin's reaction revealed nothing. I couldn't tell whether it was old or new information I had delivered to him.

He got up, saying again he'd bring the report by when he had a chance. As he started to leave, I said, "While we're at it, Wayne, tell me something, I was talking with Charlie Blacek the other day, and he said—"

Martin came over and sat down slowly. "Blacek? You talk-ed to *Charlie* Blacek?"

"That's right, Charlie Blacek. Why? What's the deal with that?"

"The deal with that is, unless you can communicate with the dead, you're going to have a tough time talking to Charlie Blacek. Blacek has been dead for over ten years."

I stared blankly at Martin, hunting for something to say. From what little I knew of him, I could tell there was no room for joking in his well-starched military mind.

"Dead?" I asked softly.

"Dead."

"We're talking about the same person? The guy who lives down the road from us, right? The guy with the old tractor and the—"

"You mean the guy who *used* to live down the road from you. That house is gone. Zelinski sold it. Peddled it and the land some years ago."

Martin stood up, shrugged, and left.

I sat for quite a while, mulling over what Martin had poured out. Although I had taken his comment about the altered perception of reality with a grain of salt, his statement about Charlie Blacek worried me to no end. Charlie was either alive or he was…or he was dead, one or the other. And if he was dead, then what?

The bar seemed darker, sadder, gloomier than ever. The music was filled with slow tales of soured love. Most of the patrons had left; only the diehards remained. The ones who arrive at five thirty or six and stay until one thirty or two. The gang that leaves foggy headed, tilting precariously to the side as they aim themselves toward the door. They climb into their pickup trucks and gun them down the country roads. These are the people you don't want to be out on the street with at this hour—at any hour.

As if in a living dream, I grabbed my keys, set a five spot on the table for Swivel, and walked out. I drove down the midnight roads past Krivac with only one purpose: to pay a visit to Charlie Blacek.

CHAPTER 29

I pulled to a stop. There, off to my right where Blacek's house should be, was nothing but a large dark pasture with blackened silhouettes of a few cattle dining at midnight. I looked down the road to our house a few hundred yards farther on. Yes, this was it—this was the place where Blacek's house had been...should be.

I climbed from the car and walked to the spot once occupied by Charlie's simple but charming home. In the grass beneath my feet were the remnants of an old gravel driveway and the walk that had led to Charlie's front porch, the very porch I had sat on with Charlie more than once, sharing a six-pack of Lone Star. The stone foundation that formed the cellar was all but filled in with dirt and sand and grass. It was barely identifiable. There was no house, no barn, no silo, no Max. There was no Charlie Blacek.

My knees felt like they were about to give out from under me as I replayed Wayne Martin's conversation about Charlie Blacek. A weary dizziness passed through my mind. I could hear Martin's last word, "Dead," as clear as when he'd said it. I knelt on the ground, wishing for the moment, the whole episode, the whole evening, to somehow pass. I wanted everything to stop.

I drove back to the house, unlocked the door, and turned on the porch light. Sitting nearly catatonic in one of the wicker chairs, I looked across the road to the field that spread out before me in the gray moonlight. The chair that Charlie Blacek always used when he came to visit sat rude and empty, forty-five degrees to my left.

Could it be that everything that had happened to me in the past two months hadn't happened? Could it be that Martin had come to the Sleazy for no reason but to tell me that? Why? What the shit did he care? For that matter, who the hell was Wayne Martin and why did he still live in Krivac? Who would live in a town if what he'd said were true? A place where reality is all screwed up? Maybe the guy is still *in* the military. Or maybe he is out, like he claimed, and he's running his own little special ops. GI Joe living on refried dreams.

I went inside and retrieved a bottle of Jack Daniel's from the shelf in the kitchen, picked up a whiskey tumbler, returned to the porch, and poured two fingers. I knocked that back and repeated it with another two fingers, and another yet again right away, trying as fast as possible to wash my mind clean.

I slept until late in the morning. The day was bleak and white. There was a grim emptiness to it. The house, walking through it down to the kitchen, felt disturbingly still. I made coffee and opened the door to the back porch to find the copy of Operation Orion that Wayne Martin had promised. It was a big document, more than an inch thick. On the cover in simple plain letters was the title: *The Report on the Findings from Operation Orion.* I brought it inside, thumped it onto the kitchen table, poured a cup of coffee, rubbed my hands over my face, and stared into the coffee cup.

Dredging myself out of the chair, I grabbed a windbreaker from the front closet and tramped across the pasture until I arrived at the path through the bushes that led to the grave-yard. Everything was precisely as it had been the last time I was there—the same scattered and collapsed fence, the same occasional granite post, the elegant gate submerged in grass. The graves rested as stock-still and motionless as ever.

But not everything was the same. Not by a long shot. Passing beyond the graveyard, I came to where the Waumtauk burial mound was…where it should have been. There was no raised mound of soil, no rim of rocks that had encircled it. There was no burial mound at all. Charlie Blacek had said the Waumtauk never die. Well, sure as hell they were gone now. Nothing remained but a spread of thin wispy buffalo grass layered on the blanched Texas soil.

I returned to the house and for several hours nurtured a hangover—the unwelcomed door prize of my long night at the Sleazy with Wayne Martin and my time afterward with Old No. 7. How does the adage go? "Beer on whiskey, mighty risky; whiskey on beer, never fear." Sure as hell proved that one wrong!

Out of sheer boredom, I opened the document about Operation Orion and began reading bits and pieces. It was dull and dry. It covered a long span of time, the first entry dating to 1953, which I knew was the year of Bud Ostermann's birth. After that, it rambled on and then stopped without an ending.

The more I read, the more I realized Martin was right: there was no coherent plan behind the government's work. Considerable time, money, and personnel had been committed, but in some areas, very little specific information had been garnered despite years of surveillance. It was surprising so little was said about the nonagrams. They were referred to as "ornamental objects," although it was clear from the description that they were the nonagrams. There was no mention of where they ended up. Regardless, they were considered to be of little importance.

On the other hand, the report revealed an intense desire to gain information about the energy, saying it was centered in a set of specific places—a description that immediately brought to mind the markers I had discovered on the property, the ones Martin had described.

Energy was indeed the overriding issue of Operation Orion. The government was certain that the knowledge of the energy—where it came from, where it was located, how to use it—would change the balance of power on the planet in favor of the United States forever. High-level meetings had been held at the White House as far back as the Eisenhower administration and continuing through the time of Bill Clinton. It didn't make sense, though. Here was a place that the government had been obsessed with for decades, and then one day they abandoned it the way a child loses interest in a toy train set. Buckets of money had been spent.

A concerted effort had been made to find out who Herman Ostermann was. Despite attempts by the FBI to track his origins and to connect him to even the most rudimentary personal information, they learned little. He lived as an almost anonymous person in the house that had belonged to Louise's family and later to her. Every attempt to photograph him had failed. On several occasions when they thought they had him on film, the images came out blurred and distorted. Remote viewing likewise yielded nothing.

Operation Orion did, however, learn much about Louise Ostermann, though they considered her to be an insignificant player in what took place on the property. There was a brief but rather detailed mention of the death of Bud Ostermann. It had happened in the school-bus crash, just as Martin had said. The date was given as September 19, 1961. Something about that date struck me as odd. Then it hit me—the month and day were the same as the one on Herman's grave. I had seen it enough times to know.

Chapter 30

As I lay on the sofa, I heard a vehicle pull to a stop on the road in front of the house. I opened the front door to find a man about to ring the bell.

"Can I help you?" I asked.

"I'm Bud."

"Who?"

"Bud Ostermann."

I was at a loss for something to say.

"I was told you were looking for me," he said.

In front of me was a man who for the most part fit the description of Bud Ostermann given to me by Ruth McDonald: hair, height, age, all about correct. But that's where it ended. He had on an old pair of jeans that were significantly too short, as though he had outgrown them years ago, and he wore a faded Grateful Dead T-shirt, something I didn't expect to find Bud wearing.

After the events of the past twenty-four hours, my interest in talking to Bud had all but vaporized. Yet there he was in the flesh—apparently. "Would you like to come inside?" I said.

"We can talk here." He went to the steps and sat down.

"Uh-huh...sure," I said, and sat next to him. "So who told you I was trying to reach you?"

"Rainey."

"That's probably true. I think I mentioned it to him once," I replied. I wasn't quite sure where to start. "You lived in the house a long time, huh?"

Bud shrugged, as if to say, "I suppose."

I talked about the room in the cellar. "If you want to come inside, I can show you."

"Don't need to." He explained that his father had closed it off and said that's all he knew. "You can ask my mother. She would know more. She's in a home somewhere, I think."

"Bud, your mother...your mother passed away a couple weeks ago."

"Oh?"

"Yeah. You didn't know that?"

There was an uncomfortable pause and he said, "My father used it."

"The room, you mean?"

"Uh-huh, the room."

"What did he use it for?"

"They did experiments down there," he said, twiddling his thumbs as he spoke.

"Who did?"

"The people who came to visit my father. I don't know who they were or where they came from. They'd go into the basement. I'd hear this sound, a humming sound that made the whole house seem like it was vibrating. That's what it felt like, anyway. They talked in some kind of foreign language. Well, not so much a language. More like noises, clicking sounds. They had figured something out that had to do with energy. They could use it in special ways to communicate and to control people, even for space travel. His knowledge of it was far beyond anything known today. Years ahead. Decades… centuries ahead. That's what I heard when he talked about it. He was a brilliant man."

"Your father, you mean."

Bud nodded. "Possibly the smartest person who ever lived, *ever*! He knew all about mathematics and physics."

"Where did he learn this?"

"I don't know. He was born with it, I think. He knew all about how the universe works. Stuff like that."

"These people who came here," I said, "did you see any of them? What did they look like?"

"I never saw them. My father made me go upstairs. I heard him communicating with them, that's all. But they were there, that's for sure."

"When you lived here, did strange things happen?"

Bud turned to me. "Like what?"

"Like bright lights out by the pond."

Bud shook his head.

"Did you ever see any little round ornament-like things, sort of round metallic objects?" I asked. "We found several of them."

"Nope."

"I can show you."

"Not necessary. I never saw anything like that."

I said, "Well, if I show you—"

"Never saw them. Lotta questions."

"Just curious," I said. "Anyway, about these things we found. Rainey said you gave him a bunch when you were kids. Were they somehow tied in with the meetings in the basement?"

Bud didn't respond. He sat on the step, staring straight ahead, now and then rocking forward and back as though he was finished with this question and was waiting for the next one.

"Would you like something to drink?" I asked.

Bud shook his head.

"So, what was it like to live out here when you were young?"

"About the same as now. The land doesn't change much. It was a good place for kids. You could play outside. Mess around in the barn. Stuff like that. You from the country?" he asked. "I mean, did you grow up in the country? On a farm or ranch?"

"No, not me. Not Audrey, my wife, either. Sort of city folks all our life."

"Growing up in the country's fun for a kid. Good place to use your imagination."

"Imagination…in what way?"

"You know, not much else to do out here, so you make believe a lot."

"I guess you and Adam liked it here as kids?"

"Who?"

"Adam, your bother."

"Oh, Adam. Yeah, Adam."

"How's he doing?" I said.

"Fine, I guess."

"Does he like California?"

"I suppose," Bud said. He looked at me. "I guess you've seen that eagle that lands on the tree every night at dusk, huh?"

"No. Which tree?"

"The one on the back end of the property by the graveyard."

"That tree?" I said, knowing exactly which one he was talking about.

"That tree. Every single night an eagle lands just about dusk. Has done it for years."

"How do you know it's an eagle?"

"If you knew birds, you'd know it's an eagle. Pretty impressive thing. They have a wingspan of eight feet or so. Big birds."

"What's it do there?" I said.

"Doesn't do nothing. Just sits there awhile and then leaves."

"And that's odd?" I asked.

"Sure. It happens every day of the year. Eagles don't live here year round. They come in the fall and leave in the spring. But this one's here all the time. Day after day, year after year."

"What do you think it means?" I asked.

"I dunno…probably nothing," Bud replied.

"It could have a nest there."

"There's no nest. Take a look. Eagle's nests are huge. You wanted to know if there is anything strange. Well…" he said, getting up, "I gotta go."

"If you don't mind my asking, do you live around here?" I said.

"Yeah, over at 8532 CR72. *That's* no secret."

"Uh-huh. Also, do you know a man named Wayne Martin? William Wayne Martin? He's a retired army colonel. He lives somewhere in the area."

"Nope."

"When you were a kid, was the government ever snooping around out here? Or in Krivac, maybe?"

Bud looked at me in disbelief. "The government's always snooping around. You don't know that? Yeah, you *must* be city folk."

"What did they want?" I said.

"They wanted to know what my father was up to, that's what. But they never learned a thing. He knew of ways to prevent that. He was too smart for them. Like I said, he was a genius. He could manipulate people, could get them to do anything he wanted."

"This Colonel Martin guy I mentioned claimed it had to do with some sort of energy out here on the property."

"Yeah, so what?" Bud said, looking down at me.

"Was it true?"

"I don't know anything about energy."

"Where's your father now?" I asked.

"He's not around anymore."

"There's a grave in the graveyard. Is it his?"

"Could be." Bud turned, walked to his truck, and drove off.

I looked at the dirt on the ground in front of me. Weird dude, I thought. Strange as hell.

CHAPTER 31

Audrey returned from Houston in the afternoon. I mentioned my encounters with Wayne Martin and Bud Ostermann and the deal with Charlie Blacek.

"Blacek. I don't remember anyone named Charlie Blacek," Audrey said.

"If you go out the front door and drive down the road near where the Clausens live, on the opposite side, what do you see?"

"Nothing, a pasture and some cattle," Audrey replied quickly.

"You're kidding, aren't you?"

"Why would I kid? I've driven past that spot countless times. I did it barely twenty minutes ago, in fact."

I said, "There was a house there when we moved in. Charlie Blacek owned it. I told you about Charlie Blacek. I used to go there and drink beer with him in the evenings, or sometimes he'd come over here."

"There's never been a house there, Michael. Not while we've been here."

"I'm sure I told you about Charlie…"

"I have no idea what you're getting at. I don't know who Charlie what's-his-name is."

I explained about Bud Ostermann coming by not more than two hours ago.

"How do you know it was Bud?"

"I didn't card him, if that's what you mean."

"It could have been an impostor. Did you consider that?"

"No, I did not consider that! Why would an impostor come by pretending to be Bud Ostermann?"

"I thought you said he was dead."

"This guy Wayne Martin who I ran into the other night in a bar, a place called the Sleazy, he said Bud is dead. That he died in a collision in the bus, the one that's out on the back of our property. And he talked about something called altered perception of reality…APR is what he called it. It's something that happens right here on the Ostermann property, right where we're standing now."

Audrey looked at me with the blankest of stares, hands on her hips as if waiting for me to drop the next bomb. And I did. I started telling her what I had heard from Martin about APR. Frustrated and getting nothing but disbelief from Audrey, I said, "I'll be back. I'm going to gas up the car. It's running on fumes."

I drove to Rudy's Shell station on the edge of Krivac. At the pump across from me was Bud Ostermann. He was driving the same dark-blue pickup truck, wearing the same faded Grateful Dead T-shirt and short jeans, wearing the same mismatched white and green socks that were evident below the high pants cuffs. He looked over at me.

"Hey Bud," I said.

"Who are you?"

"Michael Felton."

"Who?"

"Felton. Michael Felton."

"Do I know you?"

"You were just out at our place. Remember?"

He shook his head and said, "I don't know what you're talking about. I was home all morning."

"We own the old—"

He finished pumping and shook his head again.

"We were talking…just a while ago—"

"Got the wrong person," he said. He climbed into his truck and drove off.

I stood there feeling crazy. How could that *not* be Bud Ostermann? I watched the truck pull away. It had the same deep gash on the right back fender. I remembered thinking when I saw it that he must have slammed into one hell of a big pole to make a dent that big. I climbed into my car and drove down the country roads outside Krivac.

Back at the house, I told Audrey I had run into Bud at the Shell station, hoping now she might believe me. I told her he'd played dumb, pretending not to recognize me.

Audrey groaned. "Oh, for Christ's sake, Michael! Don't you see? This is all part of a little scheme they have going, and you're getting sucked into it."

"Whose scheme?"

"*Everyone's.* Rainey, Ruth McDonald, Bud, maybe even that Wayne Martin guy. They're in collusion somehow. They believe they can drive you nuts, drive us nuts. It's like what Rainey did when we ran into him out at Bell's Creek, remember? And then he claimed he wasn't there. But it *was* him, and you even proved it with his own words. Now, Bud Ostermann is supposed to be dead, but he shows up out here and then says he doesn't know you."

"Maybe this is some of that…I don't know. What if it's the altered perception of reality Martin was talking about. The—"

"Come on, Michael, you don't really believe that crap, do you?"

"I mean…well, what if…"

"*Mi-chael!*"

"Now wait, hold on. Suppose there's some truth to it. It is possible, isn't it?"

"*How?*"

"Let's say Bud never came here at all, that I only thought he did, but he didn't. And that—"

"And what? Maybe all that stuff with Rainey never happened? Or that you never found any nonagrams? Or that the whole episode with Colonel Martin at the bar never took place? The computers? *LOCUS?* You can go on forever. Then what? Are we going to question everything?"

"Well, how would we know? *What if* I just imagined it because this energy thing gets everything twisted around?"

I reminded Audrey of the confusing and contradictory information about the house I had obtained at the library. Was it a case of inaccurate reporting or a case of distorted information? Facts being turned into fiction or fiction being turned into facts? How would we know?

"Christ, Michael..."

"We don't have any actual proof. Do we?"

"Good grief, once you start down that path, where does it end? Maybe we're not here right now. Maybe we aren't. And maybe this house isn't here. Maybe it's not. And the sky isn't up above us, and that tree isn't there, and the barn isn't there, and—"

"Maybe it's not."

"Shit, *stop it*!"

"You can't ignore the fact that according to the report Martin gave me, the government had an interest in this place for a long time, and it all had to do with that APR stuff," I said.

"And maybe Operation Orion never existed. Have you considered that? Have you? And what about this Martin guy? We don't know squat about him. He could be totally fucked up, a schizophrenic nut."

"Or what if everything he said was a hundred percent true. Do you think he wrote a monster document like the one he gave me about Operation Orion for no reason at all?"

"Sure, why not? If he's crazy, why not?"

"And if he's not crazy?"

"It doesn't mean we have to buy into it. For example, take the nine poles you found in the ground out on the property. We have no reason to assume they're what Martin said they are—the source of some kind of stupid brain-wave energy or whatever nutty notion he was trying to peddle. They could be nothing but a bunch of dumb old concrete poles, property markers just like you suspected they might be."

"Or maybe they don't exist at all."

"Don't exist, don't exist! *You* found them and showed them to me. *I* saw them. Go out and look again if you don't believe it."

"That's my whole point! We *imagined* it. And what if when you go out and look at them, you only *think* they're there? It could be that for the reasons Martin described, things out here do get twisted around. Everything gets jumbled together. All I'm trying to do is make some sense of it. That's all!"

"Don't you understand? There's nothing to figure out. There's nothing to make sense of. It's a huge, gigantic, colossal mess. A fake. Don't you see?"

CHAPTER 32

Evening settled in. Still peeved about all that had happened recently, needing to clear my head of it, I took a pair of binoculars and sat in a folding chair on the grass next to the back porch. At the far end of the property, sure enough just as Bud Ostermann had told me, a large bird flew in from high in the sky. It circled once over the tree and then glided down, alighting on one of the big branches. It was an elegant creature: black feathers, sleek white head, yellow-orange hooked beak, white tail feathers. Its head jerked and turned as if surveying the area around the tree. All in all, it stayed no more than two or three minutes before it bounded into the air, spread its massive wings, dipped down, and then flew gracefully off in a smooth wide arc that carried it up into the sky.

A quiet and peaceful night lit by a gentle moon spread over the land. Audrey had hit the sack early. Later at night, I joined her. At around two-thirty, I awoke, unable to sleep. I slipped into a pair of jeans and went down to the kitchen for a glass of water. I picked up the flashlight from the counter and went out and sat in the chair on the lawn.

An ethereal fog had descended onto the fields. Trees—brown and black—were nothing more than fuzzy ink sketches outlined on a gray canvas. Everything that had happened recently passed through my mind. I tried once again to piece it together but soon gave up and merely listened to the nocturnal sounds—a bird in the distance, the cry of a far-off coyote. Sounds I would never have heard had it not been for the near-perfect calmness of the night.

Suddenly, I caught the motion of something to my right over near the barn. Seeing it only for a fleeting moment, I could make out little of it, except that it appeared human like.

I stood up abruptly, looked and listened, and then crept through the vaporous smoke-like air until I reached the barn, not sure whether or not to proceed. Peering around the corner, I could see no more than a short distance ahead. I headed silently along the side of the barn until I arrived at the end. Again I stopped and considered what to do. I continued on behind the barn, glancing around but seeing nothing. There I stood, thinking, listening. Turning to head away, I heard several sharp clicking sounds, three to be exact, one after another in succession. They came from somewhere out in the misty vague fog. I stood motionless in the darkness, waited, stepped backward five or six times, and retraced my steps until I arrived near the side door of the barn. It was slightly open, yet I remembered it being closed only moments before.

I nudged the door with my foot. It creaked inward a few inches. I nudged again. The inside of the barn was dark and bleak. I entered, moving one slow step at a time. Only a faint sliver of dull light from the outside came in through the doorway. I turned the flashlight on and panned the beam back and forth around the barn and down onto the ground in front of me. Scattered about were clusters of small irregular-shaped footprints, each about four inches long, each with two long toes. I knelt down and inspected them. Strange things. Animal? Possibly. Maybe. But unlike anything I had ever seen.

I followed the footprints across the floor until they ended in front of the hayloft ladder. As I passed the workbench, I picked up a wrench, stuffed it into my pocket, wedged the flashlight into the other pocket, and climb the ladder up to the hayloft. Looking down, the floor of the barn seemed miles below. I stepped out onto the deck. The same prints I had seen on the barn floor were scattered across the hayloft. Unless it could fly, whatever had made the prints must have somehow negotiated a tall vertical ladder.

Even with the light from the flashlight, the hayloft was in almost total darkness. I inched my way to the far end near the edge where there was no railing. I stumbled, caught my balance, but slipped and fell sideways off the loft and tumbled through the air toward the floor of the barn. My heart leaped as I twirled in free fall, bracing for contact with the ground. At the very second just before I hit, my motion was slowed and I landed with almost no impact.

I rolled over on the dirt floor examining myself—arms, legs, hands—and climbed to my knees and stood up. I was fine, completely unhurt. I looked up at the ledge of the hayloft far above me. The flashlight, which I must have dropped as I fell, lay on the ground. I picked it up. It rattled, its innards broken to pieces. The barn was shrouded in darkness. At the entrance to the side door, I saw a shiny silver-blue creature. Two stripes extended down its torso from shoulder to feet. It stared at me for a moment, then sped off in a bouncing motion. I followed it down the side of the barn toward the house, gradually gaining on it. Turning the corner of the house, I tripped and landed face first on the ground. The creature fled off into the misty field.

I plodded back to the house, went to the living room, and collapsed exhausted on the sofa. Within seconds, I was asleep.

"Michael, are you all right?" Audrey asked.

I opened my eyes. The room was filled with morning light.

"What are you doing down here? Look at you...you're filthy! What *happened*?"

I pulled myself up. "I'm not sure." I rubbed my eyes. "Something real fucking strange happened."

"What do you mean?"

"I'm not sure," I repeated.

"Look at you. Your pants are dirty. Your shoes are dirty. Where've you been?"

I shook my head. "Um...I don't know. In the barn."

"The *barn*?"

"Yeah, out in the barn," I replied, pointing in the direction.

I explained everything that had happened during the night. Little by little the whole episode came back to me the way parts of dreams are reconstructed the next day. I told her about the creature.

"You're saying you saw some kind of two-legged *creature*?"

"That's right. Something totally strange."

"Like what?"

"I'm not sure what. It was dark…and foggy as hell. I didn't see it up close. But it wasn't human. Definitely not human."

"What did it look like?"

"Short. Maybe this high." I held my hand at about four feet. "Two legs, two skinny arms, freaky face. Hard to place. I couldn't really see much."

"This was in the barn?"

"In the barn, around the barn. Yeah." I explained what had happened in the hayloft and how I had chased the creature.

"This is almost too much, Michael."

"You think I'm making it up? Do you think I went out and rolled around in the dirt or something?"

"No, of course not, but I mean…a *creature*?"

"Yes, a creature. Why is this so hard to believe. Look at all the weird-ass stuff that we saw on the video when we came back to the house from Houston…before the storm hit."

"That? We agreed it was all the doings of Rainey-the-Trickster."

"Well, this was no encore performance by Rainey-the-Trickster. Not by a long shot. This time it was real," I said, dusting myself off. "It was some kind of strange creature.

What else can I call it? Unless they have some real psycho animals out here that we don't know about. It's time to finally quit pretending this stuff isn't happening. Don't believe me? Come on, the barn's full of bizarre little footprints. I'll show you. They're all over the place. Even up in the hayloft. And anyway, how could an animal climb a hayloft ladder?"

We went to the barn. Inside were numerous footprints, all of them ours—not a single print of the kind I had seen during the night, the kind I had just described to Audrey. We looked all over the barn. I climbed up to the hayloft. Same thing again, our footprints and nothing more.

Audrey said, "I don't know what you're talking about. There aren't any weird footprints here."

"The flashlight is somewhere out here," I said, looking around the barn, figuring that would convince her. "It broke when I fell off the hayloft."

"It's in the kitchen, Michael. I saw it on the counter when we came out."

We went to the kitchen. Sure enough, there on the counter was the flashlight, in perfect working order. I said, "All right, so maybe I imagined this, too. Now who's the one suggesting things didn't happen when I know damn well they did?"

Audrey threw her hands in the air. "Let's not go there again, all right?"

CHAPTER 33

We returned to Houston and for the next week became immersed in work. According to our agreement, the Ostermann episode would soon be over. We would write it off as a terrible, woeful, unfortunate experience and try to forget it ever happened.

Sitting in the tranquil safety of my university office, looking out the window at the pleasant old stone buildings and brick walkways, at the students passing across campus with book bags, I realized that perhaps our original mistake was thinking we could find happiness in a place like Krivac. Even without its weirdness, was it truly for us? When we needed to get away, we could get on a plane and fly to the coast of Maine or spend a couple of days in the Caribbean or a week in the Rockies. Or just go down to Galveston not an hour away—walk along the Strand, spend a night at a hotel, and return invigorated. We had done it many times in the past.

I had a good feeling about our choice as I sat in the rediscovered peace of my office surrounded by shelves filled with hundreds of books. It was that moment of decision when everything was right. There was a simple clarity to it. Out in Krivac we had done things we would never do anywhere else: track people down, follow them around. What had possessed us? Why did we care about Bud Ostermann? Why did we care so much about the history of an old house? And yet, even as these thoughts rumbled through my head, I wondered why, sitting in Houston in my office, I was able to sort through everything clearly and logically, whereas out at the house I was carried off in a different mind-set. For a brief flashing moment, I thought again about Wayne Martin's comment, about the altered perception of reality. "Fuck the Ostermann house," I murmured.

I got up and headed over to meet Audrey for coffee at Salento Café on campus. Along the way, I ran into Phil Pollard, the archeologist who had examined the original non-agram. He asked what we had learned about it. I managed a feeble smile and said, "Let's see. It hums, it gives off strange light, and it has the power to blast you across the room if you get too close."

Pollard laughed deep and hard. "Just your typical archeological artifact, right? You need to get in touch with Indiana Jones."

Audrey and I sat in the café and talked about our decision to sell the house. There was little remorse. I would go to Krivac in the morning, place it on the market, and start to pack; Audrey would come out Thursday or Friday. We would bring back the most important things, close up the house, and return to Houston. Later we would make a trip to pick up the furniture and the wine. We had acquired so much wine, we would need to place it in a wine-storage locker. But that was all right. We had put together an impressive collection of good wines and a few great ones—French Bordeaux and Burgundy, an occasional Rhône and Beaujolais, and a white Muscadet here and there. Red Italian wines—Barbaresco, Barolo, Valpolicella, and Chianti—were also in the mix.

I was up and on my way to Krivac in the morning. Driving west on I-10 was easy, the outbound lanes being almost empty at that time of day. The house was exactly as we had left it. The security alarm was on; nothing unusual had been recorded by the cameras. Almost a sullen remorseful feeling permeated the house, as though it knew of our decision to leave.

I unloaded a package of boxes from the car and brought them into the house and went directly to Krivac and placed the house for sale at Jameson and Zelinski Real Estate. Ted Zelinski was once again sitting in the office reading the newspaper. He took my request in stride.

"Sorry to hear you're leaving us," he said. "Didn't work out?"

"It was fine." I had no intention of going into details of the house with him.

"I thought it was a perfect match for you and Audrey. Almost custom made."

After everything that had happened, I wasn't sure what to make of his comment. "We made some changes in the house,"

I said. "I guess you'll need to come and take a look." We set a time for tomorrow.

I stopped at the C&J Grocery and bought food for a few days and a sixer of local Shiner beer. Whatever fear I had developed for Krivac no longer bothered me. As I was about to leave, I saw Rainey walking down the street on his morning rounds of checking parking meters and writing an occasional ticket. He glanced at my car; I knew he recognized it. I waited until he was well away and then left for home. I sent a text to Audrey: Everything cool. Easy drive. Packing now. Love ya. Audrey replied almost immediately: Love ya 2.

It was amazing how much stuff we had accumulated in a few short months. Humans are indeed the ultimate pack-rats. We save everything we *might* need and accumulate piles of crap we'll never use again. I resisted the temptation to throw anything in the trash without Audrey present. She was the habitual string saver; I was the eliminator. More than once, I'd found myself saying, "Hey, honey, what happened to the…" only to be informed that I had thrown it away…"Remember?" Usually, I was glad it was gone.

I took clothes from the bedroom and hall closets and began folding them in the boxes, stopped for lunch, and started in the barn, where I packed up the large cache of tools I had accumulated over the months. This went on all afternoon and into the evening. I was happy to be leaving the house but not happy about the circumstances. Either way, it didn't matter. Audrey was adamant about getting out; I knew she was right. I sat for a while, lights off, sipping wine, and hit the sack early.

Sometime in the middle of the night I was awakened to find three strange creatures standing over me—one in front, one to my left, one to my right. I felt a blast of adrenaline rush through my body. My heart leaped and fluttered. I tried to climb out of bed but was unable to move except to turn my head a centimeter or so to the left and right. I stared at the creature in front of me. Its head and body were identical to what I had encountered in the barn. Its skin was slick and shiny, almost wet looking, silver-blue, iridescent. Its face, although devoid of features, had three large, pulsing, artery-like strands, one of which came across the top of its head and separated into two sections. There were no eyes that I could see. No ears or nose. The mouth, if that's what it was, was a thin membrane in the lower part of the skull that vibrated now and then. With this, it communicated with the other creatures using clicking sounds. The creature in front of me turned to the one on my left. A hand reached out. Two long fingers touched my forehead. I quickly faded away—that last breath on the operating table before surgery.

In the morning, I awoke late and stumbled to the bathroom. I had a detailed memory of everything that had happened during the night...up until the time I was put to sleep. I wondered for a second whether it had been a dream, one of those vivid dreams that leaves you believing everything in it really had occurred. I stared at myself in the bathroom mirror.

My skin was tender, as though lightly sunburned. There were two small puncture wounds, one on the inside of each forearm. I was exhausted. This couldn't have come from a dream no matter how real it seemed.

I showered and went downstairs and filled the coffee maker with water, but the thought of coffee repulsed me, so I slumped into a chair in the living room and may have fallen asleep for a while. I wasn't sure. Images of the creatures kept flashing across my mind. Why were they here? Why were they interfering in our lives? Or was it that we were interfering in their lives?

By noon, my appetite had come roaring back, and I needed a cup of coffee. I drove into Krivac and had a big breakfast at Carter's Café: eggs, bacon, sausage, toast, potatoes, biscuits and gravy, and coffee. While I was sitting there, Rainey came in for one of his half-dozen or so daily cups of coffee. He walked over to my table.

"Heard you're leaving Krivac," he said.

"News travels fast."

"Small town."

"Hadn't noticed," I said.

Rainey smiled a bit. "Ted Zelinski told me this morning."

"Uh-huh."

"All the spooky stuff scare you off?"

"Nope. Just leaving."

"Back to the city?"

"Yep."

"Well, enjoy your eggs," Rainey said. "They're good here."

Eggs are good here? Where aren't they good, I wondered. Sitting there in Carter's, I knew what I was going to do. We were leaving Krivac and the Ostermann house, that was for sure, but for as long as we were still here, we were going to be safe.

After breakfast, I drove over to a gun store on the outskirts of Krivac. I had never bought or owned a gun before. Had never even hunted. Had no real desire to.

The gun shop was an ominous-looking place—a sign written in huge letters across the front read GUNS AMMO. The inside of the store was even more foreboding. It was a virtual arsenal. The politics of the store owner were abundantly clear from the hundreds of signs, banners, and bumper stickers attached to the walls and counters.

I explained what I was looking for—a shotgun and two handguns of some kind. The owner, a short, middle-aged man with a few strands of hair spread across the top of his head, asked how I was planning to use the guns. Just for protection, I responded.

We started with the handguns. He laid out a vast array of choices on the counter and proceeded to explain each in detail. The majority were semiautomatic or automatic pistols with an occasional classic Smith & Wesson revolver thrown in. He gave me the nitty-gritty details of each gun. "Go ahead, pick 'er up," he said. We settled on a 9 mm semiautomatic pistol. Choosing the shotgun was easier. A nice, big 12 gauge would do the trick, he declared. It was clear this guy went for fire power.

That was it. In less than an hour, I had selected three guns. I assumed it would take several days for the necessary background checks. Not so.

"Pay cash and they's yers," he said. "You can walk outta here with 'em now."

I stared at him, thinking, isn't this illegal...even in Texas? But then, what did I care? He was doing the selling. I went to an ATM, withdrew the money, returned, paid for the guns, and drove back to the house.

Pulling into the driveway, I saw Ted Zelinski's silver Lexus SUV. I looked at my watch. Damn. I had totally forgotten about his appointment, but fortunately I was only a few minutes late. We went through the house room by room and then out to the barn. He liked the simple but effective changes we had made. The property, I explained, was exactly as when we arrived.

We sat at the kitchen table. "Let's go for one twenty-four five," he said. "That's thirty K more than you paid. Not bad for a couple months' time, huh?"

Still low for the house and the property, I thought, but if it guaranteed a quick sale, so what? We wanted to be gone as soon as possible.

"I'll get the house listed right away," he said on his way out the door. "Hope we find owners as enthusiastic about the place as you and Audrey were."

After Zelinski was well down the road, I unloaded the guns and what seemed like enough ammunition to supply the entire Brazilian Army. My plan for the day had been to continue packing, but that changed now that I had the guns. I started out the back door to go to the barn when I suddenly felt light-headed and woozy, almost to the point of falling off the porch. Gripping the railing, I sat on the steps rubbing my eyes, taking in several deep breaths. For a few seconds everything became a blur. As fast as it happened, it went away.

From the barn, I picked up a hammer and a handful of nails and a stack of boards and trudged out into the pasture. I built a crude but solid frame and nailed onto it one of the paper targets of a human body that the gun shop owner had given me. I stood back and viewed my creation. It looked ominous and evil, a black silhouette of a person. I was heading to the house when I was again hit with an instantaneous spell of dizziness. I hunched over, hands on knees.

Making my way to the living room, I slumped into a chair, picked up the phone, and called Audrey, knowing it would be comforting just to hear her voice. We talked for quite a while. She told me how her day was going so far. I mentioned the progress I had made with the packing and organizing and told her the house had been put up for sale. I said nothing about the guns or the creatures or the dizzy spells.

The rest of the afternoon and all day Wednesday, I spent with the pistols. I got better and better—to the point where I could hit almost any part of the target with considerable accuracy. The dizziness came and went sporadically. I checked my blood pressure. It was fine. Not high, not low. I became convinced that these episodes were related somehow to my encounter with the creatures.

If those bastards ever come again, I'll blow their ugly little brains out, I vowed.

The afternoon slipped into evening, the evening into night. The night was as still as any I can remember. I sat on the back porch with the six-pack of Shiner beer and looked at the barn, at the fields, at the water on the lifeless pond. Millions of flickering specks hung in the sky.

I leaned back and stared up at them, wondering what or who was out there. Were they looking up at the sky, watching our solar system blink, wondering the same thing? I would miss this part of being out here. The effects of the beer sent me into deep thoughts about the months we had spent at the house.

I went inside and turned on the CD player. My mood insisted on something soulful. Shuffling through a stack of blues CDs, I found a great old recording by Lonnie Johnson and Elmer Snowden. I knew this one well. The first song, "Haunted House," was ironically perfect. I turned out all the lights, sat on the back porch, and took a big gulp of beer. Music blasted through the screen door. Lonnie Johnson's soft sad voice enveloped me. I purred the words along with him: *Yes, my house is gettin' haunted, Blue Ghost is all aroun'...*

I stayed up late and then turned in, this time spreading out on the sofa with one of the pistols tucked under the pillow. After my encounter with Larry, Moe, and Curly the night before, I had no desire to spend another long night up in the bedroom. I fell asleep and moved not an inch until I was awakened in the middle of the night by a sound in the kitchen. I got to my feet and took the pistol from under the pillow. I could already feel perspiration collecting on my palm as I gripped the gun. Aiming and shooting at a target was one thing—*this* was real.

I entered the kitchen. Even in the darkness I could tell no one was there. Then it hit—the smell of ripe raw meat. Perhaps I had left the refrigerator door open. I flipped the light switch. The refrigerator was closed tight. On the table was a thawed chicken with the wrapper beside it. I had bought the chicken earlier in the day, planning to fry it or toss it on the grill or something. Now, here it was, pink and white and dull gray, sitting in a small pool of chicken blood, picked apart, half-eaten. But this had not been done by some animal. No way! Whoever, whatever, had devoured half of its skin and rubbery meat had done so with a knife and fork. The knife was on the table next to the bird. The fork was stuck into the bird—its prongs deep in the flesh, handle sticking straight up. Flecks of meat cut from the uncooked carcass were scattered about.

I reared back in shock. "*Je-sus H!*" It was all I could do to keep from barfing halfway across the kitchen. I stepped closer to the table. There was no doubt this hideous scene had been created by something human. Or something damn near human. Manners it had, but it liked its chicken rare.

The longer I stood there, the worse the odor from the meat became. It seemed to be rotting by the second, right in front of me. I snatched a trash bag from under the sink, picked the chicken up by the embedded fork, held my head back, and delivered the carcass into the trash bag. Taking the bag outside, I sank it into a garbage can. Searching the house would be useless. I knew it would be devoid of visitors. And yet all this had happened not more than twenty feet from me. Whatever did this stealthy deed—making its way into the kitchen, opening the refrigerator, removing the chicken, opening the package, and then taking a fork and knife from the drawer—did it without my hearing a sound.

I went into the living room and slumped into one of the big chairs that gave a wide view of the room, pistol resting in my lap. Sitting there, bathed in silence, I made a decision. In the morning I would open the grave in the wine cellar. Why the fuck not? The house was still ours. We could do any god-damn thing we wanted. I was going to find out what was in the tomb. It was somehow connected to the house, in a room of the house that had been sealed off. Was it a tomb? Who the hell would bury someone in the basement, for Christ's sake? What else might be inside it? Nonagrams? Those stupid things Rainey blathered on about. Dozens of them, hundreds of them, thousands of them, millions of them? Or was it just a big empty box? Or…or was it perhaps Herman's *real* grave? Maybe old lady Ostermann had planted him in the graveyard and then later dug him up and carted him off and deposited him in the cellar the way Norman Bates had propped his embalmed mother in a chair by the window of the old Bates mansion.

But why? And anyway, if it *was* Herman, how would I know? I'd never seen him in the flesh. If any flesh was still left on his bones—now ten years or so later—it would look like patches of burned paper, no doubt. Like the blackened hands and faces of the popes and saints that are on display in the glass coffins at the Vatican and elsewhere in Italy. Ghoulish.

Or maybe Bud Ostermann was down there—dead-alive-dead Bud. Or that other Ostermann kiddo. What was his name? Oh, yeah…Adam. Maybe he had croaked sometime along the way. There seemed to be a lot of that going on in this family—croaking. Perhaps they had planted him in the cellar, too. Someone or something was down there. Had to be. I didn't fucking give a shit who it was. I was going in.

I sat motionless and stared at the dining-room doorway. I could see only as far as that, but that was enough. If there had been a visitor in the house tonight (well, of course there had been!) and it planned an encore performance, this time at least I would get the jump on it.

I pushed the chair back so that it touched the wall. There was nothing behind me. I could see everything in the room—forward, left, and right. The lights in both the living room and the dining room were off. Just illumination from a kitchen light I had left on trickled into the dining room. The living room was bathed in the chalky grayness of the weak light that ventured in through the window from the late-night sky. I sat in the chair for a long, long time, eyelids drooping, head dipping. Each time, I pulled myself awake. Then I fell unwittingly asleep.

Chapter 34

stood in the musty wine cellar staring at the ground, knelt down, and began scraping dirt away, piling it against the wall. In little more than half an hour, I had uncovered the top. I swept it clean with a whisk broom. There were the engravings I had seen previously—the woven branches, the crescent moon, the sunlike object, the inscription predicting the enigmatic return of someone unknown. But now I saw something I had initially overlooked. On each corner and halfway across each side was a nine-pointed star, carved into the stone. Eight stars in all. Why eight and not nine? Clusters of nine seemed to be the rule—the nine spokes on the nonagrams, the nine markers I had found on the property. But here, there were eight evenly distributed stars.

I continued excavating along the sides, knowing I would need to get under the lid in order to pry it up. I wiped perspiration from my forehead. Only the dim light of the single bare bulb lit the room. I went to the kitchen, retrieved a battery-powered lantern, and returned to the cellar. What if I needed to dig several feet to get below the top of the lid? What if there was no lid at all? What if it was just a big chunk of stone that had no functional purpose?

I removed my T-shirt and tossed it on the wine rack. Digging one small scoop at a time went slowly. I stood up and stretched and looked at the stone slab below me, then knelt down and rubbed my hand along the edge of it. If there was a lid on this thing, I hadn't yet gotten to it. Another twenty minutes went by, scoop by scoop. Aha, there—finally! At last, a seam. There was indeed a lid. I estimated it to be eight inches thick. Considering its size, it would be extremely heavy. I needed to pry it up onto its side. In the barn, I found a long metal bar with a flattened end, brought it to the wine cellar, and placed a cinder block under it to use as a fulcrum.

Lifting with all my might, I managed to raise the lid a couple of inches. A short blast of air blew out, sending a fine spray of yellow dust through the room and across me. I wiped my hand over my face, cleaning off my eyes, and let the lid settle back down again. Prying even with the metal bar would not work. I needed something more. I looked around. Of course, the rings on the walls. I could use them to help raise the lid. I retrieved a long thick rope, strung it between the two rings opposite the fulcrum, and lifted the lid enough to jam a four-by-four into the opening.

I grabbed my T-shirt and swiped my face again. I took the rope and passed it under the lid and tied it snugly. Hoisting it up with nothing but manpower was not going to be as easy as it seemed. What I needed was a mule, I thought, ridiculously. I grabbed the rope and pulled on it with all I had. The lid came up little by little. Eventually, it would fall back from its own weight against the wall. I had no plans of getting anywhere near it until it was safely up lest it come crashing down and crunch me like a potato chip. Pinned like a mouse in a trap. At last, I succeeded. It tipped against the wall with a thud that vibrated through the foundation.

Below me was a deep cavernous space. A series of stone steps descended into it. Yes, it did look like a tomb, all right. I looked around the wine cellar and out to the main basement room. It was obvious that this thing, this tomb, had not been relocated to the basement from somewhere else on the property as I had once suspected. It was far too large for that. It appeared to have been in the ground for a good long time, possibly before the house had been built. Possibly even for centuries going back to the days of the earliest settlers. Then, later, the basement and the house been erected over the vault. Nothing more complicated than that. Knowing that the tomb was there, the owners of the house, maybe Herman Ostermann, had sealed off the room. Possibly, the tomb was the real reason for sealing off the room. It was all beginning to fit. Or so it seemed.

I got halfway down the steps and looked at the lid. By all accounts, it was safely immobilized against the wall. Yet that didn't stop me from considering what might happen if, God forbid, it came slamming down while I was inside. Tomb indeed—my tomb. That couldn't happen, right? So let's not go there. Just stick to the plan.

I stood at the bottom of the steep steps. The top of my head was almost even with the floor of the wine cellar, making the tomb a good six feet in depth. The air was dank and chilly. A thin layer of yellow dust, similar to what had blasted out when I raised the lid, covered the sides and the floor of the tomb. I rubbed my fingers over the powdery film. Already I could taste it on my tongue, bitter and fine as flour. I spit and blotted my lips on my wrist.

Opposite the steps that led into the tomb, well below the level of the ground, was a compartment about the height of my waist, six feet long and three feet deep—the actual burial area where the body would be laid out, I supposed. Resting there were what appeared to be human bones. I picked one up and examined it. A femur, I assumed from my minimal knowledge of anatomy. Sixteen in all, laid out in eight pairs of two set side by side. There were no other bones, no skulls, no other remnants of human life. Nothing to provide a clue about the one-time owners of the bones. Were I a physical anthropologist, I could probably have made some determination as to whom the bones had once belonged to—the age of the person, maybe even the gender. That sort of thing. But the bones revealed little to me.

Behind the bones was a small wallet. I picked it up. It was old and decrepit, the leather almost falling apart. I opened it gently. Inside was an ID with the name Jeffrey Broding typed across it and a signature below, written in the simple hand of a young teenager. Was this where Broding had somehow ended up? I tried to fit the pieces of his disappearance together. According to the information Rainey had gathered from Schneider and Robinson, all three of boys had been out by the graveyard. Broding may have been in the school bus when he vanished. It was unclear. Were Broding's bones part of the collection in front of me? Or was it that Herman had found the wallet and stashed it away down here, not wanting to be accused of foul play? Who knows?

Behind the burial platform, against the back wall, was a small narrow opening—a passage. I aimed the beam of light inside but could make out nothing. I had just pulled myself onto the platform to inspect the passage when I heard someone in the kitchen.

"Michael, are you here?"

Audrey came downstairs and stood at the entrance of the wine cellar. There I was, bare chested in my underwear, standing in the tomb. I made no attempt to climb out. I barely had enough strength to do that, anyway.

"Good God, Michael, what's going on? What did you do?"

It was obvious. "I opened the tomb."

"Look at you! How long have you been down here? I've been calling since I left Houston. You had me worried sick that something serious had happened."

What could I say? "I'm sorry. I…I've been down here for a while, I guess."

"Why did you open the tomb?"

"Look what's here," I said enthusiastically. I flashed the light across the femurs.

"Bones. What did you expect?"

"Not just bones. See, they're leg bones…sixteen bones from eight people, I think."

"So what? It's just a grave of some type."

"Don't you see? This is where they put the eight bodies Martin told me about. The ones that disappeared and were never found. There are eight sets of bones here," I said, climbing the steps of the tomb. "I don't know where the rest of the skeletons are. They must be somewhere else."

Audrey stared at me with one of those "who cares" looks. "And what's all that stuff out in the pasture?" she asked.

"What stuff? Oh…that. It's a target."

"A target?"

We went up to the kitchen. "I bought some guns. One for you and one for me."

"Guns? *Why?*"

"For protection."

"Protection? Protection from who?"

"From whoever tries to mess with us."

"What are you *talking* about?"

"Wait here, I'll show you." I went upstairs and came down with the handguns. "Come on," I said, heading out the back door.

I marched across the field, a gun in each hand. Audrey talked the whole time, demanding to know what was going on. When we were about twenty feet from the target, I set one of the guns on the ground and took the other and began explaining how it works, going over the proper way to use it.

"*Put that thing down!*" Audrey ordered.

"You need to learn how to use this. We both need to know." I aimed the gun at the target and pulled the trigger, snapping off a half-dozen quick rounds, each one ripping through the center of the target.

Audrey stood speechless, staring at me for a long while. "That's it. I'm going!" She turned and walked away.

"All right, all right," I said, taking the guns and following her across the field.

She stopped and turned toward me. "Look at you. You're standing out here all sweaty and dirty in your boxer shorts. What's going on? You're coming apart."

I rubbed my arm across my forehead. For a moment everything became a blur. Then, just as quickly, my mind cleared. We walked back to the house and sat at the kitchen table.

"Are you okay?" Audrey asked, worried. "Did something happen? Was it Rainey?"

"No."

"You were supposed to come out here and pack."

"Uh-huh. I did that. And the house is listed, too."

"So what happened? This isn't like you. We don't own guns. Don't even like them."

"Those things came back. The creatures. The silver things."

"Silver things?"

"Yeah. They have this sort of silver-blue color."

"Aren't they supposed to be gray or green?" Audrey said.

I wasn't sure if she was serious or kidding. "I don't know what color they're supposed to be, but that's what color they are. They're like the one I saw in the barn, only this time there were three of them."

"When?"

"In the middle of the night while I was sleeping. They came into the bedroom." I explained the whole episode.

"It was a dream, Michael," Audrey said.

I showed her the puncture wounds on my forearms. "And then I started having these dizzy spells," I said.

"It's from stress. We're both stressed. We just need to pack a few things and get back to Houston. We can come with a truck later and get the rest of the stuff."

Audrey was right.

"You need a shower...*bad!* And when was the last time you ate?" she said.

"I don't know. Last night, I guess."

"Well, get cleaned up and we'll go eat. And put those guns away! Upstairs, somewhere...anywhere."

I looked at myself. I was filthy. I took the guns to the bedroom, showered and shaved, and put on clean clothes.

Not wanting to encounter any of the Krivac crowd, we ate at a restaurant just outside Schulenburg. When we got back, I took a long nap while Audrey packed.

I awoke feeling better. On the nightstand was the report on Operation Orion that Martin had given me. I looked at it, thinking it was a good time to throw it in the trash. But this version was different. Stamped across the cover were the words Classified Top Secret.

I opened it and landed on a section that gave a perfect description of the creature I had seen in the barn and the ones that had paid me a visit in the bedroom. Every detail was identical. They were described as about four feet tall, some being larger. Thin and frail but highly intelligent. That the silver-blue ones might be android-like had not been ruled out. Regardless, they had a special ability to control both mentally and physically whomever confronted them. The report referred to the creatures as "Visually-Oscillating Reactive Data Systems (VORDS)," a term apparently derived at least in part from the pulsing color they emitted. They were believed to be frequently present near the Ostermann house, although they were not unique to this region. Creatures similar to the VORDS had been spotted regularly in other parts of the country, but the Ostermann property was believed to be a focal point of their activity.

Paging deeper, I came across an interview with a Colonel Martin, whom I assumed was Wayne Martin, the person I had met at the Sleazy. The interview was conducted by a Mr. Burns.

MR. BURNS: When exactly did you encounter the VORDS? The first time?

COL. MARTIN: That probably happened fairly soon after Operation Orion began. I would say within the first year or so.

MR. BURNS: Who made contact?

COL. MARTIN: It was Lt. Camberson and three others, as I recall.

MR. BURNS: And how did this happen? How did they make contact?

COL. MARTIN: It was by accident, not something we were intending to do. In fact, we had no hard evidence that the VORDS were even there. At the Ostermann place, I mean. We knew about the VORDS, of course. It was common knowledge that they existed elsewhere, but we hadn't encountered them at the Ostermann house yet.

MR. BURNS: And so Lt. Camberson did what?

COL. MARTIN: It was sometime late in the year, November or December. I'd have to look at the record. Lt. Camberson's team was assigned to surveillance of the house. We had set up a pretty good post for this from the field across from the house. There were these bales of hay. I don't think—in fact I very much doubt—that Herman had any idea we were out there. It was late in the day, around dusk or so. Suddenly they, Camberson and his group, noticed a strange form emerge from the barn. According to the record, it was short, about four feet tall. It walked to the house, went inside, and came out and headed to the front road.

MR. BURNS: The road in front of the house, you mean?

COL. MARTIN: Yes. It was not far from where Lt. Camberson's team was. Once the VORD was on the road, Camberson used his Taser to immobilize it. We had Tasers back then, but they were not used outside the military. The VORD was immediately compromised; it fell to the ground. The three men working with Camberson went out and quickly recovered the creature, the VORD, and brought it back.

MR. BURNS: What did they do with it?

COL. MARTIN: It appeared to be irrevocably damaged. As far as I know, it has never been put into working order. It was taken to Wright-Patterson. I assume that's where it is now.

MR. BURNS: Anything else?

COL. MARTIN: Yes. Lt. Camberson disappeared.

MR. BURNS: Disappeared? Disappeared when?

COL. MARTIN: He disappeared that day. We still have no idea what happened to him. He simply vanished. When the men brought the VORD back to where Lt. Camberson was, he was gone.

MR. BURNS: What happened to him?

COL. MARTIN: I have no idea.

MR BURNS: Was it related somehow to the capture of the VORD?

COL. MARTIN: Yes, probably. Lt. Camberson was the one with the Taser. There must have been some connection between the Taser energy and the VORD and Lt. Camberson's disappearance. I don't know exactly what, but there was a connection of some kind. We've never located Lt. Camberson. He couldn't have left the area. They were out in the middle of a field, a pasture. There was nowhere for him to go.

MR BURNS: Did the men look for him?

COL. MARTIN: Extensively. He was nowhere to be seen. But they had to get the VORD back to headquarters. Two of the men took the VORD. The other stayed and looked for Lt. Camberson. Then, later, several others came out and hunted for him. Camberson, I mean. There was never a trace found.

MR. BURNS: Did Herman Ostermann know about the VORD being caught? Do you think he knew about the VORDS at all? Was he aware they existed, that they were out on the property?

COL. MARTIN: I can't say for sure, but I don't see how he could not. The VORD that day had gone into the house and Herman was inside at the time. We knew that for sure from the surveillance. So Herman was quite aware that the VORDS were out there.

MR. BURNS: Did you ever encounter or see any other VORDS?

COL. MARTIN: From time to time. Usually around dusk or at night. They were mostly out by the barn or by the pond. Occasionally, but less frequently, they went into the house.

I set the report on the bed and stared at the ceiling. It now occurred to me that everything that had happened on the property from the time we had arrived was probably connected to the VORDS in one way or another. Wayne Martin hadn't mentioned the VORDS in our conversation at the Sleazy. Presumably he was restricted from doing that, the information being classified. But I suppose that didn't prevent him or someone else from surreptitiously depositing a version of it in the house.

It occurred to me that if the VORDS had something to do with the disappearance of Lieutenant Camberson, they may also be responsible for the disappearance of the Broding kid. Maybe that's why Schneider and Robinson refused to tell Rainey about it. Suppose all three of them—Broding, Schneider, and Robinson—had encountered VORDS out by the graveyard. Suppose Broding had done something to challenge the VORDS and they were responsible for his disappearance, right there before the eyes of Schneider and Robinson. Of course they'd be scared. Who wouldn't be? And anyway, who would believe a story like that? Did Rainey know about the VORDS? Maybe the kids had told him and he didn't believe them. Or he did believe them and didn't want to pass the information on to anyone else.

I went downstairs and showed Audrey the report. "Time to leave," she said, reading it. "Time to get out."

CHAPTER 35

We spent the rest of the afternoon and evening packing. Boxes were stacked in the living room and dining room. We had far too much to bring back in two cars. All day, a cool wispy December breeze filled the air. At dusk I again watched the eagle land on the branch of the tree on the far end of the property, just as Bud had described. The sun set, bringing with it a black night. It was then that I realized it was the night of the new moon. I walked into the house, checked the calendar, and mentioned it to Audrey. All I got back was a deep sigh as she continued to wrap kitchen plates.

"I'm going to Bell's Creek," I announced.

"To Bell's Creek? *Why?*"

"To get the box of nonagrams and bring them here."

"You can't be serious, Michael. That's *not* why we came here this weekend!"

I picked up a flashlight and a shovel and headed for the car. Audrey scrambled along, vainly trying to talk me out of going. It was no use. I drove through the sullen streets of

Krivac lit only by the occasional glimmer of light from houses along the road. Everything seemed unbearably quiet—no cars, no sounds.

We arrived at Bell's Creek. I parked along the road tight in near the woods, hoping no one would notice the car. We got out and went down along the bank of the creek. We hadn't gone far when I stopped and said, "What's that?"

"What's what?"

I listened. "I don't know. Footsteps. Hear them?" I waited a second. "They're gone now."

"This is *not* at all a good idea, Michael," Audrey said. "Obviously we're not alone. And we can't see anything out here."

"Not so loud. Ah...there it goes again. Whatever it is, it's moving slow as hell. There. Hear it?"

"No."

"Come on, keep going," I said. A branch with thin leaves swept across my face like the probing hands of an infant fondling my cheeks. We moved slowly forward. I stepped on a twig. It snapped, making the same sound I had heard from the footsteps behind us. Only a large animal—a bear or a person—could do that. Again, I heard another telltale noise. Always behind us, always to the left, as though inching its way along. I thought about our encounter with Rainey when we came out to the creek weeks before. I grasped Audrey's arm. We stood motionless with only silence surrounding us, listening intently.

Audrey said, "Forget it." She knew there was no changing my mind now. The only thing left to do was get the box and leave.

We headed a few steps forward. I stopped again. "Something here is odd. It doesn't look familiar at all. I don't remember the creek turning like this." Even in the torrid darkness I could tell we were going in the wrong direction. I looked around. "Ah, damn! It's back there, I think. That's where we need to go. I must have parked the car at the wrong bridge or something. Too hard to tell in all this darkness. Everything looks the same." We turned and backtracked for a short while.

"What about the creep that's following us?" Audrey said. "We're probably marching right into him."

But not so. The footsteps were once again behind us as though everything had been miraculously flipped 180 degrees. We arrived at the small bridge, crossed over, and went to where the strongbox was buried. A small patch of soil glowed, exactly as it had the first time we were there. We could see it from several feet away, shining brighter than ever in the dark night. We stood and stared for a brief moment. I jammed the shovel into the ground. The dirt moved away easily.

"Strange, for some reason the ground isn't at all hard," I muttered. "I don't know why. When I tried this before, it was like concrete. Rainey claimed we would need a code or whatever to get in here."

Audrey stood back and watched as I shoveled soil from the top of the box. In a matter of minutes, I had uncovered it and had raised it from the ground. Returning to the car was difficult. If any eyes were upon us this time, they were cold and quiet.

"You drive," I said.

Audrey turned the car around and started back to the house.

We hadn't gone far when I said, "Someone's following us."

"Where?"

"Behind us."

"Audrey looked in the rearview mirror. "There's no one there."

"Yes there is."

"Michael, you need to settle down," Audrey said and sighed. "We're the only people—"

"I can tell...there's someone—"

"You're imagining this, Michael. Just like the footsteps out by the creek. When we get back to the house, I want you to lie down and rest. Do you hear? You're exhausted. You're not thinking right. You're not."

I looked out the back window. "It's a car with its lights off."

Audrey glanced again in the mirror. A set of bright lights suddenly flashed on behind us. "Christ, where did that come from? It's right on our tail! Who is it?"

"I have no idea. It's a black car with dark windows. Pull to the side. Maybe it's trying to pass."

Audrey steered the car to the edge of the road. The car slowed but didn't pass.

"Okay, we need to get the hell away from whoever it is." As I said that, there was a hard thump against the back bumper.

"Asshole rammed us!" Audrey yelled.

"Go, go! Get onto one of the main roads."

The car hit us again, causing Audrey to swerve onto the shoulder. "Get a grip!" she roared, jamming the accelerator down and pulling back onto the road, putting distance between the two cars. We came to an intersection. At the last minute, Audrey yanked the steering wheel and banked sharply to the right. The car behind us flew through the intersection, slammed on its brakes, and did a complete turn. Soon, it was behind us and closing in fast.

"What the hell's going on?" I cried.

"It's the nonagrams, Michael. They want the nonagrams. Throw the damn box out the window."

I ignored her. "Keep going. I know a shortcut to the house. Make a left turn at the road up ahead and then get ready to make a quick right." Audrey did this beautifully, but as soon as she turned, we found ourselves blocked by a car in the middle of the road. Its headlights blazed and a rack lights across the top flashed, making it impossible to see anything. Audrey swung the car far onto the left shoulder. The wheels spun in the loose gravel and then gripped and we sped away. The car behind us crashed full throttle into the one on the road. In no time, it was on our tail again.

"We're almost home! Keep going!"

Two more fast turns on narrow unpaved roads and we arrived at the front of the house. Audrey flashed into the driveway. The car behind us came to screeching stop, waited a second, then tore off down the road. We ran into the house and locked the door.

"What the hell's going on? Who are those assholes?" Audrey demanded.

"I have no idea, but it's time to split. Get what you need— we're out of here."

I took the box and set it on the coffee table in the living room. I remembered Rainey using a key to open it when he first showed me the nonagrams out at the creek. But this box was different. It had a small rotating latch. I turned it to the left as far as it would go. The lid popped up. Streams of bright light leaped from the box and swirled around the room as though carried on strange currents, colliding and bouncing off each other, flowing past us and above us and through us.

The temperature in the room shifted from cool to warm in a matter of seconds. Audrey stood in the doorway near the dining room, her face reflecting the changing colors of the room. The light spun faster and faster. I had an uncanny sense that time was speeding up, driven by the motion of the light. The inside of the house changed. Furniture vanished. The room was empty. For a split second the entire house seemed to disappear. Then the beams of light slowed. Time began moving in reverse, returning us to the present. The light faded into thin strands and died out altogether.

I carefully approached the box and peered inside. There were eleven nonagrams, just as Rainey had displayed at the creek. I reached inside, picked them up, wrapped them in a napkin, and shoved them into my back pocket.

A flash of light filled the sky outside the house. "Lightning or something," I said. "Come on, get your stuff."

Audrey grabbed a few things from the table and crammed them into a bag. "What are you doing with the nonagrams?"

"I'm not sure," I replied. "Take them back to Houston."

Audrey stopped and stared at me. "Michael, just leave them here!" she snapped. "I don't want those things anywhere near us. All I want now is to get out of here in one piece. How did we get involved in this, anyway?"

I looked at the strongbox. It was decorated with the same cryptic carvings that adorned the nonagrams. Light continued to flash outside the house.

"What's with all this lightning?" Audrey said.

"I don't know...heat lightning or something," I replied. "Come on, let's go."

"It's December. Way too late for heat lightning." Audrey looked out the window. "There's something out there."

"Where?"

"Over by the barn. Come here! Look! That's where the light's coming from. It's not lightning at all." I stood next to Audrey. "See? There it goes again."

"Holy shit, it's those goddamn VORDS or whatever the hell they're called. A whole pack of them, a dozen or so. Maybe more. *Over there, too!* Beyond the barn out in the pasture!"

"Yeah, yeah!" Audrey said.

"We can get to the car, but we'll need the guns. Wait here."

I raced upstairs to the bedroom. The three guns I had left there earlier in the day were gone. I rummaged around frantically. They were nowhere in sight. I looked out the window. The house was surrounded by VORDS. Each one, a glowing silver-blue spot that moved in the darkness.

"The guns are gone," I said running down the stairs. "I don't know where they are, but they're not here now. Someone must've taken them when we were out. The VORDS are all around the house."

"I know!"

"The back door." I ran into the kitchen. Outside the door, not more than five feet away, were three VORDS. They peered at us through the window, their faces up close to the glass.

"We've got to get the hell out of here, Michael!"

"Call the police."

Audrey picked up the kitchen phone. "It's dead!" she said.

"Try your cell."

Audrey fumbled with her phone. "It's dead too." She picked up my phone from the counter. "Yours too. They're all out."

"We'll have to go out the front door and make a break for the car."

We raced through the living room. I yanked the door open. A half-dozen VORDS stood on the front porch, more behind them on the grass. They moved quickly toward the door, trying to gain entry. I slammed the door and locked it.

"We're trapped in, and they're trying to get in," Audrey said. "We need to find a way out."

"There's no way out now. We need a safe place in here, and we need to reinforce all the entries." We ran through the house, locking windows. I saw clusters of VORDS gathered on the lawn and heard them scratching at the front and back doors.

"Quick. Barricade the doors." We pushed furniture into the front hall. Green-yellow ooze leaked into the entryway. Audrey grabbed a tablecloth and threw it against the floor below the door. In the living room, objects on the tables and shelves began to shake. All at once, a blizzard of books, vases, lamps, CDs, and pictures shot through the air. The word *LOCUS* appeared in large red letters across all the walls, each word sporadically flashing on and off.

We ran into the kitchen. From out on the porch, the VORDS had managed to get the key and had inserted it into the lock, exactly as we had seen on the video camera weeks before. I snatched it out just as it was being turned. Other VORDS were rubbing against the outside of the door and the windows. Two peered in through the kitchen window by the sink, their large heads and thin necks turning and twisting in awkward motion.

"Try the phones again," I said.

"Nothing. Still dead."

Now, the green-yellow ooze was leaking in below the kitchen door. I had no idea what it was, but it didn't look good. We retrieved towels from the packed boxes in the dining room. When we returned, the kitchen cabinet doors sprang open. Coffee mugs, glasses, plates, cups, and saucers flew through the air. A cup hit me on the back of the head. I felt a welt thicken under my skin.

"Michael!" Audrey screamed.

I pulled open the door to the basement and grabbed a flashlight. "Come on!"

"What are you doing?"

"Into the basement!"

"*The basement?*"

"We sure as hell can't stay here. When I was in the tomb this morning, I saw what looked like a passage of some kind. Hurry!" We headed down the basement steps. I slammed the door behind us and stuck a piece of wood under the knob.

"Quick, into the wine cellar!" I heard noises in the kitchen. "They're in the house. Go!" I locked the wine cellar door from inside, and wedged a heavy wooden plank across it.

The tomb was still open, its lid tilted against the wall. I took the shovel and dug into the floor and recovered the six nonagrams and stuffed them into my right pants pocket. "Come on, we're going in."

"My God, Michael, something's moving in the tomb. It's dark; I can't see much."

I shined the light into the gaping stone chamber. The eight sets of femurs had reassembled into eight freaky living bodies. My mind flashed back to the words inscribed on the top of the tomb: "But will be back before the dawn." In single file, they stumbled clumsily out from the back of the crypt—sickly looking, dead but alive. All wore military uniforms of one type or another that hung off them like brown paper wrapped around brooms. I was right about the femurs. They belonged to the eight missing army personnel that Wayne Martin said had disappeared on the property. Here they were. The first one started up the stairs of the tomb. The others followed. I heard the scratching of the VORDS at the cellar door.

As the first of the eight climbed to the top of the tomb, it glared at me with a penetrating stare, its eyes a bilious yellow, its skin taut across its bony face. It delivered a hideous grin. The corners of its tight lips were turned upward, showing rotten and missing teeth. "You are trapped," it said in a creaky staccato voice. "You are trapped. It is all over, Lieutenant. Done. Nothing left to do." With pencil-thin fingers, it reached out to grab me.

"I'll show you what's left to do, Sarge," I said, gritting my teeth. I took the shovel and slammed the gaunt figure hard in the side, sending it against the wall. The second one, the third one, and the forth one came up, moving jerkily. I parked them one at a time on top of each other.

"I hear the VORDS," Audrey warned. "They've made it past the cellar door into the basement."

"We're still ahead of them. Hang in there. Couple more of these bastards and we're going in."

Audrey groaned.

The last two came up. Women both, wearing brown skirts and shirts that hung loose on their skinny bodies. Stringy strips of hair clung to their skulls. Women or not, they were going the way of the first six. Done! The quivering pile clustered to the left of me. I grabbed Audrey and pulled her into the tomb.

"The VORDS are in the basement now," Audrey said. "I hear them."

We started into a tunnel—a few feet wide, narrow, and barely tall enough to stand in.

"What's up ahead?"

"I can't tell," I said, groping my way ahead. "Stay close."

"The VORDS, they're at the door of the wine cellar, I think," Audrey said. "They're not far behind us. And those... those things from the tomb are back there too—moving around."

"There's no other choice. This is our only chance now."

"What if there's no way out of here?"

"Keep going." We moved through the blackness with only the pale-yellow light from the flashlight.

Audrey wheezed. "I don't feel good. I'm getting light-headed," she said.

I heard noises in the wine cellar behind us. "Take a deep breath," I said.

"Where's it going, the tunnel?"

"I don't know. It turns up ahead, I think. Are you all right?"

Audrey took several deep breaths. "I'm not sure."

"Try to go on."

The passage was getting smaller, tighter. I had to stoop.

"I can hear the VORDS. They're in the wine cellar," Audrey said.

"It's okay. We're still ahead of them." The dim rays of the flashlight barely illuminated the darkness in front of us.

"Shit," I said, "the tunnel separates."

"Where?"

"Up there. Twenty feet or so." We arrived at the fork. One branch angled to the left, one to the right. "Which way?" I asked.

"Right."

"Why right?"

"I don't know. Right."

We headed down the right branch for eight or ten feet and came to a T in the tunnel—a left turn and a right turn. This time, we went down the left tunnel. Another fifteen feet...and another choice. Straight or to the left. Straight it was. Again and again and again, more choices to make.

"We're in a maze," I said. "A goddamn underground maze."

"Look," Audrey shouted. "There's light ahead!"

We sped forward a few steps and then came to an abrupt halt. "No, don't tell me. We're back to where we started. That's the tomb where we came in from."

The light from the entrance began to fade out. *"Michael, they're sealing it off! Look, they're closing off the entrance! We're being sealed inside! We'll never get out. We'll suffocate in here."*

I grabbed Audrey by the arm. "Come on, follow me. This thing has to go somewhere."

"It's a gigantic maze. Just like you said. It could go on forever, Michael!"

"Maybe, maybe not. If it's a maze, there's a way out."

"We already tried!"

"Not very well. You get out of a maze by following the wall. Pick a wall and stay with it. Stay with that wall no matter where it goes, got it?"

I shined the flashlight in front of me. The sides of the tunnel were warm clay, sticky. The air was stale and heavy. We arrived at the first bifurcation again.

"Follow the wall," I said. "The wall to the right." We headed farther on. At each junction, each intersection, we stayed with the right wall. I could hear Audrey breathing. "You okay?"

"I don't know."

As I turned toward her, I lost my grip on the flashlight and dropped it. The light went out. We were in total darkness. I fumbled around, pawing at the dirt floor, hunting for the light. Finally I found it. I flipped the switch repeatedly, but nothing happened. Again and again I turned the switch on and off, rapping the light with my hand, hoping it would come on.

"*Fuck! It's broken!*"

I tried over and over, working the switch, twisting the cap. "Dead, totally dead," I muttered. All at once there was a flicker and the beam came back. There was a simultaneous huge sigh from both of us.

"How far below ground are we?" Audrey asked as we moved through the darkness.

"I can't tell. Ten feet maybe."

"We could dig out, then."

"No way. Too far. And we don't have anything to dig with. The shovel's back in the wine cellar. Stick with the maze."

We'd been in the tunnel a long time, a good thirty or forty minutes. I could taste the clay in my mouth. My hands were packed with slippery clay. I put both hands on the flashlight, afraid of losing it again, knowing it wouldn't tolerate another trip to the floor. We encountered scores of turns but stayed with the plan. The tunnel was getting smaller. Who had made this thing? What was its purpose? If all went well, we were going to find out.

We came to a junction of three arteries of the maze. I stood in the middle, pulling my rigid shoulders upward when a sudden blast of dizziness hit, exactly as had happened the day after my encounter with the VORDS late at night. Audrey put her hand on my shoulder.

"Are you all right?"

I shook my head. "Whew...dizzy," I replied. I turned around and realized I had lost track of which passage we had come out of. "We need to know so that we can follow the wall," I said, peering into empty darkness in every direction.

"I'm not sure. I lost track when you got dizzy," Audrey said.

There were six walls, six choices. But this was no time for guessing.

"Fuck!" I shined the light on the ground. It revealed nothing but the blackened dirt. "If we head the wrong way, we could be here forever. Not to mention coming face to face with the VORDS again." I studied the ground. I tried to calculate how many turns I had made in my dizziness. A half turn first. Then a full turn. Yes, maybe. Or maybe not. It was useless.

"I'm about ninety percent certain this is the tunnel we just came from," Audrey said. "It looks right."

I walked a short distance in and got on my hands and knees and studied the floor. There were numerous footprints. Someone else had been here not long ago, that was obvious. It must have been how they managed to get in and out of the house. That and the trafficking of the invisible creature, of course.

"You're right. Yes, I think this is it," I said, matching a print with the pattern on my shoe. I put my hand on the right wall as we headed into the abyss once more.

We hadn't gone far when Audrey grabbed my shirt and pulled me back. "Michael, listen. Shh, shh…listen."

I heard a shuffling sound in the tunnel to our left. "VORDS. That must be the direction we came from. It means were going the right way now. Quick!"

The beam of the flashlight was getting dimmer. "The battery's wearing down," I said. I aimed the light across the wall a few feet ahead of us. "*Jesus!* What the—"

"Bugs!" Audrey cried.

Thousands of them. They made the walls look like wavy curtains.

"What kind of bugs?" Audrey asked.

"I don't know. Roach-like things. Big motherfuckers." We stood motionless for a half minute, maybe longer. "We have no choice," I said.

We moved forward into a thicket of roaches. Our passing through the narrowness of the tunnel walls sent them into a wild frenzy. Roaches don't usually fly, but they can. They're too content to skit along the kitchen floor…or along the walls of a subterranean tunnel. Now, as they sailed through the air, you could hear the buzz of their large onionskin wings. They landed on my hands, arms, shirt, face, neck—all at once. I swept them off fast as I could. I heard Audrey doing the same.

Piles of moving exoskeletons crunched under our feet. As I stepped forward in the cramped dark tunnel, my foot hit a root. I took a nosedive and landed face first in a trove of dithering insects. A slew of them ran under my shirt. Back and forth across my spine they ran, as though trapped in a tunnel of their own. I no longer cared. All I wanted to do was just keep moving.

The tunnel became smaller and smaller, more and more cramped. Coffin-like. If this keeps up, we'll be down on our knees, I thought. I didn't need to mention this to Audrey. She knew it all too well. We kept following the wall to our right, countless turns upon countless turns. We were at a point of no return. Finally! Up ahead was a large opening.

"There! There! There!" Audrey all but roared. "There's a room up there. I think the tunnel ends. Hurry!" We moved as fast as possible until we arrived at an area about five feet by five feet in size.

"This is it," I said. "The end of the maze." I looked around. Multiple tunnel branches terminated here, each from a different part of the maze. The room had been carved out of the mud. A slight glimmer of light came in from up above. "We need to get up there. I'll lift you."

I stuck the flashlight into a crag in the wall and cupped my hands together. Audrey put her foot in. She was almost able to touch the ceiling.

"What's there?" I asked.

"I'm not sure. A door, I think."

"Good! Push, push!"

"It won't budge."

"Push *harder*."

"I can't move it."

"You need to use both hands," I said, setting her down. "Get up on my shoulders and give it all you've got."

I lifted her again. "It won't move, Michael. Here, hand me the flashlight."

"What do you see?" I heard clicking noises in the tunnel. "They're right behind us," I said. "Probably from one of the other branches. They're not far off."

"I think I can push the top open here. It's loose at this end," Audrey said. Giving it everything she had, the door opened a trace.

"That's it! Keep pushing! Keep pushing! Keep pushing!" I cried.

"I'm trying." Little by little, Audrey had managed to open the door a couple of feet. "I'm going up."

Once out of the tunnel, she said, "Here, quick—give me your hand."

I reached and grabbed her. "Don't let go," I said. I heard the VORDS moving closer in. *"Pull, pull, pull!"* I scratched at the muddy clay, gripping the side wall until I was able to grasp the edge at the top. I pulled myself halfway out when I felt something yank at my foot. Two VORDS were locked onto my leg. I jammed my other foot down on them again and again, hitting each on the head. They fell to the ground. I climbed out and slammed the door. Bent over, hands on my knees, I sucked in several deep breathes. "Where the hell are we?" I said in a groan.

Audrey threw her head toward the sky in relief. "The graveyard...the graveyard," she muttered almost unable to speak.

We were standing next to Herman Ostermann's grave. But the grave was no grave at all. This was where the tunnel ended, or began maybe. A rusted door hidden under a layer of dirt and grass pretending to be a grave. The house was off in the distance; our car was in the driveway near the house.

"All we need to do is make it to the car and we're out of here," I said.

We darted across the pasture. There was nothing to stop us. Perhaps all the VORDS were still down in the tunnel. Everything seemed fine until we approached the house. I saw spots of light—VORDS moving inside.

"They're in the house," I said. "Come on, just keep going. We can make it."

Several VORDS came out onto the back porch.

"There they are," Audrey said. "They've seen us."

"*Fast!* To the car!"

I fumbled with the car door, finally getting it open. Climbing in, I shoved the key into the ignition switch. Nothing. "*Son of a bitch! It's dead!* Come on, we need to get off the property. If we hurry, we can make it to the road. We tore down the driveway. On the road was a man. He stood there, watching us passively—tall and lean, hands in his pockets as a curious spectator. His face was obscured by the lack of light and the dark night. I yelled to him for help but got no reply.

Suddenly, the creatures from the tomb, eight in all, formed a line in front of us. I grabbed Audrey by the arm and pulled her toward me. In a low gravelly voice, one of them began to chant, "We are eight, you are one…we are eight, you are one… we are eight, you are one." Then all eight sang together in a hideous, cacophonous chorus. The words meant nothing. It was clear there were eight them and two of us.

"Now what?" Audrey said, urgently, looking around. "We're trapped."

I grabbed a large stick from the ground and started swinging in a wide swath, hitting one of them across the chest. It landed on the ground, then climbed to its feet exactly as had happened in the basement. I turned. The VORDS were coming in from the other direction, led by three tall metallic-looking creatures. Unlike the VORDS, their faces were rough and scaly.

We stood there, exhausted, out of breath. I held onto Audrey.

"What do you want from us?" I hollered.

A heavy resonating voice replied, "We want you to understand."

"*Understand? Understand what?*"

"We've come to your planet from galaxy M66. The constellation Leo is there. You on Earth know it by the symbol of the lion, simply made up of nine stars. This is why the nonagrams have nine spokes—one for each of those stars. The nonagrams are connected by energy to Leo and M66. On the night of the new moon, the energy here is at its peak. It is because of this that we can communicate from M66. We've been here on Earth for a long time, for thousands of years, and have watched the development of people on Earth. It has been a sporadic development, sometimes moving in a good direction, sometimes in a bad direction."

I looked around as the creature spoke. We were surrounded. There was no way off the property.

"Some people on this planet are intent on destroying life for everything. It was not our plan to interfere, but circumstances have changed now. America is the only country that can prevent the destruction. But it won't. Nuclear weapons fill the world. Soon, there will be great global disaster. The Earth's troposphere will be filled with radioactivity that will rain down across the planet. No life will be spared. The Earth and everything on it will die. Buildings and highways will be left, but life will be gone."

"We are no position to change that," I said, loud and out of breath.

"Earth people have become their own worst predators. You create cures for disease in order to keep people alive, but you don't give them the means to receive treatment. You spend vast amounts of money and time perfecting ways to kill each other, and then find better ways to save people on the battlefield so that they can go out and kill again. The irony of this has not escaped us, although it seems to have escaped your people. You let rich people and big corporations contaminate your soil and water, and you let them waste your natural resources just because they're rich, because they have money and power. Your politicians do nothing for you. They are self-serving people who don't care what the people who elected them want. They fight among themselves. And you let this happen."

"Why are you here at the Ostermann house?" I asked.

"This is LOCUS. It is the source of our communication, a portal to M66. You found the stone markers on the property. They are how we can connect to your society. I can tell you nothing more. It is all very complicated. Right now, it is more important that you understand what your people are doing than why we are here. The time has come to change the course of events before it is too late."

"Then you need to tell this to the politicians and the people who make those decisions," Audrey said. "We are university professors. That's all we are. We have no ability to change the world."

The creature continued, "People have created a media that is a tool for evil. It feeds hatred. If you look at what happened in Germany prior to World War II, you will see what is happening in your country now. The Nazis blamed the Jews for Germany's problems. America blames its problems on immigrants. Germany required the Jews to wear armbands to identify themselves. Immigrants here will soon be required to carry identification cards. In time, it will extend beyond a small segment of the immigrant population. It will include everyone who is different. It will become a type of ethnic cleansing just as in Germany. This is obvious, yet Americans fail to see it. Your media and politicians feed on the desires of your corporations to wage endless wars. Wars that accomplish nothing and only serve to turn every country in the world against each other. The world will become so polarized that war—global war—will be inevitable. Except that this time it will result in massive destruction from which the planet will not recover. It will happen sooner than people think. A cancer is growing throughout the planet that will destroy everyone. But it is not too late...and you can stop it."

The creature quit talking. From behind it, I saw the faint shape of a bird up in the sky, circling low in our direction. It was the eagle that landed every night in the tree on the back of the property. Its huge wings were open as it glided majestically toward us. As it touched the ground behind the three other creatures, there was a brilliant burst of light and it was transformed into the strangest creature of all. It was at least two feet taller than any of the others and had a dark-purple head that was bifurcated at the top, as though the brain had been split into two giant halves, each of which had a bright deep-set red eye. Above the eyes were knobby structures. The skin was rough and leathery like that of a desert lizard. It had long, thin, spindly arms that tapered down to two pointed fingers. The feet were birdlike, similar to the feet of the eagle itself.

As it stood there, the other three creatures were transmuted into human-like forms. The one who had been talking became Bud Ostermann, the other was Rainey, and the third was Ruth McDonald. They were dressed in long, green, flowing robes and had thin arms with two long and tapered fingers protruding from the sleeves. I now realized the connection of each person to the property, to the Ostermann house. They stepped aside and the large creature came forward.

It said, "Michael Felton, you will change the course of events on the planet. But I'm afraid you will have to pay a price for it. This is the message we've been given to deliver. It is not from us...it is from others. First, you must give us the nonagrams."

I realized I still had the packet of eleven nonagrams in my back pocket and the other nonagrams in my right front pocket. Somehow we must have the exact set of thirteen that Rainey told us about. I looked at the creature that had become Rainey. The expression on its face confirmed that I indeed had the necessary combination of nonagrams.

"The nonagrams must never be put together as a single set. Therefore, we must have them."

This was how we would get away. I whispered to Audrey, "When I tell you, run like hell for the street."

I pulled the nonagrams from my pockets. "Now! *Go!*" I screamed.

"*STOP! YOU MUST STOP!*", came a thundering voice from the chief creature.

We raced toward the road. The VORDS moved apart as I approached carrying the nonagrams. Suddenly, I heard Audrey scream, "*MI-CHAEL!*"

I turned back. She was being held by several VORDS. I ran toward her, dropping the nonagrams on the ground.

When I was within several feet of her, a beam of light flashed toward me, locking me in place. I was unable to move. I could see and hear everything but was frozen. I watched as a group of the VORDS took Audrey toward the house.

The chief creature spoke. "There is nothing you can do, Mr. Felton. This is the price you will have to pay. We must take Audrey."

I heard Audrey scream as they carried her into the house. The pond out in the field was transformed into a massive circular object, a spaceship of some type. It emitted bright light and began rotating in a slow counterclockwise motion. A sheath of fire descended from the sky and engulfed the house, entering into it and passing through it. The entire inside of the house was lit with brilliant radiant colors. With a blistering thunderous crash, the house turned into vapor that was sucked far up into the sky. The spaceship in the field spun faster and faster, around and around, and then snapped into the sky amid a terrible burst of noise and a flash of light that knocked me to the ground.

🜨

I awoke. The sky was bright and sunny. I stood up, dazed, looking about and blinking. The Ostermann property was spread out before me. I saw the barn to my right. There was a large patch of smoldering soil to my left. Far in the distance was an old school bus of some kind. I walked to the car, got in, and drove down the highway through Krivac and back to Houston.

CHAPTER 36

Eighteen Years Later

I stepped off the elevator on the sixteenth floor. The sign on the door across the hall to my right read: Dr. Edward A. Milscher, Psychiatrist. I opened the door and walked in. The receptionist led me into Dr. Milscher's office.

"Can I get you something to drink, Mr. President?" she asked. "Coffee, water, soda?"

"No, thank you," I replied.

Dr. Milscher's office was pleasant, somewhat lavish in fact. He got up from his chair, came over, and shook my hand. "Michael, please…have a seat."

I sat in a comfortable chair. Dr. Milscher sat to my right. His desk, a beautifully carved oak piece, was across from me. A large window behind the desk opened to a bright blue sky that held fluffy clouds. It was a beautiful day.

"How have you been since last week?" Milscher asked.

"About the same," I said. "You know, maybe I'm wasting my time. I mean, I only came here because…well, we've known each other for a long time."

"Thirty years probably. Back to our days at Hopkins when you were a graduate student and I was a resident in psychiatry."

"Yeah, a long time. A lot has happened in that time, hasn't it?" I said.

"More for you than me, I think. I've been a humble little psychiatrist."

"Humble little psychiatrist." I looked around the room.

Milscher smiled. "What do you say we back up and go over some details? Let's see...I guess you could say you've had at least three professions. First as a university professor at Monclair University. You left Monclair after the incident in Krivac and joined the faculty at Berkeley. There, you got into politics, eventually becoming a US senator from California, and finally a two-term president of the United States."

"That's right. But I have more time on my hands now that I'm no longer the president. More time to think about things."

"Well, the road to the White House wasn't an ordinary one for you, was it? Of all the people I know, you never struck me as someone who wanted to be a politician."

"I never did."

"Yet no one in the history of the United States has been more effective. Your true strength was your ability to accomplish what no one could do. Within the course of eight years as president, you brought about a permanent peace in the Middle East, for which you were awarded a Nobel Peace Prize. Then, you were able to all but eliminate nuclear weapons on the planet, for which you were awarded a second Nobel Peace

Prize—the only time that the Nobel Peace Prize has been awarded to the same person twice. I have to say, it's hard not to be awestruck sitting here with you, Michael. Even after all the years we've known each other."

I thought for a second. "Well, you don't accomplish those things by yourself. There are a lot of others, other people, who make it possible. Those are the ones you never hear about. Unfortunately."

Milscher glanced at the tablet next to him. "Let's see...last week you were telling me about the things that happened out in Krivac. About the...uh, the creatures."

"The creatures. The VORDS."

"Yes. The VORDS."

I explained again, telling him everything that had happened. Although it had been a long time in the past, it remained as vivid in my mind as if it had been yesterday. I repeated the situations involving Audrey and myself right up to the last second when everything ended—"the great conflagration," I called it. The moment when Audrey was taken. I related my emotions—our emotions, hers and mine—throughout the time we were there.

"You never talked about Audrey in your professional life," Milscher said. "It never came up, yet everyone knew you had been married to her. Have you ever wondered why that was?"

"It wasn't relevant. Not during the campaigns or at any other time. People were civil about it, I guess. I never remarried. Never wanted to after Audrey was gone. It would have been hard to do, anyway. I mean, in a sense, she was not gone. Not the way we normally think of that."

"Let's go back over what you knew about the Ostermann property…from what you learned while you were there."

I took in a breath. "We've been all through this before."

"I know, but it might be worthwhile to revisit it. It may help to bring some closure."

"Okay, fine."

"You learned from Colonel Martin that there was some type of altered perception of reality associated with the property. Correct?"

"That's right. That's what he said. More than once."

"What do you think?"

"At first I thought he was full of shit."

Milscher smiled.

"You don't believe me?"

"No, no, it's not that. I just never heard it explained that way from the president of the United States."

"Yeah, well, you were never at a meeting in the White House."

"True. Sorry, you were saying?"

"I was saying that at first I didn't believe much of what Martin told me. Back then, we got a lot of information from a lot of different people, and not all of it made sense. Rainey told us one thing; Bud Ostermann and Ruth McDonald told us something else. I had become pretty cynical."

"Was Martin trying to mislead you?"

"I'm not sure. Later though, when I thought about it, I realized almost everything he said made sense."

"As president of the United States, did you ever try to look into this? I was just wondering...you had access to—"

"Once. But nothing much showed up. Martin was a retired army colonel who had been involved in all sorts of special ops. So that was of no use."

"And Operation Orion?"

"Nothing there, either. But that never convinced me of anything. A lot of high level stuff gets destroyed in government. You end up with no leads."

"Okay," Milscher said. "Let's go back to the Ostermann property. So, you feel that everything that happened out there was as you remember it? Is that correct?"

"Where's the evidence it wasn't?"

"Right. I'm just trying to establish things here," Milscher said.

"There was stuff that happened. Strange, unusual stuff. But that doesn't mean it didn't happen."

Milscher looked at his pad. "Have you ever discussed this with anyone else?"

"Nobody. Just you. And only recently."

"So you've carried these things with you for a long time?"

"Damn long time. That's why I'm here."

"I guess the most difficult part of this has to do with Audrey. If you're not prepared to talk about this now, I understand. It's your call."

I nodded, agreeing it was all right.

"Okay. Audrey was taken by the—"

"Creatures, the VORDS."

"Right. In return for what you were to do. Correct?"

"Correct."

"But it was never actually a decision on your part, as I see it," Milscher said. "Would you concur? They decided, and you had no real choice in the matter."

"That would probably be right."

"How do you feel about it?"

"I would never have willingly given Audrey up. Not for anything. She is what I lived for. We had a great marriage."

"I agree," Milscher said. "We've known each other a long time, Michael. I knew both of you."

"I never wanted to do this political thing," I said. "In fact, I never liked it much. You need a lot of ego to do it, and that's not me. So, I'm not quite sure how I managed to succeed. I've always believed that anyone else could have done what I did."

"And, of course, you feel you paid a price for it."

"A huge price."

"Have you ever been back to Krivac, to the old Ostermann place?"

"Never. Doubt if I ever will."

"Uh-huh." Milscher got out of his chair and went over to his desk. He recovered a folder from the top of it and came back and sat down again. "Michael, I'm going to give you something. I want you to take a close look at it."

"Okay."

He handed me a reproduction of an old newspaper article from the *Houston Chronicle* with the headline, University Professor Dies in Auto Accident. I read the article. It described the death of Audrey Felton, PhD, killed in a multicar accident in Houston on Interstate 610 on a rainy night. I read the article carefully through. Then read it again word for word. I looked up at Milscher.

He said nothing. I could tell he was judging my reaction. "That was nine years *before* you went out to Krivac to buy the Ostermann property," Milscher said. "Audrey was already dead at that time, Michael."

I stared at Milscher for what seemed like an eternity.

"She was not with you in Krivac," Milscher said. "She couldn't have been." He waited for a while and said, "I'm sorry."

I turned and looked out the window behind Milscher's desk. High in the sky I could see an eagle soaring gently, smoothly. Circling, circling. I looked back at Milscher. "You're trying to tell me that Audrey was never out at Krivac? Is that what you're saying?"

"That's right, Michael."

"Then…then who was out at Krivac? With me?"

Milscher said nothing.

I looked out the window again. I saw the pale blue sky, the clouds. The eagle was gone.

ABOUT THE AUTHOR

J. R. Klein has a PhD in immunology from Johns Hopkins University. He has published widely, including over 150 articles in academic journals and mainstream magazines. He is the author of the novel, *Frankie Jones*, which came out in 2016. Klein has traveled to dozens of countries across four continents. He lives in Houston, Texas, with his wife, Jeanne.

79057354R00226

Made in the USA
Columbia, SC
20 October 2017